MW01174124

DEATH FLIGHT

HOPE SZE MEDICAL CRIME NOVEL 6

MELISSA YI

Windtree
Press

For Captain Mesaglio and Dr. PI,

with special thanks to my triple board-certified comrade.

1
___

I figured Los Angeles would be full of Botoxed, Brazilian-waxed blondes honking their BMW's through the smog, but I was surprised by how much it seemed like any other city—until it launched me directly into hell at 35,000 feet.

My name is Hope Sze. I'm a resident doctor who ends up *mano a mano* with murderers way too often, but right now I was on a different kind of mission. A Christmas mission.

I was here to surprise Dr. John Tucker.

"Excuse me. You have to check in first," called a secretary with an asymmetric white bob that was displayed to advantage by a purple backdrop framed in white fairy lights and—was that an aquarium? L.A.'s Healing Hospital sure didn't stint on its design budget.

I gave her a death stare, ignoring the tank burbling behind her. It might lower your blood pressure to watch iridescent blue fish weave their way through seaweed, but I didn't want orthostatic hypotension. I wanted my man.

Tucker nearly died on November fourteenth, when we were both taken hostage. We survived, but Tucker ended up in L.A. for definitive reconstructive surgery after Montreal doctors hesitated to reoperate. Tucker didn't tell me he was leaving. He flew off and did it.

It was up to me to drag him back across the continent.

So for Christmas Eve, I'd taken a deep breath and charged a flight from Ottawa to L.A. at the most expensive time of the year. I'd made up for it by taking the bus from the airport. Then I'd marched straight into the Healing Hospital, searching for the closest elevator amongst the sunlit marble walls, until this secretary stopped me.

"I'm here to see John Tucker." I tried to smile. Ever since the hostage taking on 14/11, I've got PTSD and a wee bit of trouble with human interaction.

She adjusted her Chanel glasses. "Let me see if I can find him."

Yeah, you do that, since you're costing him $3,000 a day, even before his surgery. The very name of the Healing Hospital made me want to smash the fresh lotus arrangement on her steel desk, but that would scare the fish undulating behind her.

"I don't have a John Tucker listed," she said.

I pushed my hair out of my face. My backpack was glued through to my skin with sweat, because it's winter in Ottawa, and I didn't leave my coat in my car and run to the airport, freezing, the way some people do. Instead, I was carrying all my belongings on my back, like a homeless person.

A combative homeless person. "Sure you do. J-o-h-n T-u-c-k-e-r. He's on general surgery. Room 4524. Bowel reconstruction three days ago by Dr. Hiro Ishimura. I'm Dr. Hope Sze." I don't usually flaunt my credentials, but if you've got 'em, flaunt 'em in the face of recalcitrant administrators.

She clicked her computer again. "No, John Tucker checked out this morning."

I paled. Not easy to do with Chinese ancestry. My hands flexed on her desk like I wanted to tear out a hunk of steel. "That's impossible."

Her eyes softened with sympathy that I didn't want to handle. I whipped out the Finding Friends app that tracked Tucker's location. I'd checked it last night, but turned off my roaming data before take-off this morning to save money when I landed in the U.S.

"We have Wifi. The password is Serenity with a capital S."

Of course it was.

And of course Tucker's little yellow dot sat at LAX, Los Angeles's main airport.

I wanted to scream.

This can't be happening.

Of course it's happening. My entire life is a Murphy's Law.

Calm down, Hope. You've had murderers try to strangle, shoot, and knife you.

You can do this.

"Excuse me," I said to the secretary, and called Tucker.

He answered right away. "Hope!"

"Tucker. I'm at the hospital." I enunciated each word.

"Yeah? Well, good thing, baby, because tonight I'm back in Montreal—"

"Tucker. I'm at *your* hospital. The Healing Hospital. I took the first flight to L.A. this morning."

After a stunned moment, he burst out laughing. *"T'es pas sérieuse."*

I gritted my teeth. "Dead serious. I wanted to surprise you."

"I wanted to surprise *you.*"

I felt like banging my hospital germ-laden phone against my own forehead, except I can't afford another iPhone. "Me too."

"It's like 'The Gift of the Magi.' You flew in to see me, and I'm flying into Montreal and driving to Ottawa to see you."

I cut to the essentials. "What time does your plane leave?"

"At 15:55. I'm on flight number 783."

I wrote that down. One thing about both medicine and confronting killers is that you spend less time wringing your hands and more time leaping to plans B, C, and D. "Okay. That's not so bad. I'll hit the airport at 1 p.m. I don't know if I can get on your flight, but I'm coming. I'm only here to see you, anyway."

"I'll buy your ticket."

"No, Tucker, you don't have any money."

"Neither do you."

"More than you." My parents help as much as they can. Tucker's might, too, but he has two sisters and negative income. "You just had surgery in one of the most expensive cities in the world. Come on. I'll call Avian Air, or the booking website, and change my ticket while I'm in the cab."

The automatic doors swooshed open. I squinted at the sunlight. It was chilly, maybe ten degrees Celsius. That was positively balmy after the snow and ice in Canada, but a little cold on my bare legs. I'd changed into shorts at the airport, partly as a "Yay, I'm in L.A." thing, but mainly so that I could show off my legs to Tucker. How embarrassin'. The only way this could get worse would be if his family greeted me at the airport. Mine would never let me fly cross-country post-op without them. I asked, "Is your family with you?"

"No. Hey—are you okay?" His voice changed.

"I'm fine." I stepped toward the taxis idling in the hospital's front circle. I couldn't wait for a bus this time.

Tucker said, "Do you need help?"

"No ... " But then I realized he wasn't talking to me.

"I can help you. It's okay. I'm a doctor."

In the background, I could hear an angry, indistinct voice. A male one.

Tucker kept talking, as was his wont. "I'm from Canada, so I don't have an American medical license, but I can do first aid and call for help."

The man rumbled again.

I didn't like the sound of it. "Tucker, just let security know. I bet LAX has some sort of medical help available. You don't need—"

A woman screamed. Even over the phone, tinny and warbling, it made me want to scream too.

2

"Sorry, Hope. I'll call you back." Tucker cut me off.

No time for Uber. I dashed for the first orange taxi, driven by a man with dark skin and a neatly-trimmed moustache and beard.

"I need to get to the airport. Stat." Unlike Grey's Anatomy, I never say stat. Until now.

Before the driver finished nodding, I jumped in the car.

Take me to Tucker. Please.

I checked my phone. His dot was still at the airport. Unmoving.

My heart thundered. I loved Tucker. We'd never managed to hook up properly. Something always got in the way, whether it was gunfire on 14/11 or me falling in love with another guy named Ryan. Yes, I have two simultaneous boyfriends. Yes, I love both of them. No, they're not okay with it. They would like to drop each other off a cliff.

I tried to make it up to Tucker by abandoning everything, including Ryan, to fly here as soon as my stem cell rotation would allow. What were the chances that everything would go pear-shaped?

Between the two of us? Astronomical.

The taxi driver signalled left and shoulder checked twice before pulling out. I gnashed my teeth as I brought up the Exploria.com website. I needed that airline ticket, because if I couldn't get on the plane with him, I wasn't going to hang around in L.A. a minute longer than I had to. I was here for my man. One of them, anyway.

"It's an emergency," I told the driver, but maybe I was speaking too quickly, or his English wasn't great. Either way, we immediately hit a stop light, and he paused, listening to his call radio squawk over some sort of Bollywood-ish background music.

"Could you turn it to the news?" I asked. That way, I could use my phone to get on the same flight and still catch any worrisome stuff at the airport. Like a shooting.

I tried to talk myself down. The chance of a shooting at the airport is minimal. They have excellent security. I was only there an hour ago. If I hustled through security and nabbed a last-minute ticket, I should be fine.

As long as Tucker was okay.

I tried to analyze the scream that had warped my cell phone speakers.

It was a woman.

She had her ABC's, because she was screaming. Airway, breathing, and circulation guaranteed, at least for the moment.

But she was unstable enough that Tucker hung up on me.

I texted Tucker. Not that he had thumbs to spare, but then he could see I was thinking of him, even though the cell phone roaming charge would kill me.

Ryan texted, *Landed okay?*

I sent him back a thumbs-up sign. I couldn't talk to him right now. It felt like I was being unfaithful to Tucker, which made no sense, but *I* didn't make much sense. Ever since Tucker and I had delivered a baby under gunfire, I had my ABC's, but also a D, for deranged.

Overhead, I could hear helicopters. That reminded me of critical cases being airlifted out of hospitals, and I flinched. Was that happening to Tucker right now?

I searched the news and checked Twitter while I was on hold with Exploria.com, waiting for a "travel specialist" because apparently you can't change tickets online. It took so long for my phone to load websites, I wanted to rip apart the seat cushions in order to de-stress. I asked the driver, "Is everything okay at the airport?"

He turned down his music. The radio crackled. "Okay," he said.

"Okay at the *airport*. Could you check on the *airport?*"

"Airport." He pointed straight ahead, through the windshield.

"Airport. LAX. Is the airport O. K." I made the O and the K signs with my fingers, to emphasize my point.

"O. K." He made the circle with his fingers and tried to imitate the K, the index and third fingers extended and his thumb pressed in the V between them.

What was up with this language barrier. I took two deep breaths and reminded myself that it wasn't the driver's fault he couldn't speak English and that I couldn't speak his language. Swearing at him wouldn't help any more than kids yelling, "Ching Chong!" at me.

I couldn't use my phone to translate because I needed it for my tickets. That was why I'd requested the radio. I pointed at it. "News. Okay?"

"News," he repeated, struggling with the word.

"News. Now. Please. Okay?"

"News," he said, clearly not understanding.

How do you explain news? How do you act it out in charades? Did he need the radio for his work?

His call radio crackled to life, and he started talking back, not in English or French, so I left him alone.

What's happening to you, Tucker?

I had to know if he was okay.

I closed the too-slow browsers and flicked over to the Finding Friends app. It reloaded. *Come on, come on.*

The driver was laughing now. Unreal. Why was he happy? What is this thing called laughing? Post-traumatic stress makes you feel like you're in an alternate universe, segregated from the rest of humanity. They're taking pretty photos of their food, and you're obsessed with breathing tomorrow's oxygen.

I forced myself to breathe today's oxygen and wait for Tucker's light to come on.

It did. He was at the airport. Same spot.

That was good, right?

Unless he was dead. That wouldn't be good at all.

Don't jump to conclusions, Hope. Just because he's not moving doesn't mean he's dead.

Yes, but you can't get to him because you're stuck in traffic with a driver who doesn't understand you.

Now I was doubting myself. I rubbed my bare thighs with my palms—suddenly, I was freezing—and clenched and unclenched my hands until I finally spoke to a woman with a Southern accent at Exploria.com. Success! I could change my ticket for a mere $275. After I accepted the usurious rate, I glared at the traffic boxing us in.

What would James Bond or Jason Bourne do?

I rolled down my window.

It was winter, even in L.A. Everyone else had theirs rolled up, but I waved at the driver in the white car across from me. "Hey!"

He rolled down his passenger window, revealing a young, black man wearing sunglasses. It was hard to tell what he was thinking. He nodded at me. "Hey, shawty. What's happenin'."

"Is everything okay at the airport? Have you heard anything?"

He frowned at the panic in my face. "Everything's okay."

"Can you check the radio?"

"Everythin's ooooooo. Kay." His window rolled back up.

I squeezed my fists hard enough that my nails cut into my palms. It was better than howling like a frustrated werewolf, but only just.

Smoggy air dried out my contact lenses. I didn't care. I'd rather feel pain than feel nothing.

My taxi driver rolled up my window and started whistling tunelessly.

Do not kill him. Do not.

3

By the time I sprinted to the Avian Air counter, my backpack banging against my vertebrae, I was sweating again.

The good news was, the airport seemed just as I'd left it: giant, sunlit bays jammed full of people and their rolling suitcases, with prominent signs directing the flow of humanity through its walls.

No one was fleeing. No one was bleeding.

I approved of that part. Well, except for the fact that my previous taxi paranoia now made me look like an overreacting, PTSD maniac.

I avoided bashing into a twenty-something woman fixing her makeup in the middle of the hallway while I texted Tucker.

I'm lining up for my ticket!

No answer. Not even the dot dot dot showing that he was writing back to me.

I inhaled, exhaled, and spoke to the sixtyish woman in front of me. "Hi, did you hear anything about a disturbance going on at this airport?"

"A disturbance," she repeated slowly. She had a short pageboy haircut, a stocky build, and what sounded like a Russian accent. "I don't know what you are talking about."

"Like, did you hear that something bad is happening here at LAX? This airport?"

She shook her head and spoke to the woman in front of her, in their language, while shooting me disapproving looks.

Crap. The wait dragged on even longer with every Russian head shake. I could ask the young, brown guy behind me, but he had his headphones on and his face down, and the last thing I needed was someone alerting the TSA that an Asian chick required extra security harassment. I'd already spotted one officer with what looked like a taser on his belt, talking on his radio.

Where are you, Tucker?

No answer. Well, the Finding Friends app showed him at the airport. That was a relief, although I'd have to recharge my phone. I was already down to 41 percent, and I had to show them my e-ticket before my battery died.

That meant choosing between supervising Tucker's dot and making sure I had access to my e-ticket. Internally, I cursed all that was good and holy, including snowflakes and homemade hot chocolate. Then I turned off my phone and breeeeeeeeathed while waiting in line for another five minutes.

Make that ten.

Jesus God. I know I don't believe in you, but if your birthday is coming up, how 'bout speeding this one up?

I tried not to think about how I'd almost lost Tucker. First during the hostage taking, second from a post-op infection, and third when Montreal doctors had played cautious about reconstructive surgery, and Tucker jetted off to L.A. Full disclosure: he probably took off faster because I was juggling him and Ryan, so our reunion was not guaranteed sunshine and cotton candy.

I finally bounded toward the agent, a Latina woman who seemed 27 years old, same as me, only she was trying to look older with her tight bun and navy uniform. I showed her my e-ticket and passport.

She clicked on her keyboard. Her bright red acrylic nails matched both her lipstick and the scarf twisted around her neck. Then she paused and frowned.

Uh oh.

"What is it?" I said, through dry lips. "Is there a problem with the flight? Or the gate?"

"No, it's ... " She held up a finger and spoke on the radio in a low voice. When she saw me trying to read her lips, she turned her back on me.

I bounded up and down on my toes before I caught myself. Something was happening. The woman with Tucker had screamed for a reason, and the gate agent knew why.

I wanted to snatch back my phone, which was resting on the counter, but even upside down, I could tell that Tucker hadn't messaged me back.

I should have skipped out on my stem cell research rotation as soon as Tucker took off for L.A. I would have failed that block—I've missed too much work, because of all the killers I've run into—but who cared? Instead, I'd failed Tucker.

I needed Tucker.

The agent stopped murmuring into the radio and turned around with a fake smile before she tapped her keyboard again. "Don't worry. Everything should be cleared up by the time you go through security."

"What happened?"

A flush tinted her cheeks. She printed out my boarding pass and shoved it toward me. "Nothing to worry about. The police have it under control."

"I was talking to my friend at the gate, and there was screaming."

"It's under control," she repeated loudly. "Go to Gate 68A, and everything should be fine. They'll take you to the remote gate by bus."

"What?"

She sighed and glanced at the Disney World-worthy lineup gathering behind me. "Just go to Gate 68A."

I didn't budge. "Was anyone hurt or killed?"

"Of course not. I'm going to have to ask you to keep your voice down, ma'am."

I understood the threat underlying her ultra-polite words. People

have been tased at airports for belligerence. A man died at the
Vancouver airport after he got tased and went into an arrhythmia.

I snatched the boarding pass, my phone, and my passport and
wound my interminable way through security. Since I only had my
backpack with a laptop, some clothes, and an empty steel water
bottle, it was maddening to watch other people protest taking off
their jacket for the X-ray. One old couple, both in wheelchairs, had
brought a bottle of medicinal oil that held up the entire line.

"'Courage,'" I muttered through my teeth, recalling a Bethany
Hamilton quote. She was a professional surfer who'd jumped back on
the waves post op after a shark chewed away her left arm. "'Sacrifice,
determination, commitment,'" I chanted as I finally cleared security
and dashed past the duty-free goods, ignoring the strange look from a
woman holding three boxes of perfume. "'Heart, talent, guts. That's
what little girls are made of.'"

Not that I was a little girl anymore, but I used to be one, and I was
building myself back up into a woman to be reckoned with.

The ticket agent had claimed everything was okay *(Ohhhhh. Kay)*,
but dread dragged my heart. Tucker and I kept missing each other,
whether it was the hostage taking, my work, his health, or my other
man. I had to find Tucker. I had to tell him that I loved him, in
person, even if he laughed and flew away from me.

"I love you," I whispered to myself. I was practicing, basically, in
between repeating to myself, "'Courage, sacrifice, determination,
commitment.'"

Please don't sacrifice Tucker.

Sacrifice the woman who was screaming instead.

It's terrible, the arithmetic you do when someone you love is in
danger. It means that you'd rather anyone else got hurt in their place.

I was running again. Gasping. My backpack thumped against my
lumbar spine.

The woman's scream replayed in my mind on a continuous loop.

Who screams like that? Nobody.

And who ignores his cell phone? Not Tucker.

What happened? What happened?

Of course 68A was at the end of the corridor. I dodged people holding lattes, a beeping cart for passengers who couldn't walk, and a slow-moving Segway.

Now I could see scads of people bunched up at gate 68A, including three wearing black uniforms. I bolted toward them with my arms in the air.

4

An officer who was about my height moved to block me. I'm only five foot two and a quarter, but he looked pretty ripped, and he had a police baton and a taser on his belt, so I wasn't going to mess with him. Except with words. "This is my gate."

"We're clearing the area. Stay back, miss."

At least he called me miss. I craned my neck. Hard to tell with the horde of people held ten feet from the nucleus of the disturbance, but I glimpsed Tucker's blond hair behind the throng. He was even easier to spot with the number 42 on both sides of his shirt.

Tucker was alive. That was the first thing I drank in. He was alive, and breathing, and talking to an older, male cop.

Thank you, Jesus, Yahweh, and Flying Spaghetti Monster for keeping him safe. I am not religious, except when it comes to survival. Then I'll take anything.

"What happened?" I asked the officer beside me.

He looked uncomfortable. His badge said "airport police," which wasn't the real LAPD, as far as I knew, but both possibilities made me swallow what little saliva I had left. Real cops have saved my life multiple times, but the real LAPD beat up Rodney King, and pseudo cops can be even more dangerous with more attitude and less training.

My airport cop said, "One of the passengers created a disturbance. He had to be ... contained."

Had Tucker fought with that passenger in order to "contain" him? Right after abdominal surgery, he shouldn't fight anyone. His sutures and staples could rupture.

Tucker, you idiot. You beautiful idiot.

I spoke fast. "My friend—the one in the 42 shirt—called me. A man came up, and a woman screamed."

The airport cop ignored my play by play. He said, "Stay here."

The crowd shifted. I saw that Tucker had taken the time to gel his blond bangs straight up. Good. He'd stopped hair styling when he was super sick in hospital. This Tucker wasn't bleeding, he wasn't hyperventilating, and he'd gelled his hair. The Tucker triad of health.

Then a man bellowed, "No!"

That man was probably 78 years old and bent over like the letter C, but still plenty big. I'd say over five foot eight and 200 pounds. Not to be trifled with.

The crowd scattered, only to snatch their phones and start filming.

Tucker walked toward him with his hands in the air. "Mr. Yarborough, everything is fine."

My cop strode toward the action, and I followed in his wake. There was no way I'd leave Tucker alone with a crazy old man, surrounded by pseudo cops with tasers.

"Excuse me," I said to a tiny, white woman with even whiter hair. She wouldn't budge, even though she hadn't figured out how to work her camera yet.

"I was here first," she said.

"I'm a doctor," I snapped, and she stepped aside.

The old guy backed up, away from the crowd and the two other cops. He was unshaven with tufty grey eyebrows. He looked like a tottery silverback gorilla, if gorillas wore suspenders.

"We've talked about this, Mr. Yarborough," said Tucker. He was calm enough that the crowd, including the cops, hovered instead of jumping in. "You're fine right here. You can't go back into security."

"They took my bottle!"

"Your water bottle was full. They had to take it."

"No!" The gorilla shoved through the crowd, stumbling at me.

Tucker twisted toward me, his eyes widening with a mix of thrill and horror.

Not exactly how I planned to make my L.A. debut with him, but *tant pis*. The rest of the crowd fell back. I didn't.

Neither did the airport cops. A female cop widened her stance and placed her hand on her taser. "Stay right where you are, Mr. Yarborough."

The male cops flanked her.

That horrible scream seared the air once more. A broomstick-thin old woman flung her ring-laden hands toward the sky, as if her gnarled fingers could halt the flow of electricity. "No, please don't!"

My cop shouted, "Stay back."

"He just wants his water bottle. Please!" the old lady called.

"Stay back!"

"He has dementia. Please don't shoot him! Harold!"

The other male cop said, "Stand back. Clear the scene."

"Out of the way!" yelled my cop.

This couldn't be happening.

Female cops are less likely to shoot. This guy wasn't harming anyone. He was an old, white man, which is a less-fired-upon demographic. And the scene wasn't "contained." There were too many of us within firing distance.

"No one has to be hurt. This is your last warning," said the female cop. She lifted the taser out of the holster and levelled it at him.

This is happening.

Tucker caught my eye. His thighs tensed. He was about to spring in between the old man and me.

5

If Tucker got tased—if she shot him with 50,000 Volts at 180 feet per second, so soon after the surgeons had sutured his bowels back together—anything could happen.

I couldn't have her tase the old man or woman into ventricular fibrillation, either.

Yet I didn't dare leap in front of them as a human shield.

You're not supposed to die from a taser. It delivers an agonizing electric shock by shooting wires that hook on to your body. Your body completes the circuit. Your muscles lock up. You may wet or crap yourself.

The pain is only supposed to last five seconds before you recover. The problem is, the old, the sick, and the drugged-out people are the least able to fight off a tase or two. Over a thousand Americans have died after a police taser.

How could I stop the airport cop from tasing one of us, without endangering anybody?

How could I halt a demented old man in his tracks?

Begging and pleading and screaming wouldn't help. It might enrage any or all of them.

I couldn't make any sudden movements, or they might tase me.

I racked my brain. What did I know about dementia? Not a lot. They like familiar people and surroundings. They have better long term memory than short term memory. And ...

I started to sing "Give Peace a Chance."

Everyone stared at me.

We don't know why, but demented patients remember music after they've forgotten their own names or how to comb their hair. Still, put on some Beatles, and they'll chime in on the chorus better than the average millennial.

I prayed that Harold could remember "Give Peace a Chance."

My voice cracked, but I didn't need to be fancy. I only needed to be recognizable to a demented man.

The female officer's eyes flicked toward me.

Come on. Don't you know this song? It's on constant replay at Christmas. They even did a remake with Sean Lennon.

Harold Yarborough paused with his fists still bunched up, his mouth hanging open.

I only knew the one line, pretty much, so I sang it again. Once a fellow med student had told me that I looked like Yoko Ono. Maybe it would help.

I beseeched Tucker with my eyes, and he joined in.

I felt my shoulders relax. My voice grew stronger, merged with his.

Our gazes fused together. I hadn't laid eyes on Tucker in weeks. It was the first time we'd sung to each other, and I could feel the melody resonating in my chest before it floated through the airport bay.

A few passengers turned their phones on us like we were a pop-up flash mob instead of two people trying to save an old man.

Harold Yarborough's mouth opened.

The female officer tensed, taser ready. Their radios crackled.

Then Harold started to sing, too.

He was slow. He was off tune. He fumbled the words and rhythm. But by God, he was singing. And no one was going to shoot this old, white man singing "Give Peace a Chance" on Christmas Eve, in front of a dozen cameras.

The officer lowered her taser.

We sang the line twice more, and then Tucker and I stopped. I was still breathing hard. My chest heaved.

Harold kept singing, off-key and alone, before he paused, still confused, but the energy had shifted. He was puzzled, and the officers were wary but not angry.

I exhaled, and for the first time since I landed in L.A., everything really was Ooooooooooh. Kay.

Tension seeped out of my body. I could have laid down on the cool tile floor for an hour, waiting for my heartbeat to return to normal.

Except for one thing. My skin prickled. Tucker's eyes flamed at me from six feet away, eyebrows drawn together, mouth tight with concentration. Without him saying a word, I knew what he was thinking: *You are brilliant, and I want to rip off your clothes.*

I allowed myself a tiny smile and a wink, because I was thinking the exact same thing.

The rest of it was noise. The police officers gathered all of us in for a debriefing of sorts (*Who are you? What were you doing? How dare you interfere? How do you spell your name? We need to ask you more questions. Spell your name again*). But all I could see, and feel, was Tucker.

Tucker's looks don't hit me in the stomach, the way Ryan's do, but his face is more friendly. Approachable. Guy next door. His mouth's a little big, in more ways than one. His upper lip is a bit thin, and now that he was post op, not only were his T-shirt and jeans on the baggy side, but his cheeks looked a bit gaunt, which hurt me.

And yet when he smiled, nothing and no one else in the world mattered to me.

Tucker and I have done many things, but at this moment, simply standing next to him was foreplay. Even though we were inches apart, the heat from his skin and the intensity of his gaze made me blush and struggle to focus on his words.

"Mr. Yarborough wanted his water bottle," said Tucker. "He couldn't accept that the security officers had thrown it away. It had sentimental value because his daughter, Kim, had given it to him.

When they called him to the desk, he tried to go back for his water bottle. He grew quite combative—"

"I tried to stop him," said the old lady. Now that I could breathe again, she looked to be in her sixties or seventies. She was about five foot four, with excellent posture, wearing some sort of drapey black tunic and those enormous rings. Seriously, one ring looked like 24 carat gold, with a ruby bigger than one of my nostrils.

"Yes, Mrs. Yarborough did her best. But he was ... quite insistent." Tucker looked at me as if he knew I could be insistent, and he was looking forward to me begging.

I didn't realize I'd licked my lower lip until Tucker's eyes zoomed in on it, and I had to snap my mouth closed.

"He knocked over luggage. He threw a bag at the counter," said the female officer.

"Yes, but he didn't hit anyone!" said Mrs. Yarborough. "Please, officer. He wouldn't hurt a soul. We're trying to visit his daughter for Christmas in Montreal."

"Kim," Mr. Yarborough put in.

The officer shook her head. "The counter agent had to call for help. We had to clear the scene."

"No one was hurt," said Mrs. Yarborough. "It was our bags he was throwing. If there are any damages, I'll pay for them. Please, officer."

"I have to file the report."

"By all means." Mrs. Yarborough cast anxious eyes on the female officer, who stepped into the corner to talk to yet another officer.

I reached for Tucker's hand. I thought that was legit. Even the Beatles wanted to hold hands, to make another retro music allusion, and I couldn't stand not touching him.

He grasped my fingers and squeezed. No hesitation, no pulling back, no self-consciousness that we were in front of a crowd who might still be filming us.

This is what Tucker would be like in bed. Uncompromising.

His grip loosened so that he could caress the edge of my hand with his fingertip. Such a small thing, but I sank my teeth into my bottom lip.

" ... right, Doctor?"

Doctor. That snapped me out of my sexual haze. Someone was either talking to me or Tucker. "Yes?"

The older male police officer, the one with grey hair, gazed at me with deep suspicion. "You'll sign a report?"

"Oh, absolutely. I can do that right now, if you want."

They produced a whack of papers. Tucker and I sat down next to each other with our forms while the Yarboroughs continued playing 200 Questions with the officers.

"Officer, I assure you, I'll take wonderful care of him," said Mrs. Yarborough to the female officer, who had rejoined them, along with a fourth airport cop. "I already do. I take care of all his meals, all his cleaning, all his bills and all his pills—why, he barely makes it to the bathroom without me! And sometimes, not even then!" She nodded and winked at the officer, like that was a great joke.

I looked up from my form. Every officer looked repulsed, as would anyone who doesn't wear a diaper.

"It's because we're at the airport. He's fine at home. We're going to have so much fun in Montreal at Christmas. They have the best food. It's the gourmet capital of North America."

I was impressed that Montreal's culinary reputation had reached Los Angeles.

"So," said Tucker. His knee pressed against mine. He was not contemplating Montreal bagels.

"So." I couldn't look at him. My cheeks were already incandescent. I would lose it in front of everyone.

"All this paperwork is going to delay our flight. I heard them talking about it. Our flight is already complicated because it's at the west gate, with the bus—"

"What is that, anyway? I thought they said remote gate, but I had no idea what they were talking about."

He waved his hand. "Same thing. It's the overflow part of LAX, on the western side of the airport. They hardly ever use it except for parking overseas aircrafts between flights."

"So why are we ... "

"Because it's Christmas. Everyone's winging around the world to eat turkey with Grandma right now. They're using every section. They'll load us on a bus and take us to the west gate, or remote gate. No big deal, except it was one thing too many for Mr. Yarborough."

Poor Mr. Yarborough.

"The bottom line is, I figure we've got minimum twenty, thirty minutes before they sort this out." His knee burned against mine.

My heart hammered as I leaned in toward him. "You sure we're not going to miss our flight?" I'd do anything for this guy, but I didn't need to pay for a whole other thousand dollar flight when we could join the Mile High Club instead.

He gave a low chuckle. "Nah. Marina will text me if our plane boards before then."

I frowned. "Marina?"

He nodded at the agent at the desk, a brunette cheerleader type who grinned back at Tucker from behind a line of angry customers.

I ground my teeth together. Of course Tucker had not only prevented a demented old guy from decapitating people with his luggage, he'd also made friends with the perky ticket agent who filled out her navy uniform better than I would've.

"Hey, I wanted to get to you as fast as possible. Making friends is free, right?"

I checked his face out of the corner of my eyes, too embarrassed to face him head on. "Sorry."

"It's okay, Buffy. I like you jealous and possessive. Puts us on equal footing." He put down his pen. He'd managed to fill out his form by writing big and messy.

"Just a minute," I said. I'd listed out my name and contact information. I didn't have much to add in my statement, since all I'd done was show up and sing.

"That was very impressive, by the way," he said, as I signed the bottom of the last page.

I gazed up at him.

"How you saved that guy's life. I thought I was going to have to tackle him, or take the tase for him—"

"Don't even joke about it."

"—But you came and defused the whole sitch. You're like an evil genius."

Evil? Genius? I burst out laughing. After all this foreplay in front of the airport police, who were finally letting the Yarboroughs go, he was equating me with Dr. Evil?

"An extremely hot, sexy, formidable genius."

This time, I gave him my best attempt at a smolder. "Prove it."

6

As soon as we hustled out of eyesight of Gate 68A, I stopped and wrapped him in my arms. I could feel his heart banging against mine, shielded by ribs and muscle and pericardium.

"I love you," I mouthed against his chest.

Saying the words, knowing he might not say them back, hurt. But we were alive. Alive, alive-o. I had to tell him the truth right away, even if it flayed me.

I could feel his lips move on my hair, whispering the same thing back to me, as if the words were nearly too precious to release into the air.

Tears stung my eyes. I both do and don't like being mushy after 14/11. I had to tell him how I felt, because otherwise, when the planet exploded in a ball of hydrogen in 2.2. seconds, I'd regret it. Yet it was almost too much, too rich, to hold him now. I peeled my mouth away from his skin enough to peer up at him. "You couldn't get operated on in Canada, eh?"

He slanted a smile and tilted his head down to kiss me. "God, I missed you, Hope."

I pecked him back, suddenly shy, but he leaned into me, stronger than ever, and somehow, his mouth tasted like summer rain before it devolved into something spicier. When he took a moment to breathe, I tucked my face into the spot where his shoulder met his neck and muttered, "Me too." My hand brushed against the numbers on the back of his shirt, which gave me another excuse to change the subject. "What's with the number 42?"

"It's the answer," said Tucker.

"To what?"

"To life, the universe, and everything."

That rang a bell. I'd never read Douglas Adams, but I'd heard of that quote. And right now, Tucker was my life, my universe, and everything.

I hid my face in the crook of his neck again. I blinked away some more tears. Then I inhaled his skin and kissed the curve of his neck before I licked it.

His hands seized my shoulder blades. He exhaled, and I could feel the tension in every part of his body.

I was glad. Sex was easier than love. "Do you know any good hiding spots?"

He touched my hair. "Nowhere that's as good as you deserve, but..."

"Yeah," I said. Words. No good no more.

He grinned at me. "Give me your phone."

I didn't know why he wanted my precious iPhone, or why he was delaying our hook up, but I handed it to him.

He handed it back. "Unlocked, if you please."

I punched my passcode in. It's a long one, in case I lose my phone and accidentally have any patient information on it. I offered it back, eyebrows raised. It was sexy to have Tucker take charge. I licked my lips.

He flicked his way through my phone alerts and made sure it would ding and vibrate if I got a text. "So we don't miss the plane," he said, and he took my hand. His were warm and not sweaty. In other words, perfect.

I tried to be thoughtful too. He was only wearing a backpack. I said, "Do you have a suitcase?"

"I checked it. Let's go."

I lingered a little behind him, taking deep breaths. I wanted to do this. It was time to do this. I sent a quick mental apology to Ryan. *We who are about to fuck, salute you.* And then I followed Dr. Tucker into what turned out to be the family bathroom.

Bathrooms don't turn me on. Family bathrooms especially, with their built-in change table and their urine smell. The lockable door, though? Genius.

Tucker unzipped his backpack, whipped out a fat, pink candle, and set it on the edge of the sink.

"A candle? Where did you—?" Where did he have time to find a candle, in between catching a plane and battling a lost, old man?

Instead of answering, he struck the match on a folded matchbook cover. Scritch. The flame caught, casting a warm, yellow light on the room.

"You can't bring matches on the plane," I said. My voice echoed off the grey tile walls. It sounded hollow, like my resistance. I relished the smell of wax as the candle caught, flickering its light on both of us. I was smitten with this man.

He propped his phone on the counter, behind the faucet. It started playing "I'm in the Mood," by John Lee Hooker.

I burst out laughing. "Tucker—"

He kissed me. Now the spicy taste of his mouth was stronger, almost like pepper. I liked it. It reminded me of him. Edgy, unpredictable, a little wild.

Then he turned off the lights and started stripping off his clothes in the glow from the candle and his phone. Shirt, pants—always a problem to do it gracefully, when you've got to get them off your feet, and they get stuck on your socks, but somehow, he managed.

I found myself reaching for his belly, careful to avoid his bandages, as if I could heal his scars with my fingers. He pushed my hands south, humming along to the song, and I laughed.

I'd imagined sex with Tucker hundreds of times, but I never expected this.

He tugged the edge of my shirts. I threw my arms over my head to make it easier for him to pull them both off at the same time.

I knew we shouldn't get naked for sex in a public place. I've heard enough war stories to know that you should leave your clothes on so that you can make a quick getaway. Yet Tucker had created the opposite vibe with his candle and music. He could create romance out of a cube of bouillon and a piece of string.

He wrapped his arms around me so closely that I could feel his heart beat against my bra-clad chest as he breathed in time with me.

He made it sacred.

Even so, when his hands stirred and he stripped me completely naked, except for my socks, my first instinct was to step back and cover myself up.

This proved impossible when Tucker applied his mouth between my legs. I always feel a bit awkward about this, like I'm too exposed, but the man knew what he was doing, so I leaned against the cool plaster wall and let him do his work until I was a gasping, shuddering mess.

I took a deep breath. I started to drop to my knees to return the favour, but Tucker grabbed my arms to keep me upright. He lifted me up, pressing my back against the wall, and even though I knew he shouldn't lift anything post op, let alone me, I automatically wrapped my legs around his waist as he sank into me.

He wanted to look into my eyes, and I wanted to look into his.

We had loved each other for so long. This moment was sacred, too.

Then he figured out *exactly* how to hit my G-spot. I threw my head back and tried not to cry out, especially after he bent forward to taste my neck. He drove so hard that my vision blurred. I thought I was on the ceiling for one glorious second.

Afterward, while my eyes refocused, he lowered both my feet down to the floor gently, so I wouldn't slip in my socks. I tried to sound coherent. "That was ... you're so ... "

He grinned.

"Are you okay? You're not supposed to lift."

He raised an eyebrow at me, only slightly breathless. "Never better."

I blushed.

He whipped off the condom. Somehow, he'd magicked one on without me noticing. And it didn't take him long to get ready for take two, especially when I got on my knees and did my best to apply the second condom with my mouth. That's harder than it sounds, no pun intended, but he enjoyed the effort.

He pushed me back against the cool wall as we faced each other, this time with both feet (mostly) on the ground, and I didn't care that someone had started shouting outside. If anything, it made us even crazier.

This time, I marvelled at the small things as well: the soft skin under his arm, his smell, the tenderness in his fingertips before he lost control and rammed into me. It was sex, but at the same time, it felt holy. Almost beyond words or thought.

When it was over, he said, "You're so beautiful."

I started crying. I couldn't explain it, but he didn't ask me to. He only smiled down at me and brushed my bangs out of my eyes with such gentleness, it made me cry harder.

Eventually, I wiped away my tears.

I would have gone a third time, but a woman on the overhead speaker intoned, "Attention, please. Attention."

I froze.

7

"We regret to inform you that all departures and arrivals in Terminal 6 will be delayed."

Tucker's hand stilled. I could feel each fingertip pressing into the skin on my side. "That's our terminal."

"Of course it is," I said. At this point, I'd be stunned if a natural (or unnatural) disaster occurred more than fifty feet away from me.

We both threw on our underwear. If we were going to die, we'd rather it wasn't buck naked. And I, for one, would not tend to gunshot wounds as a nudist.

Airport shootings happen. LAX had one in 2002 and another in 2016. But they beefed up their security since then. They're one of only two American airports with their own police force.

I remembered the police officer raising her taser, and I thought, *Maybe that's the problem.*

But they wouldn't delay the airplanes for another taser. This was something that had affected the entire terminal.

Still, I was calmer now that I was with Tucker. Even if we faced Armageddon, at least it was together.

"Please stand by for further details," intoned the overhead voice. Not very dramatic for Armageddon. Maybe it was something boring like high winds, but I wouldn't relax until I got level I evidence to that effect.

Tucker scrolled through his now-quiet phone, wearing only his black boxers. "Twitter hasn't picked up on this yet."

"Why don't you try Marina?" I said, less waspishly now that I'd finally had a taste of Tucker. I climbed back into my black star T-shirt and long-sleeved, V-necked cobalt shirt.

"Already tried," he said. "No answer." He grinned at me. "Love the shorts, by the way."

I smiled back at him. The first day we met, at resident orientation, I'd snuck in late, wearing red hibiscus board shorts, and he'd admired my legs. "Glad you noticed. But now that you've seen 'em ... " I unzipped my backpack, stuffed in the shorts, and grabbed a pair of mauve jeans.

"Boo," he said.

"You'll see my legs again." If I had to run onto the tarmac, I wasn't about to do it in shorts. There is a limit to vanity, especially mine.

"Yeah, but I want to see them all the time." He ran his hand down my ass and legs, undeterred by denim. "I waited forever for you."

"Less than six months." I donned my trusty red fleece jacket. Even less sexy than jeans, but the zip up pockets were big enough for my passport, wallet, and a pair of disposable gloves. I stopped carrying a purse in first year med school, when I had nowhere to lock it up in the change room during an anaesthesia elective.

"That's forever." He went back to his phone. "Wait, there's something here about a dog. Yeah, one of the pre-boarders on our flight had a dog. Maybe that's it."

I frowned. "A dog shut down the whole terminal?"

"Maybe if it ran onto the runway."

"Oh, no. There was a dog in New Zealand who wouldn't get off the runway." My throat convulsed as I tried to swallow. "They shot it."

Tucker's mouth flattened. "That wouldn't happen here. They love animals. Remember how Pink freaked out when they coloured horses with non-toxic chalk for a Selena Gomez video? They'd never shoot a pet on a runway."

"Yeah, but LAX is one of the busiest airports in the world. They're not going to stop long for a dog." I shouldered my backpack. "Let's go."

He kissed my ear and blew out the candle. The music had already been silenced. Our interlude was over. Chaos had begun.

Still, we stalked back toward the gate like we owned it. I'd found Tucker, we'd stopped an old guy from getting tased, and we'd ravished each other. Next stop: save a dog, save an airport—who knew?

Tucker kept refreshing Twitter, but I watched the people around us. If this ended up as a shooter scenario, I needed all senses on alert. I surveyed for sudden movements or bulky clothes that might conceal a weapon.

Although people looked annoyed as they scrolled their phones, no one was panicking. Yet most of the crowd flowed in the opposite direction, away from our gate, while Tucker bounded toward it. Who was the smart one around here?

I searched for cover in case of gun fire. I'd never realized before that airports have no place to shield yourself. It's designed for the free flow of people, not shelter from an active shooter. You could dive under rows of benches, but I wouldn't count on their flimsy metal and wide open spaces to stop a bullet. The walls on the tarmac side are made of glass. The hangar-like hallways are designed only for pedestrian traffic. The public bathrooms don't even have doors; you roll your suitcase behind curved walls that maintain privacy from peeping Toms, not assault rifles.

I kept my ears attuned for screaming or for any further announcements.

My nose twitched, ready for smoke or other suspicious scents. I wasn't a sniffer dog, but I'd do my best with my limited equipment.

I scanned the TV screens. They still broadcasted national news instead of actually, you know, informing us of what was going on in Terminal 6.

Tucker noticed the way I was casing the place. "We're going to be okay."

Why did everyone keep saying that? I glanced at him out of the corners of my eyes before I shook my head. There was no guarantee either one of us would make it out of LAX with our body and brain cells intact. Sure, 99.999999999 percent of people do, but that's not a hundred.

On the other hand, I shouldn't prematurely drag Tucker down. I forced a smile.

"I mean it, Hope. We've got this." He grabbed my hands, interlaced our fingers, and winked at me.

I pressed my lips together so hard, my bottom lip cracked. If two long-lost lovers finally hook up at the beginning of a movie, you know doomsday cometh. It makes for maximal emotional impact when you slam one or both of them down to the ground.

Tucker started singing "Give Peace a Chance," only he changed it to "Give Hope a Chance," which made me laugh out loud. Ah, the irony of someone named Hope not believing in hope, especially at this time of year. Game point: Tucker. He was so bizarre and cheesy, not to mention brave and tongue-meltingly good in bed/bathroom/beyond. I never knew what to make of him.

So I was laughing when we heard the distant sound of sirens.

And, being doctors, we both sprinted toward gate 68A.

Even if I fled, Tucker would blow me a kiss as he careened toward the sirens, the fire, and gunmen, so I matched him stride for stride.

Tucker's first target was the counter agent, Marina. As she spoke on the phone, she shook her head at both of us, although her glance lingered on me.

"It's not here," a short guy with intense brown eyes told Tucker. "I think it's at the west gate."

"Yeah? What's going on, Neil?" said Tucker. Of course he knew his name.

"All I know for sure is that they pre-boarded people from here. Loaded them on the bus and brought them over to the west gate. Maybe twenty minutes later, we got the warning that the terminal was shut down, and ten minutes after that, we heard sirens, same as you."

"They've blocked off all of the west gates," said a woman with a German accent, setting off a free-for-all.

"Because of the police!"

"Isn't it an ambulance?"

"I heard a helicopter," said a young woman with a Santa Claus hat atop her elbow-length, sleek black hair.

In other words, no one knew what was going on. I glanced out the windows while they speculated. No obvious sirens or emergency vehicles. The first guy, Neil, was right: gate 68A was dead, no pun intended. We needed to get to the action.

"We're doctors. We've got to help," said Tucker.

"They've got paramedics," said Neil.

Tucker ignored him. He cut to the front of Marina's line. I hung back while a few people whispered "Thank you" to me for singing to Mr. Yarborough.

Marina looked from Tucker to me, biting her lip. "There's nothing you can do now. They said it's too late."

"What happened?" Tucker demanded.

She lowered her eyes and touched the knot of the red scarf around her neck. She didn't want to tell us, but we carried the M.D. card, and she was in such distress, the words broke out of her throat. "One of our support staff ... passed away. A baggage handler."

"No!" called a woman behind us.

I sucked in my breath. We'd worked so hard to save one man from a taser, and now another man had died on our watch.

8

Tucker paced in the terminal.

Every so often, he'd check his phone, or pass by Marina's desk, but mostly, he paced.

He reminded me of this lion I once saw at a tiny zoo in Costa Rica. The lions were held in a grassy area no bigger than your average living room, with no place to hide from gawking humans. While the lioness lay down and stared back at us, the male lion paced the perimeter of the territory. He could not rest. He could not eat or lie down with our probing eyes latched onto him. He couldn't escape, either. So he paced.

I wanted to talk to Tucker the lion pacer. Mostly, I wanted to tell him that it wasn't his fault. If they'd already declared the baggage handler dead, he must have died in a pretty spectacular way. At first, Ontario paramedics weren't able to declare people dead unless the mechanism was obvious, like a beheading. L.A. paramedics might have more leeway to declare at the scene, but chances were, it was far too late for us to help.

The young, Santa-hatted woman cocked her head at Tucker and adjusted the cherry scarf around her neck. "What's wrong with him?"

"He wants to save lives," I said.

"But he wasn't even there. It was at the west gate, right? And he helped save that other guy."

I shrugged. "Doctors feel guilty about everything."

She pursed her Angelina Jolie lips. "I guess that's why I'm an actor instead." She tugged at the green minidress she was wearing over silver leggings and thigh high red boots. When she noticed me noticing, she said, "OMFG. ShapeR. Love it. Hate it. You know?"

"Yep." Shapewear's not my thing, but my mom wears ShapeR when she goes out with my dad once a year, to keep her tummy looking toned and her butt high. "You look amazing, though."

"Thanks." She flashed me a white-toothed smile. In L.A., even the average person on the bus was hot, so an actor was stunning. She looked like Santa reborn into a sexy young thing. "I wanted to look good for my ex. Plus, I heard Trina's on our flight. You know, the singer? I'd die to get in one of her videos. But this thing is killing me. I have to get it off before I'm stuck in it for five hours!"

We both burst out laughing, and I remembered how much I used to like talking to strangers. It cheers me up. I stopped doing it since 14/11, but here in L.A., maybe I could let down my guard.

Our laugh seemed to wake Tucker up. He marched to my side.

"They still won't let us on the scene," he said. "Hi," he added to the Santa ShapeR girl.

She shrugged and walked away with a little twinkling of her fingers.

"Their own doctors are probably on the scene now," I told him.

"Yeah, but they're not us! We might have been able to save him!"

We're resident doctors, formerly known as interns, licensed in a foreign country, who were having sex in a different part of the airport when he died. "You can't save the world, Tucker."

"You have," he said quietly. And then he started pacing again, along the window.

Bam. I'd prayed that Tucker had mostly escaped PTSD. He'd insisted he was fine, and I'd wanted to believe it. He'd appeared relatively unscathed compared to my misanthropic, panicky, I-hate-the-world, I-can't-even-eat-meat-anymore kind of post-traumatic stress.

Now I realized he'd overcompensated. Tucker had made it his mission to save every single person he met from any disease or discomfort.

In other words, he was as deranged as I was, and much more likely to fail. We made an incendiary combination.

I shadowed Tucker, pacing alongside him for a minute. I wanted to point out that he'd kill himself if he tried to save everyone. *It's too late to rescue the baggage handler. Why torture yourself? They have doctors in Los Angeles too.*

Was he worried that the baggage handler had died under suspicious circumstances? It was statistically unlikely. We should take comfort in that.

Yet I'd defied probability every other time I'd run down a murderer. If the poor baggage handler had been a victim, Tucker would never rest. My brain warped, imagining him as an actual lion, roaring with rage and leaping over suitcases until he'd dragged the killer away.

I stopped trailing Tucker and traced an R on the white plaster wall. I missed Ryan. He is sane. He detests death and drama. We could hit it and then he'd play video games while I'd cry with happiness over a Virtue and Moir video or force him to read *Sarah, Plain and Tall*. Ryan wouldn't obsess over not saving someone on the other side of the airport. Still, I couldn't text Ryan right after consummating my relationship with Tucker, even if that made no sense to anyone else. Instead, I beamed my thoughts toward my engineer in Ottawa. *I love you. I'm thinking of you. No matter what.*

Half an hour ticked by. In between pacing, Tucker scanned his phone and muttered things at me like "Someone took a picture. It looks like a body bag," or "Another ambulance showed up."

Even though I cruised Twitter too, I didn't find much except people posting holiday pictures and GIF's.

Tucker cheered up. "You should search for hashtags. #LAX is trending right now."

#LAX mostly netted me complaints about the delay. The glass half-full types (literally) took pictures of themselves at the airport bar.

Others moaned about family dinners they'd miss or the stockings they wouldn't fill. I also managed to hit a lot of ads.

Tucker cracked a smile. "Do you want to scroll through my phone?"

I took it, frowning. His was bigger and heavier than mine, but more importantly, he'd managed to filter out the junk.

#LAX RUNWAY DOG (accompanied by a blurry photo of what did look like a dog on the runway, dwarfed by a plane)

    Trouble at #LAX. 1 fatality reported. Details to follow.

    Baggage handler reported dead at #LAX

    #LAX reports delays of 2-5 hours. #delayed #3bottlesdeep

"THESE ARE like newspaper headlines with no articles," I said.

Tucker laughed. "Yeah, totally. It does give you an overview of what's going on, though, right? I've been checking Facebook and Instagram too, and the LAX official Twitter account, and the police account, and the news outlets, but Twitter's the best of all of them."

I raised my eyebrows. "It's not telling us anything we didn't already know. Except the dog."

His grin widened. After a minute, I figured out it was because he was better at social media than me. Tucker's competitiveness was going to drive me berserk. Ryan never lorded his computer superiority over me, and I didn't brag about my medical prowess to him. We were a team.

Tucker and I were a team, too, but he wanted to lead the team. The problem was, so did I.

An old man's voice broke into my irritation. "Well, get me some more water, then!"

I locked on to the disturbance. The demented man and his wife, the Yarboroughs, were arguing at the window, her in a hushed voice, him at high volume.

"I gotta get out of here!" Mr. Yarborough stood up and jabbed his finger at the airplanes idling outside. "I got a plane to catch."

His wife held up the water bottle and pointed toward the fountain, obviously trying to distract him.

Tucker hustled to her side. Good. He was like a sheep dog. He needed to work, or he would go mad. He raised his eyebrows, silently asking if I wanted to accompany him to the water fountain.

I shook my head. I'd watch our backpacks and make sure Mr. Yarborough behaved. The old man had sat down at the prospect of water, so he seemed mollified for the next 60 seconds, but his wife could use an extra babysitter.

Two other people had joined us at gate 68A. One was a Pakistani-looking mother who'd sat down in the corner near a garbage can, with a scarlet poncho over her hunched shoulders, nursing her baby.

The other was a fat woman clumsily patting a grey, shaggy dog wearing a blue jacket. This dog was as big as Roxy, the affectionate Rottweiler that Ryan is fostering, but much fluffier. It reminded me of Farley, the dog in the For Better or For Worse cartoons, who was basically like a stuffed animal blown up to dog size.

Who were these newbies? Since Tucker was helping the Yarboroughs, I searched for a familiar yet knowledgeable face and landed on Neil, who was thumbing through his phone. "I thought you said they did the preboarding. Wouldn't these people preboard?"

Neil nodded. "They came back after the sirens. I guess the bus brought 'em back."

Curiouser and curiouser. "Did they just get here?"

"Maybe ten minutes ago."

Huh. I'd been too focused on Tucker the lion, who was now bounding back toward the Yarboroughs with not one, not two, but three bottles of water. When he handed me the third one, I didn't explain how I carry a steel water bottle to cut down on plastic; Neil was within earshot. "Thanks, Tucker. I heard the Yarboroughs were on the plane when the ... event occurred. Why don't we talk to them? They'll know what happened better than some randos on Twitter."

Tucker was going to investigate this death anyway. We might as well fact-check properly.

"You're right." Tucker hoisted both our backpacks from the chair, ignoring me as I swatted him away, whispering, "Don't lift!"

He was already calling out to the Yarboroughs, "Crazy that we're stuck here."

Mrs. Yarborough had sunk into a chair and pulled out her tablet while Mr. Yarborough guzzled his first bottle. She shook her head and glanced up from her screen. "You are absolutely right. Thank you for your help, Dr. Tucker."

"My pleasure," said Tucker. "Have you met Dr. Hope Sze?"

It felt eerily formal, like he was introducing me to his grandparents soon after we'd jumped each other. "Pleasure," I said.

"Call me Lena," she replied.

I still have trouble calling grown-ups by their first names, but I nodded. Tucker set our backpacks on the floor, and I smiled at him.

"It was so brave of you to sing." She folded her tablet in its embossed black case. "I said to Harold afterward, 'Now, that is one brave girl!' You make the perfect pair. Are you doctors at the same hospital?"

"Absolutely." Tucker switched on his nicest smile. "We're more worried about what happened on the runway just now. Did you see anything?"

"Not too much."

"Much!" echoed Mr. Yarborough.

We paused to see if he'd add anything, but that seemed to be it.

Mrs. Yarborough tried to touch her husband's shoulder. He twitched away from her, muttering under his breath. She explained, "He's angry because of the ruckus with the police and all the paperwork. We got on the bus and boarded the plane, and then we sat there for 30 minutes before they took us off again."

"Gosh, that's terrible. What happened?" said Tucker.

She frowned. "I'm not sure. Harold wanted his water bottle, so I was trying to persuade him that mine was as good as the one from Kim. Of course hers was a nice one, made out of glass, with a special blue plastic cover. I forget who makes them, but they're quite expensive."

Good Lord. We have a medical term for overly detailed conversation: circumstantial speech. What did a water bottle have to do with a dead baggage handler? Tucker managed to look interested, though, so I imitated him, right down to the head tilt.

"I was trying to figure out if I could get a new bottle online and have it shipped to Montreal. Then Kim could bring it right to the airport, and he'd be less upset."

Tucker maintained his smile. "So you didn't see anything?"

"No. Well ... " She glanced at the woman with the fluffy dog. "The animal caused quite a ruckus."

"What happened?"

"That woman lost control. It ran right onto the runway. She was screeching because it wouldn't come back to her. It was quite the scene." Mrs. Yarborough spoke with distaste, even though she had screamed during the taser incident. It was quite all right for her to yell when her husband was in danger, but not okay to "screech" when your dog might get run over by an airplane.

Still, she'd confirmed that the dog had run out on the runway. That was something.

"Can you give us any more detail?" Tucker said. "Did you see what happened to the baggage handler?"

"I'm afraid not. Harold knocked my tablet on the floor, and I had to tend to it. I'm having trouble turning it on. I can't check my orders. See?" She showed us her tablet's screen, which lit up, but as soon as she changed the angle, the screen blanked out. "I have to talk to one of my people in Shanghai, if you'll excuse me." She pulled out her phone and dialed. *"Ni hao.* Yes, Clinton. The warehouse didn't answer my e-mail. Did you ... "

Strange. She sounded completely in control. I wouldn't have pictured her freaking out if I hadn't heard her myself. It seemed like she was quite the businesswoman at work and a mess at home. I sympathized.

Tucker moved on to the dog woman. She was sixty-plus years old, 200-plus pounds, and my height, with a greying brown bowl cut and wrinkled white skin. Her bulk was emphasized by a green cardigan with a Christmas tree stretched across her chest and an elf embroidered on each lumpy pocket. She won the ugly Christmas sweater contest this year. She carried three bags, one in her left hand and two ringed around the right, the same arm as her leash. If you counted her dog, that was four "personal items." She studiously avoided eye contact.

The dog stared at me. It looked harmless, but I kept a few feet away. I have a healthy respect for dogs. I only trust Roxy.

Tucker beamed. "Everything okay with you and your dog?"

"Fine." The woman's lower lip jutted out. She was not attractive. I know that shouldn't matter, but she was a contrast to the tide of effortless youth and beauty of L.A.

Tucker bent over the dog before I could stop him. "He seems like such a good boy. What's his name?"

"Gideon." Her voice softened noticeably.

"May I pet him?"

"He doesn't like strangers."

But Gideon was snuffling at Tucker's closed fist, then licking him, and Tucker was laughing. "I love dogs. Our family dog died two years ago, and I miss him every day. We have a new one, but it's not the same."

I didn't know that. I stared at him.

"You're a good boy, Gideon," Tucker cooed. Gideon wagged his tail. Tucker added, "I wish I had a treat for him. It must be tough, waiting with a dog."

"I have liver treats," the woman said slowly. It was almost like she had a speech impediment. I had to listen more closely than usual. "I can't give him a lot, though. He might poop on the plane."

"Can't have that!" said Tucker. "Did you already give him some?"

Her head dipped toward her chest. "Well. I had to get him to come back."

"Where did he go?" Tucker sounded curious as he held Gideon's head with both hands and enthusiastically rubbed the fur around his ears.

The woman almost smiled, now that he was paying attention to her dog instead of her. "Well, he was ... exploring." She chewed her bottom lip and tugged on the leash, bringing Gideon closer to her. "I don't want to talk about it. I have anxiety."

"That's tough," said Tucker. "That's why you have Gideon, right?"

Although he was guessing, she nodded several times, as if he'd said something profound. "He's my ESA. I'd die without him."

European Space Agency? That couldn't be right.

"Emotional Support Animal," the woman explained.

Ah. That pinged a memory in my brain. Emotional Support Animals had made the news—and provoked outrage on Facebook—when someone ignored the rules and tried to sneak a peacock on board the plane, but this was the first time I'd encountered one at an airport. I don't get out much. However, I did know that most ESA's were *not* the equivalent of highly trained guide dogs. They were basically pets that made people feel better, and the ESA designation can be an excuse not to pay to store your animal in the plane's cargo hold. As long as you get a doctor to sign off on your letter—saying, for example, that you have anxiety—you're good to go.

Gideon stared at me before glancing at his owner. I got the feeling that he wasn't crazy about being in an airport, surrounded by strange people, smells, and noises. That made me edgy. He could probably feel it. I forced myself to relax and tune into the owner's complaints. "Even my brother told me, 'Gladys, don't bring 'im.' But I said, 'Lee, I have anxiety!'"

Now I knew her name. And her brother's name, for whatever that was worth. I glanced at the poncho mother with the baby. Even post-partum and sleep-deprived, I bet she'd make a better witness than Gladys.

Tucker soldiered on. "I hear you. Because you can't see anxiety, like a broken leg, people don't seem to understand it. They think that you're okay, even when you're not."

"Especially when I'm going on an airplane. I have anxiety!"

"So you had Gideon," Tucker prompted her gently.

"Yes! And the bus driver was giving me a hard time, even though I had all my papers and booked this flight six months ago. He didn't want Gideon on the bus. He kept asking me if Gideon was going to make a mess. I said, 'He's trained,' but he kept asking me anyway."

Tucker clucked and shook his head.

"He liked that woman's baby, and you know the baby is going to make a mess."

Tucker made sad eyebrows at her. He was good at it.

"But when we got off the bus, the bus driver was yelling at me, telling me that I had too many bags, and I wouldn't be allowed on the plane with four carry-ons. I said that Gideon was allowed to have carry-ons, too, and the driver got so mad, he was radioing people."

I bit back a smile. I could picture it.

"He made me so upset that I almost fell down the stairs, getting off the bus, and Gideon ran onto the runway!"

Pay dirt. Tucker's shoulders yanked to attention.

"I dropped all my bags. I was trying to pick up the stuff that fell out, and Gideon was running around, and the bus driver ended up calling up all those people, you know, the ones with the carts that move luggage?"

"The baggage handlers," said Tucker.

"The bus driver was shouting at them. 'Get that dog!' I told them that if they'd calm down, I have liver treats in my pockets, I can give them to him, but they were running and shouting and calling on their radios. It was making Gideon more and more upset. He ran under a plane and started barking at them whenever they got close."

I closed my eyes.

"The bus driver said he'd call the police and they'd shoot my dog. I started crying. Those baggage people were running and yelling at each other in Spanish, and one of them was scared of dogs, so he kept away, but the first one was diving at Gideon and trying to grab his leash ..."

My teeth clamped together. Poor dog.

"The bus driver ended up jumping in a baggage cart and trying to run Gideon down! I was screaming and chasing him, but you know, I can't run fast. I have osteoporosis."

Osteoporosis doesn't stop you from running, but I nodded anyway. *Keep talking.*

"What happened to him?" said Tucker.

"He came back to me," she said. "I knew he would. He loves me. I gave him a liver treat."

I cut in. "No, not Gideon. The baggage handler who died."

She stared at us with big eyes. "I don't know. I was trying to get on the airplane, I almost dropped my bags. No one would help me. It took me so long to get on the plane. I almost fell. And then they made me get off again!"

"Did you see anything?" Tucker pressed.

"Gideon was pulling."

"I mean, did you see what happened to the baggage handler? Were medics on the scene? Or even an ambulance?"

Her hand trembled as she moved to stroke Gideon. "I have anxiety," she whispered at him, and then she refused to say another word.

Tucker kept trying to talk to her. After more sympathetic murmurs, more sad eyebrows and zero information, I stood up, searching for the nursing mother. She'd been pushing a stroller and had been wearing a bright red poncho, so she should be easy to spot.

Yet her seat was now filled by a white mother and toddler daughter. The girl crawled in her mother's lap, dangerously close to showing off the pull-ups under her black and green skirt, as the mom struggled to blow a blue latex balloon. I frowned at the balloon, not only because of the latex, which is allergenic, but because air expands when you take off. That balloon might pop at a higher altitude, although maybe they'd throw it away before we boarded.

And then I glommed onto the baby mom. Her newly-donned khaki jacket hid her poncho, but she couldn't move too fast with a stroller.

The mother whirled around before I'd gotten within ten feet of her, placing herself between me and her baby. "What do you want?" She had a slight accent, but her intent was clear.

"Nothing." I was too startled to come up with a good answer. After she nodded and tightened her grip on the stroller handles, I added, "I was going to ask you a few questions."

She shook her head, a curt, angry movement. Her eyes burned at me, tearless and silent.

This was not the Hallmark version of a mother. This was a woman who was willing to fly solo, cross-continent, after delivering a baby. She was probably on her way to meet family over the holidays and was in no mood to talk to a nosy stranger. Maybe I should have waited for Tucker to charm her, but ten to one, she'd be even less likely to talk to a man. I opened my mouth.

She held up her hand. It trembled in the air, and I realized that not only was she furious, but she was afraid of me.

That was what made me let her go. I had spent too much of my time living in nightmares to create more for somebody else.

9

"That was useless," said Tucker, at 5:35, as we waited in line to board in Terminal 3. He stood so close that only I could hear him as the pre-boarders made their way on the plane.

I nodded. I got a thrill out of his voice in my ear. *My cochlea vibrates for thee.*

"Mrs. Yarborough didn't see anything. The dog owner only saw her dog. And the mother ... "

"She was scared of us." I frowned. I hadn't been good luck for mothers in labour recently. But this mother had already delivered, and her baby, swaddled up and sleeping, had looked small but healthy. There was no way I'd endanger this baby.

We stepped aside as Gladys and Gideon belatedly joined the pre-boarding line. He sniffed the air, and she struggled to rein him in, her bags swinging on her arms. I was surprised Tucker hadn't bought her a carry on and wheeled it on for her. He'd probably refrained only because that would violate the question, "Did you pack your own bags?"

An elegant black flight attendant reached out her hand for Gideon's leash, but Gladys shook her head, even though her own right arm stretched all the way in front of her, trying to restrain the dog. She almost dropped the bag she was holding in her left hand.

The guy in front of us, eyes shaded by a shabby red baseball cap, started talking on his phone. "There's a fuckin' dog getting on the plane. We're never going to get out of here. Yeah, it should be in a carrier. I don't know what people are fuckin' thinking nowadays."

The couple behind us sipped their coffee, their paper takeout bags crunching in their hands. How long was this pre-boarding going to take, especially with the Gladys and Gideon show? My backpack's straps cut into my shoulders. The laptop was heavy.

Tucker read my face and reached forward to grab the straps off my shoulders.

"I've got it," I said, shifting to the side and evading his touch.

"It's not true that I can't lift after surgery," he said. "I looked it up. It's not based on any randomized control studies—"

"Because they'd never do studies on humans post op and risk popping their sutures. That doesn't mean you should bench press."

He laughed. "Wrong muscle group."

"Right concept. *I* should carry *your* backpack."

"Over my dead body." He looked like he meant it.

I remembered him lifting me in the bathroom, and my cheeks reddened even as I willed them back to normal. "For the next six weeks, anyway. Then you can carry my backpack all you want."

His eyes glittered, no doubt picturing a thousand things he'd do to my "backpack," which didn't help my blushing situation. I've never felt so fiery in my life. I busied myself with buckling the strap across my hips so that Tucker couldn't yank my backpack onto his own shoulders out of sheer stubbornness, before I changed the subject. "By the time we land, we'll have more information about the baggage handler, if you still want to pursue that."

"I sure do." His expression turned grim again. Someone had died on his watch, which was completely unacceptable.

Gideon barked at one of the gate agents, who jumped.

The business class people shifted impatiently. Their carry-ons were already stacked on their rolling suitcases, and they held out their passports, ready to rock and roll.

"Excuse me," said a woman with a low, throaty voice, and everyone turned.

She swept to the head of the business line without asking for permission or forgiveness. She was even taller than most of the men, with such abundant yellow-blonde hair cascading down to the small of her back that I suspected extensions. Her oversized sunglasses slipped down her aquiline nose, revealing her arched eyebrows and on-point eyeliner. The stilettos alone added five inches in height. She was wearing an all white pantsuit that I would have avoided, for fear of a visible panty line, a period stain, or a stray dust ball, but of course she magnetically repelled any such evidence of human frailty.

A man trailed in her wake, talking on his phone. "Yeah. Yeah. I hear ya. Don't worry about it. Hang on, we're boarding." He had a New York way of dragging out his vowels. He was much less physically impressive than her, like a six instead of a nine on ten on the looks scale: short, stocky, skin spray-tanned darker than my own, thick lips, fake-looking black hair, but his massive sunglasses and black button down shirt probably cost more than my monthly salary.

I couldn't help wondering who they were and what they did. I don't have time to keep up with celebrity gossip. I've never watched the Kardashians. But these two looked like someone I should have heard of.

The Santa brunette, recently freed from her ShapeR imprisonment, raised her eyebrows at me, and I resolved to ask her later. No doubt she was much more plugged in than me.

Then I remembered that the guy beside me was a walking pop culture magnet. I tugged his hand.

Tucker shook his head even before I asked. "She looks familiar, though," he said under his breath.

Huh. Another mystery. I wished I could do something high tech like take a picture of their faces and run it through facial recognition software. Ryan could probably do it. He's a computer magician compared to me.

The blonde snapped her fingers. A slender young man hustled in front of both of them, carrying their bags plus three passports open to the correct pages. He murmured to the gate attendant.

"Hurry up, Alessandro," said the blonde.

Alessandro. Kind of like the Lady Gaga song. He was wearing a well-cut white shirt and silver tie, but the pants were a bit baggy on him, as if he'd lost weight. When he turned around to check the bags, I noticed dark circles under his eyes, even though his brown hair was beautifully highlighted, and his teeth and the whites of his eyes were clear.

There was something familiar about him. I found myself holding my breath, watching him more than Mr. and Mrs. Money.

"What is it?" Tucker said.

I shook my head. I wasn't drawn to Alessandro sexually. If anything, he gave me a flutter of alarm. "I don't know."

"Okay," Tucker said, but a crease remained between his eyes. He didn't like me staring at another guy. I refused to calculate what that meant for me and Ryan after we landed in Montreal. Instead, I took Tucker's arm, and he cheered up.

No one criticized Mr. and Mrs. Money or redirected them to the back of the line. The gate agent scanned the trio's passports and waved them through. They acted like king and queen of the world, and everyone reacted accordingly.

Mr. Money's aftershave was so strong, I could still smell the musk lingering in the air.

10

When we finally stepped on the plane, it was gridlocked. I heard barking ahead, and we only had one aisle, so it didn't take too many brain cells to figure out why.

I glanced at the people ensconced in first class, or whatever it's called when you only have two seats on either side of the aisle, so the dreaded middle seat doesn't even exist. I recoiled slightly from the Yarboroughs immediately on my left, in seats 1D and F. It felt like I couldn't get away from them, but she was only showing him how to tighten his seat belt. They weren't causing any trouble.

I told my heart to calm down and focus on something more important, like being able to afford first class when I'm 75.

The next passenger, to our right, must have paid for two seats, since his body overflowed from the window seat into the aisle one. He'd already put on his eye shades and slipped his ear buds in. Smart man.

Mr. Money was two rows behind the Yarboroughs, talking on the phone ("Yeah. Absolutely. One hundred percent") while flipping through a tablet that I bet he could hardly see from behind his sunglasses. He did the man spread, legs akimbo, taking up a few crucial inches of the aisle, so that people had to wheel their suitcases around his left knee.

In the window seat, Mrs. Money stretched her legs so far that she looked like she might encroach on the leg room of the passenger in front of her, even with the more generous proportions of upper class. Speaking of proportions, if she leaned forward, her breasts threatened to rub against the seat back of the woman in front of her.

Alessandro had established himself behind them. His laptop's background photo showed a line of baggage-laden people silhouetted against the sunset. He kept glancing at Mr. and Mrs. Money, waiting for their next order. He noticed me watching him and hastily opened a finder window.

Across from him was a very slender woman. Although most of her face was hidden behind her shades, I suspected she was lovely, with light brown skin and blonde-brown ringlets. She wore all-black, close-fitting, expensive clothes and a large opal between her breasts.

I shook my head. We were doctors earning a pittance on a resident's salary, and it felt like we'd never make it to first class. It sucks to be a student who won't even buy gum after a night shift of saving people's lives (I don't love gum, and it's overpriced at a hospital; I either brush my teeth or occasionally save candies from restaurants) while politicians and movie producers can assault women by day and make a trillion dollars by night. But I had my bae, or my boo, or whatever I was supposed to call Tucker now, and he was worth more than a trillion dollars. I grinned over my shoulder at Tucker, and he smiled back as we lollygagged our way to the cheap seats.

Maybe we could interview the Richie Rich later. If they'd preboarded at Gate 68A, they could've picked up on something that Gladys didn't. But how on earth were Tucker and I going to interview them when we were stuck in cattle class?

I heard a gasp, and even though I was short and five people back, I glimpsed some already-seated economy class people shying away from G&G. "Watch out for the dog!"

Gideon yanked his head to the right. Gladys tossed her non-dog arm into the air. One of her plastic bags nearly clipped the red ball cap off the guy's head.

"Hey, watch it!" he snapped. Americans are not known for quietly enduring insults. Well, I hear Midwesterners are polite to a fault, but not the denizens of L.A., or tourists, or anyone whose flight was delayed by two hours.

"Sorry," said Gladys. Her dog reeled her forward. She grabbed the nearest seat back to steady herself, but her hand accidentally twisted the hair of a businesswoman sitting in the aisle seat.

"Ow!" The businesswoman pushed the dog owner's hand away from her shiny, brown bob.

"Why do you have a dog here, anyway?" said the man in the middle seat.

"Gideon's my service animal," gasped Gladys.

Was an Emotional Support Animal classified as a service animal? I wasn't sure, but I belatedly remembered a really good one from a PTSD meeting. Ted was a cute, well-behaved yellow lab who wore a jacket identifying his role. He focused entirely on his person, a war veteran, for the duration of the meeting, even though we all smiled and cooed at him. Ted made us relax instead of worrying about how screwed up we were. Ted ended up helping everyone at that meeting. I have zero issues with real service dogs.

Meanwhile, Gideon's fluffy tail nearly swished the balloon girl in the face. To be fair, the girl had been rooting around on the floor, instead of buckled in her aisle seat, 14C, but she started to cry. Her mother heaved her into her lap, glaring at Gladys.

"I have—a letter," puffed Gladys. "I have—anxiety."

Hmm. I have anxiety, too. Should I have borrowed Roxy for my flight?

Next, Gideon sniffed a skinny boy, maybe seven years old, who was clambering in the aisle seat opposite the balloon girl. The mother reached forward, but not before the dog gave a good, sharp bark, and the boy gasped.

"He—won't—hurt you," said Gladys.

The mother embraced her son and started speaking to him in another language, like Spanish but not. Portuguese, maybe.

The father stood up, although he was hemmed in the window seat. "You need to control your dog," he said, his English slightly hesitant, but his anger evident.

"Gideon is—my service—animal."

"You need to control your service animal," said the father.

"Gladys, I can help you," said the flight attendant who waited ahead of us, mid-plane. She had plain but pleasant features, dark blonde spiral curls, and a low, gravelly voice.

Gideon barked.

"Just keep moving!" yelled a guy behind us.

Gladys waved her hand, dismissing the riffraff without turning around. It would have looked cooler if her bags hadn't fallen down her arms and banged against her own sides, making her say "Oof." She urged Gideon forward. "Go on, boy. Go on."

Gideon barked again.

"Do you need help with Gideon?" Tucker raised his voice, naming the dog and, ideally, calming down the mob.

"No. He only likes me," Gladys said, and so we inched our way forward. Somehow, it was worse when even my seat at the back of the plane was literally in sight, but we were hemmed in the aisle because of a human impediment.

"We're not going to leave for half an hour," said a woman behind me.

"Yeah! We were already late before this fatso and her dog—"

My hands fisted. Gladys was annoying me, too, but I whipped around and glared.

A line of fed-up travellers glared right back.

I couldn't figure out who had spoken, but their malevolence was clear. A chill snaked down my spine. They were pissed, and if they couldn't take it out on a fat woman and her dog, they'd make me their target. Anyone would do.

Tucker touched my shoulder. He didn't want me to get into fisticuffs with anyone. He called down the line, "Merry Christmas, eh?"

"Merry Christmas," Neil muttered, from where he stood near the Yarboroughs. Even he looked ready to stake someone.

I exhaled and counted the reasons why they were justifiably pissed. A demented man had attracted the police, a baggage handler had died, all the planes were delayed, and we'd scored the slowest-boarding plane of all time. But I was lucky to board the plane at all. I had to remember that.

"I'll take the dog," the throaty-voiced flight attendant was saying. "Excuse me." She grasped Gideon's leash.

"No. Gideon can't be away from me. Gideon!" Gladys screeched like the highest note on a rickety old piano.

The flight attendant's shoulders twitched. She took a breath, obvious through her thin, navy uniform, as she relinquished the leash. "Okay, then. But move along. We have people trying to board within 15 minutes."

"That's why I need extra time to board early. I have—anxiety." Although Gladys huffed a little, she spoke better at rest. That meant she seemed in no hurry to get to her seat.

The flight attendant manufactured a smile above her red scarf. "Let's keep moving, shall we?" She urged Gladys and Gideon forward. "These are your seats. Sir, could you stand up to let them in?"

"Thank God," someone murmured.

"God is dead," a man said behind us.

"No, He most certainly is not!" snapped the Portuguese woman, nearly clapping her hands over her son's ears.

When I whirled around, everyone was staring at a 20-something white guy whose T-shirt said Straight Outta Compton. His face was mostly obscured by brown, scraggly hair.

"But Mama—" said the Portuguese boy, in English, before his mother swiftly cut him off in their own language.

Compton gazed past people's heads at the back of the plane, oblivious.

Goose bumps rose on my arms. I don't like to be trapped in enclosed spaces since the hostage taking, and soon I'd be hurling through the air with a bunch of angry nutjobs.

Tucker kissed my ear. I shivered and rubbed the goose bumps, trying to warm up my flesh.

11

Two ice ages later, G&G settled into 16AB, with Gideon flopping onto what was supposed to be the leg room for three different people. The man in 16C already looked like he needed a drink.

I glanced at my ticket. I was 33C, whereas Tucker was 18A, the window seat in the second exit row. No doubt he'd worked his magic on a booking agent to get that choice arrangement. We'd spend the flight half a plane away from each other, with me ensconced directly in front of the toilets. "See you in six hours."

Tucker shook his head. "I'll follow you."

I smiled. Maybe he wanted to kiss me before takeoff.

However, when I stooped to stow my backpack under 32C, Tucker stuck his head in the little kitchen behind the toilets, at the very back of the plane. "Excuse me. Magda, right?" he said to the gravelly-voiced flight attendant, turning on the charm so widely that I could practically feel the blast of it.

Magda certainly did. She blinked and nodded.

"I had abdominal surgery, and my girlfriend flew to L.A. to be with me, but now her seat is here and I'm in the exit row."

Magda nodded and said softly, "This flight is sold out."

"Of course it is, because Avian Air does such a fantastic job. But I was wondering if you might be able to help us sit together. We're both resident doctors in Montreal. Maybe you've heard of her. Dr. Hope Sze?" I would have elbowed him if he hadn't just had surgery, but he prompted, unrepentant, "The hostage taking at the Montreal hospital last month?"

"Oh, my goodness. That was terrible. The woman who was in labour with a gun to her head—"

Lightning would have shot out of my eyeballs if I'd been a cartoon. People mostly respected my silence and PTSD and left me alone in Montreal, but Tucker had outed us for an airplane seat switch.

"—And you! You're a hero, Dr. Tucker."

"Dr. Sze did most of the hard work," he said.

His modesty inflamed Magda even more. "I didn't realize that she was—that you were ... and you're on our plane! Of course you have to sit together. Let me see what I can do for you."

"That's okay," I said, shoving my water in the back pocket of seat 32C.

"No. Absolutely not. You want to be with your hero, don't you?"

I glared at him. He smiled at me and all but batted his eyes at her. "Magda. May I call you Magda?"

"Of course." Her cheeks tinted a delicate pink.

"You are a rose among women. Dr. Sze and I have been apart for a month, and this would make our Christmas."

Her glow flickered. "I'm not sure I can find someone to trade with row 33. It might be easier if you moved to the back."

Of course it would. Toward the toilet seats.

Tucker's smile never wavered. "I don't care where I'm sitting, as long as it's with Dr. Sze." He squeezed my hand.

I squashed his fingers right back, hard enough to hurt him. He kept on grinning anyway. Dink.

After she hustled up the aisle, I shook my head at Tucker. "Never do that again."

"What?" he smiled back at me, innocent.

"Cash in on 14/11."

"All I did was identify us."

I eyeballed him. "No. She didn't recognize my name."

He waved his hand. "She needed a little help. As do we all. That's fine."

"That's not why we did it."

"Of course not. But listen, Hope, what's the point of us being separated for five, six hours when we could be together? Don't you want to be with me?"

"Of course. But not if—"

"And whoever we're trading with wants to make new friends. That's my favourite part of airplane rides, sitting with a stranger and ending up with a beer buddy in Kuala Lumpur. It's win-win!"

Yeah, right. We say we'd like to meet up on a plane, but what we really want is a neighbour who won't hog the arm rest, barf all over us, talk, drink, and/or play egregious music the entire flight.

"People are good, Hope. They want to help us. When they hear the news, they feel helpless. They're not the police, or firefighters, or hospital staff. They can't do anything. They feel impotent. But here's their chance to help a couple who's been through so much. And who doesn't want to help young love? I sure would, if I were given a chance. It's good karma! It'll come back tenfold."

"Excuse me." said a high, breathy voice from 33B.

My eyes widened. I couldn't concentrate on the woman's cute little brown pixie cut, fawn-like brown eyes, or the D cups she displayed under a white mesh top, because ... what was up with her nose?

It was too small. Sounds ideal if you've been bugged about your too-Asian nose your whole life, as I have, yet the mini bump in the centre of her face made her nostrils look gargantuan as she whispered, "My name is Topaz. I couldn't help hearing what you had to say about karma. That was beautiful."

Oh, no. Brains to match the nose. I tried to smile, but probably looked more like a psychopath imitating a normal human expression.

Tucker, however, beamed his delight upon Topaz. "I'm so glad you understand."

"I always think it's important to increase your karma. My guru says it's like a bank account, almost? Like, you have to make a lot of deposits, because you never know when there will be a withdrawal? Good karma, good karma. He's always talking about that."

My temples started to pound, but Tucker said, "Cool. Who's your, ah, guru?"

Her dark eyes lit up, and her slim body angled toward him. "Devaguru. You've heard of him? His website got a million hits last month."

"Congratulations," said Tucker. "No, I've never heard of him, but he has an interesting name."

"It means teacher of gurus."

Dear Lord. What an egotist. I heard L.A. was flaky, but I couldn't believe when she followed that up with, "I can see your aura."

"Oh, yeah? What's it telling you?" He sounded genuinely interested.

"You've been through a lot of turmoil."

No shit. He'd just told Magda that we'd been through a hostage taking, and that he'd had surgery.

She kept holding his eyes with hers and talking. "That's the dark part of your aura. But you're very ... vigorous."

OMFG.

"I see red and orange—"

"Vigorous. That's me," said Tucker, squeezing my hand again. I snorted audibly.

"—but there's a lot of danger. I think it's ... " Her eyes shifted over to me. "Yes. Your girlfriend is swimming in darkness. Lots of passion, of course. She's as passionate as you are—"

I gave a curt nod. She'd acknowledged me as his equal.

"—but she's in trouble. It's almost like she's ... " She hesitated.

I didn't want to hear any more. I cleared my throat. "I feel fine."

"—cursed."

Screw you and your miniature nostrils. One at a time. Full frontal. On HDTV.

"That's why I have to sit with her," said Tucker, also unamused.

Topaz surveyed him over her mini nose. "Of course. That's what I was going to say. You should sit together. You can have my seat."

"He can?" The words leapt out of my mouth. I regretted staring at her nose.

"Oh, yes. He should protect you from ... " She glanced up above my head again. "Fire. I see fire coming for you."

I was almost willing to put up with her aura-reading if she actually got out of her seat. "Thank you." It took me an extra second to urge her name out of my throat. "Topaz."

"Very kind of you, Topaz. Do you want me to help you with your bag?" Tucker held his hands out, palms up.

I shook my head at him, but Topaz was already shouldering a small, opal-coloured purse. "This is all I have. I travel lightly. Devaguru says that if you travel with a light heart, you don't need as many possessions."

I said brightly, "That's cool. I only brought a backpack, too."

"Yes." Her eyes rested on the Mountain Equipment Co-op monstrosity that I'd barely wedged under the seat. "Wonderful."

Her Lilliputian ass finally left 33B, and she pointed to my boarding pass. "Seat 33C. I like that number. The 3 looks very nurturing, like a mother's breasts."

My eyes popped, but I managed to keep my mouth shut and give a sharp, silent nod.

When Magda returned, Topaz told her, "I'm ready to go to 18A," and floated down the aisle.

Tucker swung himself into 33B, the middle seat.

I stopped him. "I'll sit there. I'm smaller than you." In our family, the small person always ends up in the middle seat. My little brother, Kevin, protests mightily, but the fact is, he fits better. And Tucker had already given up his exit row seat. No need for him to be squished between me and a truly enormous black man who was doing his best to keep himself contained on his cushion.

I smiled, silently thanking my new neighbour for his thoughtfulness, and he nodded back at me, headphones already in his ears.

I clicked my seat belt into place. I'd never been so eager to watch the seat belt demonstration. You could feel the energy in the airplane as everyone willed it to levitate into the air.

"Hello everybody, and welcome to Avian Air. This is Captain James Mesaglio speaking. Our flight time today will be five hours and two minutes, and our estimated time of arrival in Montreal is 2:09 a.m. local time. Thank you for your patience while rearranging our flight on Christmas Eve. Our thoughts are with the García family."

Now we had a name, or at least his last name. No one had named the baggage handler before.

Under my breath, I said a quick blessing for Mr. García and his family. It didn't surprise me that he had been Hispanic. No matter how much the U.S. president railed against foreigners for stealing our jobs, like a protest sign pointed out, IMMIGRANTS GET THE JOB DONE. Which reminded me of another protest sign: WE LOVE IMMIGRANTS. EVEN MELANIA.

The pilot continued, "We're expecting some significant tail winds, so we'll try to make up some time on our flight. We hope to arrive a few minutes ahead of schedule despite inclement weather. The temperature at our destination is now minus 24 degrees Celsius, with light snow. We wish you a pleasant flight. On behalf of all our crew, thank you for choosing Avian Air as your airline this holiday."

Tucker smiled and kissed me, a big smack on the lips that made me laugh. How lucky was I to get Christmas off, in L.A., with this guy, even under the shadow of death?

He turned his head abruptly, breaking off our kiss, and when I opened my eyes, I realized why.

Straight Outta Compton, the "God is dead" guy, unbuckled his seat belt and clambered from the middle seat into the aisle, about five rows ahead of us.

We all stared at him. This was the moment for the flight crew to "arm and crosscheck," whatever that meant, not for passengers to get up and boogie. Plus the jeans sagging halfway off his ass did not inspire confidence.

"Sit down," someone called, but not with any real conviction.

Compton ignored him and waved at a flight attendant who was poised to demonstrate how to place a yellow oxygen mask over your nose and mouth. "Hey. Hey!"

She turned to face him. She looked fifty-ish, with shoulder-length greying hair and a trim figure. Not someone to be trifled with. "My name is Linda. How may I help you?"

"I need a lighter."

I grasped Tucker's hand. He didn't move. His nostrils flared, watching Compton.

Linda maintained the pink-lipsticked smile on her face. "No one is allowed to use a lighter on the plane, sir, in case of fire. May I assist you with something else?"

He shook his head. "I really need a lighter."

"I must remind you that all aircrafts are non-smoking, sir."

"I know that."

Tucker and I exchanged a look. Everyone should know that, in the 21st century. And this guy must not have been born back when they did allow smoking on flights. So why did he need a lighter?

Yet another candidate for the crazy list on this plane.

Linda stared him down with a schoolmarm expression.

Compton didn't say a word, but bent over and started pawing around the legroom of the guy in the aisle seat. The guy stood up, disgusted, and a minute later, Compton stood up and tried to mash his luggage into the overhead bin.

"Sir, your bag is too big," said Linda.

"No, your shelving is too small!" he said, which might have been funny, except one man was already dead, and we'd waited too long for this flight. We couldn't end up grounded because of some wing nut.

"We'll sky check your bag," she said, already holding a label in her hand.

"No one touches my bags except me," he said.

Tucker's breath escaped in a sigh. This was definitely going to be a problem. He stood up.

I grabbed his thigh. "Don't you dare."

"Hope, show of force."

This is a psych term. Psych patients—or any patients—can rebel and turn violent on you. You try to de-escalate them in a few ways. One of them is basic human kindness. Dr. Mel Herbert suggests that before you shoot them up with drugs, let them go to the bathroom and give them a baloney sandwich. Compton was free to go to the W.C., but I didn't have a sandwich, and he'd much rather I handed him a lighter.

The next way of dealing with them is a show of force. A group of people—men, women, doesn't matter, but the more individuals the better—stand up and make their way toward the patient together. I imagine it's some evolutionary thing, but 90 percent of patients will back down in the face of a group.

I sighed. "Fine."

I got up, too.

"You don't need to."

I'm not a big Bible-quoter. I silently endure every time Ryan does it. But I was not letting Tucker go into Crazytown alone. "Tucker, wither thou goest ... "

" ... so do I." He beamed as he took my hand. "Okay, Doctor. Let's go."

12

H e kept holding my hand as he led me up the aisle. Some people turned to look at us. Tucker nodded back at them.

Linda turned toward us, irritated. "Please take your seats and buckle your seat belts."

"We thought you could use a little help," he said.

"When we need your help, we'll ask for it."

Tucker's mouth opened. I knew what he was thinking, namely, *I'm a doctor. You'll be begging for me within the hour.*

I replied, "I'm glad you have everything under control," and pulled Tucker back toward our seats.

Tucker didn't move.

He's bigger than me, so I wrapped his arm around my neck and leaned toward the rear of the plane. "Let's goooooooooo," I muttered, which is what Kevin used to say when he was small and our mom was trying to get him to try on shoes at a store.

"We can leave, but first we wanted to let you know that we have medical training in how to handle recalcitrant people," Tucker said. "Dr. Hope Sze and I are both medical residents."

Crap. Outed to the head flight attendant. I leaned harder.

Compton said, "Doctors, huh?"

We all turned to look at him.

He flicked his own nose with his index finger, a peculiar thing to do. I stiffened, but Compton said, "You don't like smoking."

I shook my head, staring into his unblinking brown eyes. *Sometimes you can smell the crazy.*

Tucker said, "Hate it."

Compton shrugged. "Yeah, cigarettes suck."

Then he climbed over the aisle guy to clamber into his seat.

And that, rather anticlimactically, was that. We paused for a moment, but Compton buckled up his seat belt and blended in with the rest of the human furniture while Linda tagged his bag.

"You're welcome," Tucker told her. "If you need anything further, you know where to find us," he added over his shoulder as I towed him to row 33.

I took a sip of water while the screens on the back of the seats showed plastic-looking people who relished buckling their seat belts and using their seat cushions as personal floatation devices.

My heart banged uncomfortably in my chest. Whenever I get on a plane, I figure I'm lucky to get off with all four limbs. Add in Tucker confronting or comforting anyone with a pulse, and I could rocket into a full blown panic attack.

For some people, the plane's like taking a bus. *Ho hum. Wake me up when we get to Atlanta.* But if there's one thing I've learned from death and doctoring, it's that I can't take anything for granted. Am I breathing? Cool. Might not be happening two seconds from now.

The plane rolled toward the runway. Planes are slow and lugubrious on the ground, like penguins waddling until they hit their natural element.

But when this plane finally started to accelerate, it hit the air at such an angle that I involuntarily grabbed the arm rest.

Tucker reached across the arm rest to rub my leg. "Everything's going to be okay!"

Ooooooooo. Kay.

I nodded, unconvinced. I gazed out of the small, oval window, past the silent colossus on my left. I swallowed to release the pressure in my ears. Most of all, I gripped Tucker's hand.

The plane levelled out. I headed to the bathroom to switch from my contact lenses to my glasses when the seat belt sign pinged off. And then I nodded off.

When I woke up, Tucker was missing.

I rubbed my eyes and checked my watch. We'd only been airborne for thirty minutes. He couldn't have gone far. I stretched my legs and checked my phone, even though it would be neurotic to have him message me because he'd stepped into the john two feet behind us.

The bathroom. That reminded me of the airport's family bathroom. My thighs flexed involuntarily. I've never wanted to join the Mile High Club. Airplane stalls smell like urine, and there's zero room. And yet five hours was a long time to go without my new man.

I twisted around to eyeball the bathroom behind me. The light was on, so someone was in there. He should be back soon.

I tried to read, but it wouldn't hold my attention. I unbuckled my seat belt and checked my watch again. I'd been awake for six minutes.

You can't be one of those twosomes following each other around. Remember when you laughed at the Saturday Night Live skit about the "love toilet" for needy couples?

I need to know where he is.

You're on an airplane. He can't have gone anywhere.

Still, I stood up to gauge if there was any obvious kerfuffle. Compton was my first guess, but he seemed to have settled into his seat, lighter-free.

Tucker's white blond hair tends to stick out. Maybe not as much in L.A., where platinum is fairly common, but I should be able to spot him from a distance.

No one was in the aisle, so I stretched out my hamstrings and verified that the other toilet across the aisle was occupied. It was. I decided to stand outside the bathroom behind our seats while texting him. *I'm up now. :)*

Yes, I added the smiley face to make me look less psycho. It might not work, but then Tucker knew what we'd been through. He'd almost chosen psychiatry instead of family medicine. He wouldn't judge me.

My neighbour, the quiet mammoth in the window seat, cleared his throat and pointed straight ahead of him, which was behind me, since I was facing the bathrooms.

I frowned at him.

He pointed toward the head of the plane again.

I shook my head.

He pulled the earbuds out of his ear canals. "At the front."

"What is?" I was starting to think that everyone was insane.

"Your boyfriend. They called for help."

"What? I didn't hear anything." I'm not that good a sleeper, especially with PTSD. I would have woken up for an airplane announcement.

"The stewardess came up and asked him."

Damn it. Guess it's true that if they know there's a doctor on board, they'll quietly ask for help instead of broadcasting their plea, in order to reduce passenger panic.

I arrowed toward the front of the plane. Whatever was going on, Tucker would be in the thick of it.

13

All the way up the aisle, I cast my eyes right and left.

The Santa girl curled up under her sleep mask and a blanket.

On my left, Compton watched a bloodied Japanese woman shriek on-screen. Horror wasn't my first choice for him, but at least he was quiet.

I passed row 18. Topaz pointed further toward the front of the plane and mouthed something I couldn't catch. I nodded at her anyway.

Gideon was lying on the floor while Gladys munched on something. She'd placed her hair in a bun on top of her head, and she was covering her mouth as she ate, as if she were ashamed of herself.

None of the flight attendants were in economy class, which was very unusual. Somebody should be rolling a cart up the aisle.

Then, from behind the curtain separating me from business class, I heard someone bellow, "I want to go home!"

I ripped aside the flimsy, blue curtain. Sure enough, the demented old man at the front of the plane tried to climb past his wife, from the window seat into the aisle.

Tucker used his body to block the Yarboroughs in their seats. All three flight attendants hovered in the aisle like he was their human shield, unaware that he should be recuperating after surgery, not performing hand to hand combat with an old man.

Tucker had his back to me. He hadn't noticed me closing in on them. "Hang on, Mr. Yarborough. I've got something for you right here." He reached for the briefcase of medication held open by the black flight attendant, who was sandwiched between himself and the cockpit.

I didn't like the layout. Tucker had planted himself at the epicentre of this mess. Mr. and Mrs. Yarborough were still technically at their seats, 1F and 1D, on Tucker's right. The black flight attendant had her hands full with the medical kit, so she couldn't help if Mr. Yarborough went ballistic, and the other two flight attendants blocked him from me.

I advanced up the aisle, past Alessandro, who avoided my eye. Mr. Money flipped through his phone, and the Missus wiped her nose. None of them could be arsed to help.

Mr. Yarborough's face scrunched up with distrust. "What is it?"

"This is Gravol, or Diphenhydramine." Tucker held up a pink pill.

"I don't need pills!"

Tucker nodded. "You want to see Kim, though, don't you?"

"Kim?" His tufted grey eyebrows wriggled. "You got Kim?"

"Yep, your daughter's waiting for you in Montreal. You'll see her soon. You just have to take this pill, okay?"

No. Didn't they have anything better in the medical kit? Maybe Tucker was playing it safe, trying not to give him anything too strong, but it could backfire. Kids can get sleepy with Diphenhydramine ("Time for your medicine!" one of the residents, Stan Biedelman, had once crowed to his niece when she was too hyper at a wedding and had developed a rash from her dress), but a few of them go berserk instead.

I needed to get at that medical kit, or possibly inspect Mr. Yarborough's own pharmaceuticals for something more appropriate. If he wouldn't take anything by mouth, an injection would do.

"He's fine," said Mrs. Yarborough to everyone in the aisle, including me. "He just needs a nap."

Yeah, right. If he was so fine, why had he provoked a near-tasing? We'd saved him from it, but now Mr. Yarborough was up in the air with us, with no real police, no pseudo police, and no weapons.

"For fuck's sake. I'm Joel J. Firestone. I'm trying to get some work done here," Mr. Money called out from 3D, at my right shoulder. "Shut that guy up."

"Joel ..." murmured Mrs. Money, but she broke off in order to sneeze, a high pitched 'choo! that would have been comical anywhere else.

"My wife has allergies. Get rid of the dog while you're at it." Mr. Money, or Joel, snapped his fingers at Alessandro, who rose reluctantly from the seat behind them.

"May I be of assistance?" Alessandro called to the flight attendants over my shoulder.

"When we need your help, we'll ask. Sit down," snapped Linda. Then she remembered to add, "Please."

Under an hour into our flight, and we were all on edge.

Alessandro crouched over his seat, not fully standing, but not sitting, either. Evidently his fear of Mr. Money was greater than his fear of Linda.

I wasn't about to sing again, but I did need to distract Mr. Yarborough so he'd be more in the mood for meds. I pitched my voice to carry to his wife. "Mrs. Yarborough. What do you have that reminds him of home?"

Tucker wheeled around. "Hope!"

I passed him a thin smile, focusing on Mrs. Yarborough. Her lower lip trembled. "He misses our cat, Misty."

I wasn't about to start meowing, although I made a sympathetic face. "What else?"

"Ah ... he usually has steak and onions every Friday at 5 p.m."

Bingo. The business class equivalent of a baloney sandwich. I turned to Magda, who seemed more reasonable than Linda. "Do you have steak?"

"Yes." She scurried off to make it.

"There," said Tucker, as if he'd orchestrated the entire thing. "That sounds delicious. Sit down, Mr. Yarborough, and you can have some steak. Would you like some water?"

"Beer," he said.

"Uh ... "

Mrs. Yarborough said, "He's allowed one beer per day on his trip."

"All right, then," said Tucker.

The black flight attendant, whose name tag said Pascale, hustled for that one.

When they reappeared a few minutes later, Magda unveiling a plate of steak and rice, and Pascale offering him a glass of beer, Mr. Yarborough consented to sit in 1D.

Mrs. Yarborough mouthed a thank you at everyone, but Tucker wasn't done. "Here's your medication, sir."

Mr. Yarborough washed down the pill with beer.

Well, at least he took it. I swerved around Linda for a good look at the medication kit. Most of the real estate was taken up by a blood pressure cuff, a stethoscope, IV equipment, and a blood sugar monitor.

The drug choice was pathetic: no sedatives, but two kinds of Epinephrine, one for a cardiac arrest and one for anaphylaxis, so if he were allergic to the steak, or his heart stopped, we had choices. Atropine for bradycardia. Dextrose for diabetics. Lidocaine, although we don't use that so much for arrhythmias anymore. Nitro and aspirin for heart patients. And the Diphenhydramine that Tucker had given in tablet form, also available by injection.

So we had a few basic medications for a heart attack, we could give fluids, we could give sugar, and we could run a code for a few minutes (only two doses of each kind of Epi, though, so you'd want to land the plane ASAP). This was not good.

On the other hand, Mr. Yarborough was now smacking his lips and slicing into his steak. He was no longer standing and brawling. That was a plus.

"Could I see his medications?" I asked his wife. Although I haven't done my geriatrics rotation, I knew I'd have to rule out polypharmacy, which means they're having problems because we're giving them too many drugs.

Mrs. Yarborough looked startled. "Oh, dear. I packed his medications."

"Well, you can get them."

"No, I mean I packed them in his main bag."

That seemed odd. "You mean they're checked in his main luggage?"

"Yes, I didn't want to lose them, and we had too many things to carry. He made such a fuss over his water bottle."

I sighed. "Do you have a list of medications?"

"Harold, did you bring your list?"

It took him a while to answer as he masticated on his steak. "What?"

"Your list. Could you show this nice doctor your list of medications?" She stage whispered to me, "He keeps them on his phone."

Why would you let a demented patient take charge of his meds list? Sure enough, he grumbled, "No."

"Come on, Harold."

"No!" He started chewing with his mouth open. Steak and rice don't look good mixed up together.

I gave up on him and asked Mrs. Yarborough, "What are his diagnoses?"

"Well, he has diabetes."

Great. "High blood pressure? Coronary artery disease?" I lowered my voice. "Dementia?"

She nodded warily, eyeing her husband, but he chewed cheerily enough.

"Anything else?"

She tried to laugh. "That's enough, isn't it?"

Tucker tried a more conciliatory tone. "Have any of his medications changed?"

"Not for the past six months."

"And the dosages haven't changed?"

She shook her head.

"Did you check his sugar recently?"

She hesitated. "This morning, it was 270."

I glanced at Tucker. That sounded high to me, but Americans use mg/dL instead of mmol/L, so it always sounds dramatic. He punched it into his phone. "That's like 15 for us."

It was high. Normal is more like 4 to 6, certainly under 10 for a diabetic, in our units. But I'd rather he ran high than low for the next five hours. Low sugar, or hypoglycemia, means your brain is deprived of sugar, and you can and will die from this.

Hyperglycemia is hard on your organs, but you won't die from it right away. Your higher risk for strokes, heart attacks, and other complications accrues over years. As long as he didn't cause a ruckus on the flight, he would soon be someone else's problem.

"You probably shouldn't drink," I said. He'd not only finished his glass of beer, he'd filled it back up with a can and emptied that, too.

"Did he take all his pills this morning?" I asked Mrs. Yarborough.

She nodded. "I keep track of his medication. We had to wake up early for our flight, but otherwise, everything was quite as usual."

"Is he on insulin?" I asked.

She shook her head. "He hates needles."

"Should we do an Accucheck?" I whispered to Tucker.

"He's eating," he whispered back, and I nodded. He'd been hyperglycemic this morning, and he should go higher with food, not lower. I didn't want to prick his finger when he was poised to tumble into a post-meal snooze.

"Is his sugar normally well-controlled?" I asked Mrs. Yarborough.

She nodded. "Oh, yes. I take very good care of Harold, and I have to keep things organized because Kim has so many questions."

"What does his sugar normally run at?"

"It's usually between 72 and 180."

Tucker checked his phone again. "That's like between 4 and 10."

It was pretty textbook. I only dwelled on it because hypoglycemia is a reversible cause of confusion. We do A-airway, B-breathing, C-circulation, D-dextrose (check the sugar). If you're in doubt, give glucose.

I cast one last look at the medication kit. "Let's keep this handy, but he seems good for now." Good enough for our flight, anyway.

"Yes, Doctor," Mrs. Yarborough said with such humility that I cracked a smile, and Tucker winked at me.

Four more hours. We could get through four hours. No sweat.

14

B*ing!*
      The seat belt lights came on.

      Linda placed an apologetic hand on my sleeve. "I'll have to ask you both to take your seats. Thank you for your assistance. Avian Air is grateful for your services."

But not grateful enough to bump us up to business class, or even past the toilet seats, on a sold out flight. Tucker and I grinned anyway as we headed down the single aisle, back to row 33.

"Another life saved," he said.

"Or at least tempered," I said, thinking of the Gravol and alcohol Mr. Yarborough now had on board. *Please, please, go to sleep, Mr. Yarborough. Then Kim will greet you with a brand new water bottle at the Montreal airport, and we'll all have a holly, jolly Christmas.*

Tucker and I buckled up. The plane jostled so hard that a couple called out; they'd been playing cards on their tray table, and the cards had started to slide.

A high, young woman's voice came over the intercom. "Ladies and gentlemen, this is your Co-Captain Andie Phillips speaking. For your own safety, please keep your seatbelts fastened as we make our way through a large northern weather system. We're already making all necessary arrangements to provide you with a pleasant and comfortable flight through these weather patterns. Please stay in your seats until the seatbelt light is extinguished. Thank you."

I made a face. The double speak is terrible on airplanes. Why can't they say "We're flying around some bad weather"? Also, not to be mean, but a helium voice isn't as comforting when you're going through turbulence.

On the other hand, I sympathized with Andie. Patients gaze past me, searching for the "real doctor." My friend Tori, who's very soft spoken, once ran a code where the male respiratory therapist complained about "that bossy nurse." Tori had to pull him aside to explain that she was the highest-ranked physician and his foot dragging had put a child's life at risk. Luckily, the patient pulled through.

I became hyperaware of the plane's walls shaking in the wind. I have never fully understood how planes become and remain airborne. I gripped Tucker's hand and tried not to grind my teeth. A dentist had recently suggested that I buy a $500 mouth guard.

"It's okay," said the clean-shaven giant in 33A, on my left.

I turned to look at him.

The corners of his lips twitched. "I'm an Aircraft Maintenance Technician." Since I looked blank, he added, "An airline mechanic."

"Oh. That's cool. In L.A.?"

"In Texas."

He didn't drawl, so I wouldn't have guessed his location. Before I could ask more, the plane shuddered again, and I peered out his window. The small oval of sky told me nothing except that it was a dark and cloudy December evening.

"This is an Airbus 320," said Tucker, on my right side. "It has a pretty good safety record."

I glanced at him sidelong. "What does 'pretty good' mean?"

Tucker shrugged. "I haven't had a chance to do much research, but most of the problems I saw were pilot error, like the suicidal copilot who deliberately crashed a planeful of 150 people into the French Alps—"

My eyes widened.

"—but also the good one where they ran into a flock of Canada geese near LaGuardia, which disabled both engines—"

"This is a good story?" I cut in.

He nodded. "The pilot landed in the Hudson River. All 150 passengers and five crew members were saved, although one person was seriously injured."

"Five," said the airline mechanic.

"Five people. Sorry," said Tucker, with a flash of irritation. He didn't like being wrong. Normally he could laugh it off, but even he was on edge today.

The mechanic shrugged.

I did vaguely remember the story. I was studying at the time, so I missed the details, but that was true of 90 percent of my life.

Tucker continued in my ear, so that the mechanic couldn't overhear. "Even though the post-crash investigation raked Captain Sully through the mud, they concluded that he'd done everything right. Sully ended up retiring afterward. He had PTSD."

I shuddered. I had PTSD—heck, both of us did—and doctors get investigated all the time. The investigation for our hostage taking was still ongoing. I didn't want to retire at 27, though.

Tucker wasn't done. "For 42 years, Sully said he'd been making deposits in his bank of experience. Then when the crash came, 'the balance was sufficient so that I could make a very large withdrawal.'"

Medicine was like that, too. Except it wasn't small deposits. More like a relentless onslaught of disease requiring non-stop deposits. Residents would never leave the ATM machine.

"Fascinating guy. He had a Mensa-level IQ, but his life wasn't easy. His dad killed himself when Sully was 44, without leaving a note. And Sully and his wife had infertility. But they adopted two daughters. Sully spoke out against suicide. And this is my favourite part: at 'the miracle on the Hudson,' he abandoned a library book underwater in the cockpit. When the library got it back, they waived the late fee. The mayor gave him a new copy of the book, along with the keys to the city."

I digested this. It seems like we hear about all the broken people with PTSD, but none of the heroes. I wanted to hear more about the heroes. "How do you know all this?"

"He wrote a memoir. Plus there was a movie about him. Didn't you know that?"

I shook my head. You want to talk about medicine, or reminisce about children's books, preferably while eating delicious ethnic food, I'm your woman. News, celebrity gossip, and the rest of the world? Not so much. I'd look Sully up when we reached solid ground and free Internet again. I'd research the rest of the crew too. The media like to lock in on one person, but it's almost always a team event.

The plane sailed smoothly through the sky. The seat belt light was still on, but I leaned on Tucker's shoulder and dared to think, *We're going to make it. We really are. We're going to have a future.*

15

I dozed off with Tucker as my pillow. Because I'm short, I could curl up like a baby with my legs on my seat and my head and arms on his lap. It was the first time we'd slept like that. He stroked my hair, and I thought he fell asleep too.

I jolted awake when Tucker started to rise.

"Shh," he said, but I was already placing my feet on the floor. I shook the heavy fog out of my brain.

"What is it?" I had the feeling it wasn't the bathroom.

He pointed toward the front of the plane. I stuck my feet in my shoes, loosened my seat belt to the max and crouched, still technically belted but better able to see above the rows of seats between us.

Alessandro was bent over Gladys, in row 16, trying to talk to her. From the look on his face and his apologetic open palms, he was almost pleading with her.

Because Gladys was also short, the seat backs blocked my view even after I released the seat belt, but she was shaking her head.

Tucker stood up.

"Not our circus," I said, placing a warning hand on his hip (*yay, I get to touch his hip now!*). Even if he didn't understand the reference to "Not my monkeys, not my circus," meaning none of our business—he could see as well as I could that no one was in medical distress. I placed my fingers just above his bum, in case Tucker would key into my touch and go back to sleep, or initiate some more interesting activity.

Instead, he gently moved my hand back to my own side. "I'll be a minute."

"You will not."

He sprang down the aisle.

I stalked after him like a tiger.

" ... hundred dollars. Cash," Alessandro was saying. "That would buy a lot of liver treats."

The Italian man was good. He'd probably only been talking to her for a few minutes, but he'd already figured out the liver treats.

"I have liver treats. See?" said Gladys, rooting around in one of her oversized pockets. "Too many things in here. Hang on. That's only crumbs."

Gideon jumped up on his feet, sensing the crumbs. He dislodged the passenger in 16C, a sixty-ish, balding white man who harrumphed and locked his tray table away before Gideon knocked it over.

Alessandro stood back involuntarily. "Good dog," he said, but even I could tell that he wasn't comfortable with canines. Maybe handbag-sized ones, but not one that was half his body weight and poorly trained. Alessandro reached into his jacket's breast pocket for his wallet. He counted out ten bills. "Two hundred dollars. How does that sound?"

Gideon leaned against his owner's legs, yawning. Gladys licked her lips and dropped her hand to rub his head. "You want me to move?"

"Yes. Trade seats. Get as far to the back as you can."

Right. Bribery's a classic way that the rich make sure they get what they want.

Then Tucker grinned in a way that made my stomach plunge.

Oh, no. This request made us relevant, because our real estate was at the back of the plane. I could no longer tell Tucker to mind his own beeswax.

Magda made her way from the front of economy class, where she'd been helping the Portuguese boy. "May I help you?"

Alessandro turned toward her with a practiced smile. "I believe this young lady and her ... companion are interested in seats at the back of the plane."

"I didn't say that." Gladys rubbed Gideon's neck. He leaned into her, turning away from everyone else.

"What's the problem?" Magda barely glanced at her, preferring to gaze up at Alessandro.

"One of the passengers in front is allergic to this young lady's companion," said Alessandro, grimacing when Gideon crouched and barked. "I've asked this young lady to move to help reduce her allergies."

He kept calling Gladys a young lady, even though she obviously wasn't. It reminded me of a nurse in the ER who often coaxes 90-year-old gentlemen forward by calling them "young man." I think it's a way of flattering old people when you don't know their names. Alessandro certainly knew how to read people and how to whip out his wallet, but judging from Gladys's face, his skills were less effective on someone who had built up a resistance to charming young men.

Gladys's lower lip jutted forward. "He's tryin'a give me money because he doesn't like us."

Gideon barked in agreement.

Alessandro exhaled, but he kept his eyes on Magda. Even under the yellow airplane lights, he was a handsome man. "Surely when a woman's health is being affected, you have to make accommodations?"

"Let's talk about it," said Magda. "Perhaps we could all go to the galley to discuss this, where it's a bit more private?"

"Of course," said Alessandro.

Gladys shook her head fiercely. "I'm not going nowhere. I paid for these seats because they're right near the exit. He's tryin'a kick us out for someone in first class. Well, we're not *in* first class. She's all the way over there, behind a curtain. Gideon and I are staying right here."

She flopped back into her seat, nearly hitting the bald passenger in the aisle seat, while Gideon tried to stand up with his tail tucked under. The 16C passenger tilted his body into the aisle, looking pained.

Tucker raised his voice. "Maybe we could help." He ignored my *Wait, what?* look. When I reached out for his arm, he caught my hand and pressed it against his midsection. "Dr. Sze and I could check on the patient in first class, to make sure that she's breathing as easily as possible. We also have seats at the back of the plane, if anyone would like to trade."

"We're not going anywhere. That woman should be the one who moves," said Gladys. "I have anxiety."

Whew. I was almost glad she'd said it. We'd gone a whole three minutes without her diagnosis.

Magda blinked and manufactured a smile. "Yes, I understand that anxiety is very difficult, so it's wonderful that Dr. Tucker has offered to help." She turned to Tucker. "Please, if you and Doctor, ah, Zee could assist us, we would be so grateful. Why don't you take a look at the passenger who's feeling under the weather, and we'll advise you if we require your seats?" Although she sounded calm as she stepped in front of 16D to get out of our way, her neck flushed under her carefully-tied scarf. She was not enjoying this.

I raised an eyebrow at Tucker, who sauntered toward the blue curtain separating us from business class. "Of course! This will give us a chance to check on our other patient, too." He ripped open the curtain and gestured me ahead of him.

I couldn't say why, but dread made me linger on our side of the curtain until I felt Tucker advance, trying to nudge me through. At last, I took a deep breath, squared my shoulders, and searched for our patients.

The first one didn't take much sleuthing.

The leggy, busty blonde sneezed vigorously. Her eyeliner was smeared around her now-puffy eyes. She looked less like the cartoon

Stripperella, more like Ursula, the sea witch from the Little Mermaid.

Pascale, the flight attendant, offered her a white plastic bag for her used tissue. The blonde shook her head and sneezed into it again before she lobbed the tissue at the bag and snatched another one out of the packet in her lap. "I can't—stand it," she said to her man, sounding a little nasal.

Her airway and breathing were congested but intact. Phew. No Epi and no intubation needed. I admit it, I felt a flash of schadenfreude at her transition from femme fatale to Snuffleupagus before I pushed the thought away. She was my patient now. We had the same goal: survival and symptom improvement.

Her man craned his neck. "Can't send a boy to do a man's job. Where the hell is Alessandro? What's taking him so long?" He shook his head at us. His sunglasses didn't stir off his nose. Maybe they were custom made, although if he really cared about his wife, he would have taken them off so he could see her better. He scowled at us. "What the hell? Aren't you in cattle class?"

"I'm Dr. Tucker, and this is Dr. Sze," said Tucker. "We're here to help your, ah, friend."

"My wife, Staci Kelly. Don't you know anything? Christ. Her face alone is insured for a million dollars, and it's blowing up because you people are too stupid to get rid of a dog that she's allergic to."

Tucker's torso jolted in recognition of the name. It didn't mean anything to me, so I said, "They're trying to move the dog. Why don't we see if we can help Ms. Kelly?"

He eyeballed me. "How old are you, twelve?"

I wanted to hit him. Instead, I ignored him. His aisle seat meant he was in my way, so I tried to make eye contact over his head and her tissue. "Hi, Ms. Kelly. I'm Dr. Sze and this is Dr. Tucker. We're resident doctors from Montreal."

"Resident doctors? What does that mean. Like, are you real doctors, or are you naturopaths or something?"

I kept talking over Mr. Money. "We're medical doctors doing postgraduate training in family medicine. I understand you're allergic to dogs. What's bothering you the most today?" It wasn't my smoothest segue, but Mr. Money's glare seared its way up my nostrils.

"Are you having trouble breathing?" Tucker put in. "Are you wheezing, or having trouble swallowing?"

Yes. Good. Zero in on the anaphylactic symptoms. I shot Tucker a grateful smile. Pascale had reopened the medical kit, and he grabbed the cheap, red stethoscope from its depths. He held up its diaphragm, ready to examine her.

She nodded yes, but it wasn't clear which symptom she was answering.

"Short of breath?" said Tucker.

She nodded, and now I could hear her wheezing, a high pitched noise coming out of her throat.

Honestly, I've never seen anyone anaphylactic to dogs before. Patients sneeze, and their asthma worsens, but I've never seen anyone lose their airway.

I glanced at the medical kit. I knew they had one adult and one pediatric endotracheal tube. Before we resorted to that, we only had a few medications for allergies, which made our decision-making so much easier. I grabbed them.

"I'd like to examine her now," said Tucker.

"Christ," said Mr. Money, but he stood up.

Tucker and I both migrated toward the seat. Good thing we were both skinny. He ended up kneeling on the seat, facing her, and I placed my right knee on the cushion and kept my left on the floor.

Tucker eyeballed her airway and started listening to her lungs. "Are you on any medication?"

She shook her head.

That was weird. If she was so allergic, why didn't she carry her own puffer? Maybe she'd packed it in her checked luggage, or relied on Alessandro to cart it around for her. On the other hand, a lot of people say they had asthma as a kid, they outgrew it, and never carry meds anymore.

Good thing the airplane supplied one. Americans might call it

Albuterol instead of Salbutamol, but it was the same medication. I shook the blue puffer and handed it to Tucker.

"You know how to use this?" he asked her. "It opens up your airways. You're going to feel a lot better in a minute."

She shook her head, and he coached her on how to inhale the medication into her lungs while I drew up the Epi. This was our big gun, and I had to be ready to use it. It will bring down airway inflammation like nobody's business, but it won't last forever. And we only had two doses.

If it got to that point, we'd have to land the airplane.

Right now, she wasn't so bad. She was taking lungfuls of Ventolin, and I thought she was breathing a little better. Although no one wants to admit it, anxiety makes asthma and allergies worse. You have to treat the head as well as the lungs. Actually, you should always treat the head. As Sir William Osler pointed out, "Ask not what disease the person has, but rather what person the disease has."

"You're doing great," said Tucker. "You're a superstar."

She gave him a tremulous smile behind her puffer.

Then we heard shouting from economy class.

16

"**O**FF the plane!" Mr. Money roared from behind the curtain.

We all froze in place.

Staci Kelly stilled mid-inhalation, her cartoonish breasts arched forward and the puffer resting in her mouth, like Jessica Rabbit with the world's worst carrot.

We could hear the flight attendants trying to placate Mr. Money. He must've charged into the cheap seats and commandeered the "man's job" of forcing Gideon and Gladys to the back of the plane.

Tucker jumped to his feet. "I'll take him."

"Tucker, no!"

He looked at me, and he didn't have to say a word. I knew what he was thinking. Mr. Money was one sexist SOB. He'd listen to a white, male doctor before a supposed twelve-year-old girl.

He had a point, but he was post op. I wasn't.

"Stay with the patient!" I snapped, edging ahead of him.

"You do it. You already have the Epi." He strode to the curtain and yanked it closed behind him.

I placed the Epi back in the medical kit, needle capped, careful not to depress the plunger. The Epi could stay with our allergic patient. Then I shoved the flimsy curtain aside.

Mr. Money grandstanded in the aisle of row 16. Magda was closest to me, but she, Tucker, and then Linda all clustered behind his back, trying to get his attention as he pontificated. Alessandro faced him from row 17, nodding painfully along.

"Two hundred is nothing. Chump change. You need a little more than that, am I right? Especially when you're on vacation." Mr. Money nodded in agreement with himself. He placed his fingers in his belt loops and patted his own stomach. "You and I understand each other. We're both used to getting what we want. I like that in a woman. So we got a deal? Three hundred bucks. Cash."

Gideon barked throughout his entire speech, unimpressed.

Gladys gaped at him, looking more gormless than ever. "I booked this seat six months ago. I need room for Gideon. I have to be near the exit. I have anxiety—"

"My assistant booked our seats a year ago. Let's not quibble." Mr. Money reached into his pocket and slowly revealed a fat roll of cash. I've never seen so much moolah at once in my life. It looked very impressive as he peeled off bill after bill after bill. "Look. That's 360 bucks. I need the rest for my wife. You got me over a barrel. You're a good negotiator. Now can Alessandro escort you to your new seats?"

Gideon tucked his tail under his bum, but he never missed a beat in his barking. In dog, he was saying, *Hell, no.*

Gladys bent her head and crooned, "You're a good dog, Giddy. Yes, you're such a good dog. I love you, good dog."

"Right. He's a good dog. So couldja move it?" Mr. Money's neck flushed under the spray tan, visible to me even with Tucker and the gang interspersed between us.

The "good dog" barked for the 360th time, never taking his eyes off Mr. Money. *Danger! Danger!*

Gladys shook her head and said to Gideon, "Do you want a liver treat? Huh? Oh, yes, you do. Hang on, baby. I got lotsa stuff in here." She fumbled with her pockets.

"Lady, you do not know who you're messing with." Mr. Money snapped his fingers. "Alex, get her out of here."

Alessandro sneaked another scared look at the dog as he inched toward row 16. He didn't want to touch Gideon or Gladys, but he had to obey his Massa, which meant he gazed from his boss to the dog, searching for a clue.

I kept my mouth shut. For once, Tucker wasn't running interference, and I wanted it to stay that way.

The passenger in 16C, who had endured the three of them arguing over his bald head with Gideon planted at his feet, quietly slipped to the back of the plane, past Alessandro, removing himself from the equation.

Alessandro reached for the sleeve of Gladys's cardigan.

Gideon's ears twitched backwards, and he flattened more toward the ground.

"Please," Alessandro whispered, trying not to look at Mr. Money. This was his job, and he hated it. Poor guy.

Gladys shooed his hand away. "If you touch me, Gideon will bite your balls off."

Gideon growled.

Alessandro hopped away from him. "Call off your dog!"

"I didn't say anything!" Gladys protested.

Mr. Money backhanded Alessandro across the face.

I heard the crack against his skin from where I was standing. He'd swung that hard.

Everyone gasped. Alessandro sucked in his breath. Both his hands winged toward his cheek, like he couldn't believe it.

Don't send a boy to do a man's job.

"Stop it!" I snapped. Just because this idiot had money didn't mean that he could start whacking people and throwing them around the airplane like my grandmother's Mah Jong pieces.

Mr. Money ignored me. He told Alessandro, "Go check on my wife. That's all you're good for." He turned back to Gladys. "Okay, lady, there's an easy way and a hard way. You want the hard way."

He literally began rolling up his sleeves. This required him to unbutton his left cuff, then his right. He rolled each black sleeve up, slowly exposing his forearm muscles for maximum dramatic effect.

Tucker maintained a calm voice. "There's no need for physical violence. I hope you're all right, Mr. Alessandro. Dr. Sze and I can check you over."

Alessandro shook his head. The imprint of Mr. Money's hand still burned across his left cheek.

Tucker nodded and shifted toward Gladys. "We also have seats in the last row. We're happy to exchange them. Gladys, Gideon might be more comfortable in the back, where there are fewer people around. What do you think?"

She shook her head. Gideon's short, sharp barks reverberated around the cabin, making my temples pound. I winched my teeth together.

Tucker crossed his arms. He wasn't used to people saying no to him. Before he could negotiate further, Alessandro rushed past Mr. Money and the rest of us, toward business class and Staci Kelly. Pascale met him at the curtain.

One good thing: Alessandro was now out of hitting range. I wanted to thump Mr. Money in return, but Magda, Tucker and Linda clumped up the aisle between us. They'd turned sideways to let Alessandro get by, though, so I got ready to thread through the slipstream.

Magda swung her hips to bar me. I bit back a swear.

Linda placed her hands on her hips, drawing herself up to her full height, even though she was shorter than everyone except me and Gladys and Gideon. She stood the closest to Mr. Money now. "You have to go back to your seats. All of you. We can't have you brawling in the aisles."

"Right. Exactly. Go back to your seat." Mr. Money glanced at Tucker. "Where are your seats?"

Tucker pointed at row 33.

"I know you're at the back, numb nuts! Which row?"

Numb nuts. Who was this guy? He insulted doctors, he hit his staff ... Compton had unnerved me, but the real danger was from business class. Tucker had been rendered momentarily speechless, so I called out, "She didn't say she'd trade with us, but we're in 33B and C."

Mr. Money leaned over Gladys and Gideon and said in a low, ugly voice that nevertheless carried across the airplane, "Okay, bitches. Time to go to 33C."

Maybe he thought that was a good joke because of the dog, but Gideon was male. The guy couldn't even insult them right.

Gladys ignored him. Gideon stiffened, staring at him.

Mr. Money clapped his hands together. "Let's go. Chop chop!"

Was that a Chinese slur? Gideon barked at him even louder than he had at Alessandro.

Good dog, Gideon.

"What the fuck," said Mr. Money, scanning the plane. Everyone ogled him right back. He was the live in-flight entertainment for over a hundred silent passengers, one of whom was conspicuously filming him.

Mr. Money jabbed a finger at the camera. "Stop filming. Now!"

The camera slowly lowered, revealing a terrified, white-haired man with glasses.

Mr. Money nodded in satisfaction. "I'm going to make sure you delete that. Right after I move these bitches." He snarled at Gladys, "Go on!"

"She didn't agree to the move," I pointed out.

Mr. Money's head wrenched frontward to see who'd spoken. Spotting me, his face knotted up. He looked so ferocious that Tucker instinctively took a step backward to protect me.

"Shut up, you little gook," said Mr. Money.

The plane gasped.

I didn't. Par for the course. Because racist patients have been filmed demanding "white doctors who speak English and don't have brown teeth," it's becoming part of our training. I even looked up their lame slang. Gook was an ancient one, from the Vietnam War, and didn't shock me as much as some of the others.

"You can't talk to her like that," Tucker snapped. "You can't talk to any of us like that."

I expected Mr. Money to object or to belt Tucker. Instead, he threw back his head and issued a long, dismissive laugh.

I cut him off. "Shut up yourself, you old fraud. Why don't you look after your wife instead of hitting your employees and cursing at physicians?"

Tucker sucked in his breath. Doctors never lose their tempers. Never, ever, ever. Nurse Jackie can do it on the small screen, but in real life, doctors get dragged off to our disciplinary college faster than this plane could crash to the ground.

On cue, the plane started to rock back and forth.

"Everyone, please, stay calm," said Magda.

Her voice broke. It did not foster calm.

"Yes, please," said Linda, although she grabbed a seat back in order not to sway with the plane. "Everyone, return to your seats and buckle your seat belts until further notice."

The lights flickered.

"Daddy, are we going to die?" The little Portuguese boy's voice rose into the air. He sat in the middle of a nearby row, close enough for me to see his dilated pupils and his cowlick sticking up in the air.

Yeah, kid. We're all going to die. But I held that one back while the father's voice murmured useless, soothing things and handed him an iPad.

The boy glanced at me again, uncertain, but he took the iPad and stopped questioning our mortality.

"Go to your seats!" said Linda, straight into Mr. Money's face.

Even if we wanted to obey, Tucker and my seats were at the back of the plane. We'd have to mow down both Linda and Mr. Money to get to them.

Tucker took a step forward.

Mr. Money jerked his hands up in fists, one leg planted in front, the other behind and ready to kick.

I stared at him. This was a fighting stance. I recognized it from when my parents had forced Kevin to go to karate class.

Holy crap. Mr. Money had martial arts training, and he was prepared to use it on us.

17

"Sir, why don't we go back to your wife. I'm sure she'd appreciate your help," said Linda, although her voice trembled.

Mr. Money didn't reply. His eyes flickered between me and Tucker, fists ready.

Magda darted into the leg room of 14C, startling the balloon girl, but Magda only snatched the in-flight magazine out of the pocket of the seat in front of her. She raised it like a shield. "That's enough!"

I nearly laughed. Satan had boarded the aircraft, and a flight attendant thought she could defend herself with *Avian Times*.

One upside: Magda had taken herself out of the aisle. That left only Tucker and then Linda between myself and Mr. Money.

"Sir." Linda reached forward, as if to touch his elbow.

Mr. Money snarled and knocked her arm away with one hand. His other fist raised to strike.

Tucker's arm streaked into the air to block him.

"No!" I shouted, but Linda was already stumbling backward as Tucker surged past her to meet Mr. Money.

I jumped into the Portuguese family's leg room. The woman yelled something like mayo day-os.

"Sorry," I breathed, but I was giving Linda room to fall out of the way so I could spring back into the aisle and take Tucker's back. That was the crucial part of the equation. I would die for him, I would kill for him, and now I was literally and figuratively behind him. I growled, "Don't you *touch* him!"

"Hope!" said Tucker. He heard me seething behind his shoulder blades and whirled from Mr. Money to face me, guarding me with his body.

"Get back!" I was ready to take on Mr. Money with my bare hands. I started to slip sideways between Tucker and the seats—I can basically fit into the space between atoms—

"Get out of here, Hope!" Tucker grabbed my shoulders, thrusting me backwards.

"No!"

Gideon barked. Gladys started to hum tunelessly. The airplane shook and dinged its seat belt alarm, adding to the chaos, but I was louder than the bell.

"Don't you touch him. Don't hit anyone, don't swear at anyone, don't evict any dogs," I raged at Mr. Money over Tucker's shoulder, who was manhandling me toward the cabin while the two flight attendants ducked out of our way. "I can treat your wife's allergies, as long as you stay calm and stop attacking people—"

"Hope. Hope, I'll handle this. Go back to Staci Kelly and Mr. Yarborough. I can do this. They need a doctor up front—"

He was trying to get rid of me. Part of me understood that. We did not need a brawl. We needed calm. But I was beyond singing "Give Peace a Chance." More like *You want a piece of me.*

"You think you can tell me what to do?" Mr. Money spat back, sneering at me from behind Linda and Magda and Tucker. "You couldn't act in one of my movies if I put a paper bag over your face and used a ten foot dildo."

What? A dildo? I was confused enough to stop knocking Tucker's arms aside, although the rest of the plane gasped, and Topaz piped up from row 18, "You can't talk like that. My guru says we have to show harmony—"

"I'll talk how I want, you little whore. You're all whores. I could buy and sell every one of you and still have enough change left over for a Caribbean island. Now get that bitch and her dog to the back of the plane."

A seat creaked. My giant neighbour, the airplane mechanic from Texas, strolled toward us from 33A. He was so tall that he seemed to fill the aisle side to side, and his head extended toward the airplane cabin's ceiling.

Mr. Money paused in mid-threat. Pro tip: if anyone ever asks you if you'd rather have a physically imposing avatar or a miniature one, in a crisis, always pick the Hercules.

"Hercules" didn't need to speak. He stood at row 18, arms at his side, feet planted, and Mr. Money shut up.

This was a real show of force. It made me realize how stupid I'd been.

Tucker was right. One of us had to stay with our patients. I would have sent him, but he refused, so it was up to me to be the sane one.

As soon as Mr. Money backed off.

I crossed my arms and peered over Tucker's shoulder, ready to enjoy Mr. Money's parade of shame back to his seat.

Mr. Money kept his eyes on Gladys and Gideon, not wanting to look up at Herc, although his stillness signalled his awareness that he was no longer the biggest man within arm's reach.

Gideon barked louder than ever, but also wagged his tail, which was confusing.

Linda opened her mouth and extended her hand toward Mr. Money's back. She was the closest to him again. "Would you like a beverage?"

"Absolutely, sir," Magda piped up. "I can help you with that."

Tucker and I twisted so that Magda could skedaddle past us toward the business class cabin, saying "What would you like to drink?"

Instead of doing a 180 and marching back to business class with a martini, Mr. Money stood his ground, audibly breathing in and out, like a bull in a field deciding where he should charge. Then he said, "I gave you your chance." He pounced at Gladys's feet.

Her feet? What would that accomplish?

As if in slow motion, I watched his fingers seize Gideon's collar.

"No!" I shouted, trying to push past Linda, but she grounded herself like a concrete wall, holding back me and Tucker.

Gideon barked and snarled, stiffening his front legs. He tried to plant them in the carpet, but his claws ripped through the fabric as Mr. Money dragged him into the aisle.

Gladys screamed, a high, thin, rattly scream even more terrible because she couldn't get any air behind it. Then she tried to beat Mr. Money's back with her fists. It was more like flailing.

"Stop!" Tucker shouted.

Linda pivoted toward him, her mouth ajar—why does it always work better when a man bellows?—and Tucker leapt past both of us. The cords stood out in his neck.

"Tucker, no!" I snatched for him but missed as Magda grabbed my shoulders from behind, murmuring, "It's okay, it's okay ... "

How the hell was this okay?

Before he made contact, Linda yanked Tucker's arm, spinning him sideways. "Don't touch him! He'll charge you."

"That dog doesn't belong to you," the red baseball cap guy called from his seat. Other people near us rose out of their chairs and fled toward either end of the plane, even though Linda called, "Stay in your seats!"

Mr. Money huffed, dragging Gideon a few inches backward. "You know what—belongs—to us? The air. *Clean* air. That we—can —*breathe*."

Gideon choked as Mr. Money tried to drag him directly by his collar. *He* couldn't breathe.

"Stop it!" I knocked Magda off my shoulders, but she clutched my right elbow like a too-high handcuff.

"Sir, I can help you," said Linda. Her voice trembled as she struggled to clamp both of Tucker's wrists.

Tucker said, "Let me go. I can do this. Linda!"

"Fuck you and fuck your fuckin' dog, too!" Mr. Money roared.

The airplane shuddered and gave a big bump that made me grab the nearest seat to hold myself upright.

Even Herc steadied himself with a palm pressed against the seat back of a thin-nosed woman who looked like Margaret Thatcher, her eyes wide behind her tortoiseshell glasses.

Linda bumped the back of Tucker's knee like a seventh grade douchebag boy.

Tucker stumbled. With his arms pinned, he had trouble balancing.

"No!" I shouted, tearing myself away from Magda.

Tucker had already wrenched both wrists free and caught himself on a seat back, although Linda whacked him in the shoulder. "Sorry, sir! I mean doctor!"

Whose side was she on? I called, "Are you okay, Tucker?"

He nodded, still gripping the seat.

"Please, doctor, come up front with me," Magda said.

I ignored her. My life was Tucker.

"Gideon!" wailed Gladys.

Mr. Money had lost his grip on Gideon during the big bump, falling on his hands and knees. Now the dog tried to wiggle his way back to Gladys, past Tucker and Linda and me and Magda.

Tucker sprang for his collar, but Mr. Money, still low to the ground, looped his arms around Gideon's hind legs and towed him backwards.

Tucker's fingers slipped on fur and accidentally caught Gideon's ear.

Gideon yelped. Tucker let go.

Mr. Money chuckled. He captured Gideon's collar and hauled himself to his feet, grunting only a little. The man was in freakishly good shape. He probably worked out by killing and eating toddlers for breakfast.

Then he began whistling.

Goosebumps rose on my arms. I recognized those five

monotonous notes, but it took a second for my brain to place the title: "Who let the dogs out."

Mr. Money glanced at the exit sign. There were two exit rows, 17 and 18.

He fixated on his left. Then he barked the chorus as he dragged Gideon down the aisle.

I realized aloud, "He wants to throw Gideon out the exit door."

"No. He can't do that," said Linda.

"So stop him!" I shouted.

Herc straddled the aisle from 18C to 18D. That exit row was sealed off.

I breathed a little easier until Mr. Money leaned into 17D and hissed at Margaret Thatcher, "Get up."

Her lips trembled. Her dyed-red hair barely moved, but she stared at him, hypnotized, like he was a viper.

"Get out of my way, you stupid bitch!"

She pressed on both arm rests to propel herself into a standing position, breathing so hard that her burgundy polyester scarf trembled, and Mr. Money yelled, "Get on the seat. Stand up on the seat, all of you! Move it, move it!"

Although Herc had dammed up one exit row, Mr. Money would tunnel his way through the other, past three passengers, and force open the exit door while we were in mid-air.

Impossible. Every step of it was ludicrous. He couldn't drag Gideon six inches, let alone another two feet, although the way Gideon was whining and digging his claws into the carpet made me want to scream.

Margaret Thatcher tried to edge into the aisle instead of clambering up on her seat. Mr. Money, Gideon, and Herc had taken up all the real estate, which made Mr. Money even more furious. "You stupid bitch! What part of *On. The. Seat* do you not understand?"

This was a senior citizen. He wanted her to hop on an airplane seat. More evidence of his insanity.

But he might hit her, and her quavering form impeded Herc from grabbing Mr. Money. I gestured for her to come toward me.

She turned sideways and tried to step over the dog.

"No, bitch! On the seat, you dried up old gash!"

She clambered on the seat cushion, clinging to the seat back, and looked so unsteady that Tucker hurtled forward and grabbed her around the waist

"No, Tucker!" I hollered, to no avail. *Don't carry her!*

Herc reached forward to grasp her. He was the one facing her.

She shied away from Herc, peeping like a mouse. He checked himself, and Tucker ended up carting her up the aisle, with some belated assistance from Linda, while the rest of us clambered out of their way—Gladys squished back into row 16 while I shot back into the leg room in front of the little balloon girl and her mother.

"Hey!" said the mom.

I apologized, but was immediately distracted when they dumped Margaret Thatcher on her feet in front of me.

"Are you okay?" I asked Margaret Thatcher.

She nodded, but her lip trembled.

"Go to the front. You can always stand in business class," I said, steering her on the other side of me as kindly but as swiftly as possible. I needed her gone so I could snatch Tucker out of harm's way. He'd already rocketed back toward row 17.

"Hey!" protested Gladys, who'd been turtling her way toward Mr. Money until I blockaded her with Margaret Thatcher.

"Sorry." *#Sorrynotsorry.* I shot past Gladys plus every flight attendant except Linda. Once I punted Linda aside, and dragged Tucker back to safety, I'd be in pole position.

Mr. Money stepped into Margaret Thatcher's previous leg room and heaved Gideon after him. It was so tight that when he bent over to drag him, his butt jutted into the aisle.

Then he hollered at the other two exit row passengers, an elderly black lady in the window seat and what looked like her petrified daughter in the middle seat, "On your seats, slaves! Get out of my way!"

Everyone gasped.

Tucker snatched Mr. Money's left elbow, dislodging his hand from Gideon's collar.

"Don't touch him!" Linda shouted at Tucker.

"Fuck off, kid." Mr. Money kicked backwards.

Tucker twisted, evading the kick, but dropping the arm.

"Tucker!" I fought my way forward. Linda was only a few inches taller than I was. I could take her.

"Sit down, doctor!" Linda widened her stance and threw her arms out like a star.

"No!" I tried to dive between her legs. Not my smoothest move, but as Tina Fey pointed out, if there's an obstacle, take a cue from Sesame Street and try "Over! Under! Through!"

Linda screamed and snapped her legs together before I could get my head between them. "Stop it!"

"Just get out of my way!" I started to rise, pushing on the floor for extra leverage, but at this low vantage point, I had an excellent view of Tucker, who'd also gone low, grabbing Gideon's collar.

Mr. Money thwacked his hand.

His hand. As doctors, our hands and our brains are our livelihood.

I opened my mouth.

"Gid-ee-*onnnnnnnnn!*" Gladys's shriek Dopplered toward me.

It was like a linebacker hit me in the kidneys. I sprawled left on a diagonal, onto a lady's white tennis shoes.

"You okay?" I gasped.

Gladys continued to lumber forward—after I got flattened, Linda had enough warning to fly to the right, into the opposite bank of passengers—and Gladys reached over Tucker to hammer on Mr. Money's right shoulder.

He kicked backwards once more.

I screamed. Tucker sprang out of the way, toward Herc.

Mr. Money made solid contact with Gladys's knee.

She dropped like a de-stringed puppet, emitting a faint "Oof."

My own back twinged, but I could still haul myself up, using the tennis lady's arm rest. "You okay?" I asked again.

The tennis lady nodded, which was good enough for me to turn back to Tucker.

I'd have to vault over Gladys first. Since it looked terrible for a doctor to hurdle over an injured human in order to save a dog, I glanced down at Gladys to make sure she could breathe without spinal injuries.

Somehow, Margaret Thatcher had battled through the throng and crouched over Gladys's head. Gladys seemed to be talking back to her.

Cool beans. Aside from the kidney punch, Gladys had actually done me a favour by knocking Linda out of the way before immobilizing herself. Now I could do battle with Mr. Money without the head flight attendant or the doggy defender obstructing me.

I launched into the aisle, back issues be damned. I landed right into the spot between Gladys's splayed legs, which encouraged her to wriggle out of the aisle, toward Linda.

Linda cowered away from both of us, covering her torso with her arms. The woman kept thinking I was attacking her. "I'm *saving* you!" I yelled.

Meanwhile, Tucker pitched himself at the ground. Toward Gideon. He yanked the collar, so his hands still worked. He was trying to wrench it out of Mr. Money's grip.

That was the smart thing to do, save the dog without assaulting the rich guy. Smart Tucker.

Except Gideon was crying and choking again.

And Mr. Money said, "Oh, no, you don't," and booted Tucker in the stomach.

In his recently-repaired stomach.

My turn to scream.

18

Tucker folded in half and pitched on his ass, trying to catch himself with his non-dominant right hand.

Herc heaved him backwards, out of the fray.

And I sprinted forward. I must have looked pretty fierce, because Mr. Money's eyes widened in the split second that he saw me coming. He started to raise his arms.

I kicked his abdomen.

Seemed like quid pro quo. Most middle-aged guys, no matter how much they work out, develop cushioning. I kicked him so hard, he crumpled toward Margaret Thatcher's seat.

Gideon snarled and shot across the aisle.

Someone grabbed my right shoulder from behind. I shook that off.

Tucker lunged toward my face. "Stop, Hope, stop!"

How did he get past Herc? And why should I stop? If anyone should stop, it was this maniac trying to throw a helpless dog off the plane while smashing any humans who got in his way.

I launched myself at Mr. Money again.

He slammed me with an uppercut under my chin.

I bit my own tongue. I fell backwards on the blue carpet, jarring my head hard enough to knock off my glasses. I lay there, stunned.

"Hope!" Tucker shouted.

My tongue throbbed. The jaw pain was flatter and more diffuse, but omnipresent. My skull ached, and the blood pounded in both my temples. My back still twinged. So five different sources of pain competed for receptors.

I didn't move while my brain tried to compute all that sensory input, plus the most important factor.

He hit me. That bastard really hit me.

I couldn't see anything except blobs, and yet I knew I had double vision. The person to the left of me had four blurry shoes instead of two. Damn it.

Terrible time for a concussion.

"Ouch!" I yelped. Two people had grabbed my arms and started dragging me toward the front of the plane, giving me rug burn on top of everything else. The one nearest my face—Pascale—was asking, "Are you okay?"

"Don't touch her! Don't move her!" said Tucker.

They immediately abandoned me in the aisle, stepping over my body to get back to Mr. Money, whom I vaguely realized was still causing a ruckus, but I had more important things on my wobbly mind.

"My glasses." I tried to focus.

I needed my glasses before someone stomped on them. "My glasses!"

I crawled forward, despite the nausea, and located my glasses to the right, under an aisle passenger's seat, precariously close to some tan loafers. My hand snaked forward.

It took two tries because of the double vision, but I snagged my specs. I breathed a little easier, propped myself up on my elbows, re-hooked my glasses over my ears, and yelled, "Tucker?"

He was already leaning over me. He tilted his head to avoid casting a shadow on my face as he gauged my pupil size. "Hope. Hope!"

"I'm okay," I said, although I had to close my eyes and lie down on my back because now everything was spinning, including Tucker's anguished expression. I should cover one eye at a time and see which eye was causing the diplopia, or if it was both, but I wasn't up to self-diagnosis at the mo'.

"You hit your head. How many fingers?"

I clamped my eyes shut. "I can't do it right now." People stepped over us—more civilians fleeing the brawl—which made my brain sway. Then another thought struck me, and I snapped my eyes open. "Is the dog okay?"

He twisted to look over his shoulder. "He's—oh, Jesus."

"What does that mean?"

Tucker didn't answer. I tried to keep my eyes open, but the yelling and the pushing and the lights made me feel sicker than ever. How was I going to save Gideon when I couldn't even see, and Tucker was too busy rescuing me to knock out the bad guy?

"You go," I told him. "I'm okay. It's just a concussion."

He swore under his breath. He reached around my neck, checking my C-spine with firm fingers, top to bottom. "Does that hurt?"

"No! I didn't break my neck. Go get the dog!" I shook my arms and legs to show him that I had no obvious neurological injury.

The plane bumped again, making my temples shriek and a few people gasp. Someone stepped on my arm. "Ouch!"

Tucker braced himself on the floor over me.

I will not throw up. I will not.

Although if I do, it'll be on Mr. Money.

"Go back to your seats!" Linda hollered. Then she added, "Stay in your section!"

I took a quick peek. The worst of the exodus had already occurred. Some passengers had spilled out of the front rows of economy class, bunching up at the curtain. A few passengers remained barnacled to their seats, although the Portuguese kid was standing on his, clinging to his iPad.

Margaret Thatcher bobbed into an aisle seat near my feet, which was closer to the action than I would have liked for her, but since some people had cleared out, we did have more room to fight, once I could stand up.

Gladys seemed to be blubbering now, and Gideon was whining in a high-pitched, piteous way that made me push a reluctant Tucker aside and drag myself to my knees, then my feet, only to disbelieve my own confused eyes—

—I shook my head again, dizzier than ever, trying to figure out what was going on.

While I'd been flattened on the ground, Herc had taken down Mr. Money.

Mr. Money had also been knocked on his back, although the method looked different. Maybe Herc had snatched his right leg out from under him, because Herc grasped that ankle and forced the extended leg up to 60 degrees while Mr. Money snarled, "I'm gonna sue you! I'm gonna sue every last motherfucking one of you!"

Herc struggled to secure the other leg, which was actively kicking toward his face.

The flight attendants did battle with the arms. From what I glimpsed, they got in each other's way, and they were losing.

Also at Mr. Money's head end, jammed into an aisle seat, Gladys wept, "You're a bad man! You're a very bad man! You're going to hell!"

Some men had stood up, filling the aisle beyond Mr. Money's kicking foot, around row 19, but they watched Herc and the flight attendants instead of jumping in.

Then Compton, the weirdo, pushed himself to the forefront of that useless crowd. "Do you need help?"

"Get in there!" I shouted at him.

Since Herc was blockading the entire aisle, Compton attempted to scale the back of the aisle seat in row 18. It was too tall and awkward for him, so he stepped on the arm rest and tried to wedge his way through seats 18B and C. "I'm coming, man!"

Topaz, who was still in 18A, shrieked in protest and batted him back.

A woman cried out in Portuguese behind me. I bet that the dad had stood up, but the mother had forbidden him to help.

Linda started to kneel on Mr. Money's left arm and grab the right. The other two flight attendants fled up the aisle, letting the more senior attendant deal with it, but Mr. Money tried to sock Linda with his free arm.

She tumbled to the side.

"Get his arms!" I shouted, wincing at my own voice. At least my double vision had improved. I was still spinning, but not spinning with two different views of the world.

Tucker shot down to the ground.

"Not you!" I screamed at him as Linda sprang further out of his way, into the abandoned seat opposite Gladys.

Too late. Tucker grasped one of Mr. Money's wrists—no, both—no, one again—

Mr. Money cast his head from side to side, mouth opening, as he flexed his arms despite Tucker's best efforts.

"Get his head!" I screamed.

Mr. Money sank his teeth into Tucker's right forearm.

Tucker's entire body stiffened, but he didn't loosen his grip with his right hand. He hauled off and socked him in the eye with his dominant left hand.

Mr. Money gagged. Tucker wrenched his right arm out of Mr. Money's mouth.

"Someone else take the head!" I shouted.

Gladys stumbled out of her seat.

"Not you!" I yelled, but Gladys held a dark red polyester scarf in her fat hands. She looped it in Mr. Money's mouth and tied it behind his head while his eyes bulged in fury.

"Got another one of those?" said Tucker.

Linda touched the scarf around her neck. "We need zip ties, but —" She swiftly unknotted her scarf and handed it to Tucker.

"Tie his wrists together," he said, in a tight voice, "and then get me another one for my arm."

Even with the lame lighting and my concussion, I could see the circular bite marks imprinted above his wrist. Despite them, he controlled the beast's arms until Linda had secured them, both with her scarf and by kneeling on them.

The good news was that the bite was hardly bleeding, so Mr. Money hadn't managed to tear out a chunk of flesh. The bad news was that human saliva can carry up to 50 different types of bacteria.

We had to wash out Tucker's wound ASAP and cover him with antibiotics when we hit the ground. But first we double-checked that Linda felt safe.

"He's not getting away this time," she said.

"I'll get the zip ties," Pascale called over her shoulder as she rushed toward first class.

Magda handed me her scarf. The airplane bounced. So did my head. I still moved Tucker further up the aisle and bound his wound. It was superficial, but Mr. Money had broken the skin. The spectres of hepatitis and HIV danced in my head.

I heard distant barking. Both Tucker and I snapped to attention. I grimaced while my brain tried to follow suit.

"Gideon!" called Gladys, clawing me and Tucker aside. We both sprawled into an empty row.

Gideon broke through the wall of men toward the back of the plane. I could see better than Tucker, since I'd bounced out of the aisle seat back into the aisle itself and was the first in Gladys's slipstream.

"Get the collar!" one of them shouted.

"I can't!"

"Ow!"

A kid yelled, "Mommy, a doggy!" in an amazed voice that made me choke back a laugh—*yes, kid, a doggie, that's what we've been fighting over for the past ten minutes*—and Mr. Money roared behind the gag while Gladys stood up and mewled, "Gideon! Come back!"

She started to walk toward her dog, directly over Mr. Money's body.

She bowled Linda out of the way, into the rightward row of seats. Since Linda had been imprisoning Mr. Money's scarf-bound arms, this freed him up to sling both fists upward at once, in a vicious chop between Gladys's legs.

Gladys staggered into the next bunch of seats on her left, knocking into Margaret Thatcher, who'd been crouched over Mr. Money, perhaps nerving herself up to flee toward business class.

Margaret Thatcher flattened herself on the ground like a startled cat before she snaked her way toward the window seat. Since she was moving all four limbs, and so was Gladys, who looked like an over-turned beetle, half on the seat, half on the floor, I figured that the two stooges had once again miraculously escaped serious injury.

The only problem was, even though Herc locked down both of Mr. Money's knees, throwing his hands as well as his own knees into the mix, the bad guy lifted his still-bound arms to hammer on Herc's head.

"NO!"

We had to pin him down. He could not escape.

I leaped just as the airplane swerved.

I stumbled over Mr. Money's head and arms, crash landing on all fours. My wrists slammed into the carpet. One knee landed on his torso instead of the ground. My head was jarred by impact. I looked like a human-sized bug squatting over him, with my face too close to his crotch and my nether regions over his face.

Gross. I sat down fast, thumping my bum down on his chest hard enough to make him gasp.

I perched on his torso with my back to his head. I couldn't see a damned thing behind me, including Tucker.

I didn't have time to turn, because once Mr. Money caught his breath, he bucked like a bronco, yowling behind his gag. My wrists and ankles ached from impact, and whoopie, my vertigo and nausea started up again. But I couldn't do a 180 when I was acting like a human lap belt.

When you restrain someone in psych, you don't restrain only their wrists and ankles. You also bind their bodies to the stretcher with a waist strap. Then you might clamp a face mask on them to stop the biting and spitting, before the drugs kick in.

I was the body restraint.

I was sitting facing Mr. Money's groin, almost like the reverse cowgirl sex position, but better than a near-69.

Mr. Money bucked some more. My head spun. I tasted bile and swallowed it back down. I would cheerfully barf on Mr. Money, but Herc was right in front of me, sitting on the knees, and I didn't want to spew all over him.

I did need Mr. Money to stop moving, though, so I punched him in the crotch.

His limbs stiffened. He howled behind his gag.

I felt like hurling again myself. I'd never bagged a guy on purpose before, and I felt like his flesh had been imprinted on my knuckles. But if it saved Tucker and Gideon, I'd do whatever it took. And he was lying more still.

Behind Herc, Compton shouted, "I got him! I got him!" Presumably he meant a foot, which was only borderline useful, but he was trying.

A doughy-looking man told Compton, "I'll take over."

Phew. Compton was too much of a loose cannon.

I was also reassured by Herc, who quietly adjusted his weight on Mr. Money's knees, provoking a fresh moan from behind the gag.

"I have the zip ties!" cried Pascale's French-accented voice behind me, and I recognized Linda's lower pitch saying, "Good. Start with the wrists."

"I got them!" said Tucker, and I could breathe again. Tucker was alive, albeit in the thick of things.

Then Mr. Money jostled me worse than airplane turbulence. It felt like I bounced a foot into the air before I fell back down again, although it was probably only a few inches. My head begged to differ. It spun like a Tilt-A-Whirl.

"Get his feet!" Linda again.

Herc shifted. He stretched forward, scooping the zip ties in his Jack Reacher-sized hands, but the doughy guy did the actual lassoing so that Herc could remain in position.

Once Mr. Money was properly tied up, I could get off his torso and loosen the gag. It would only take a few minutes. The doughy guy looked competent as he worked, ignoring the peanut gallery shouting instructions to him. Soon Mr. Money would be contained.

The Portuguese family gave a fresh cry of alarm.

And Tucker swore.

"No!" bellowed a man's voice, and everyone looked up except me. I didn't dare turn around, but I could identify the timbre and slight accent: Alessandro, the good-looking Italian assistant, back for more punishment. What an idiot.

An idiot who made the flight attendants scream as he cast himself upon Mr. Money. "Let him go!"

Mr. Money's upper half arched. I had to know what was happening, had to orient myself toward the circus going on behind me, so I twisted to glare at him over my shoulder.

Alessandro grabbed me from behind, babbling, "He'll hurt you, you have no idea ... "

"Fuck OFF!" I shouted at him, before Tucker bear-hugged him around the waist and wrenched him aside. Alessandro tripped and fell to the right, nearly crushing Pascale, who'd ducked into an aisle seat, and Linda said, "Leave us alone! You get out of here!"

Now it was Herc's turn to grab Alessandro and spin him toward Mr. Money's feet.

Doughy guy ducked out of the way, releasing the ankles.

Mr. Money peeled himself off the carpet again, this time rocking his shoulders from side to side, trying to dislodge me.

No help for it. I rose into the air faster than him. Then I landed hard, on his belly, knocking the wind out of him. I felt his torso jolt in response. This was dangerous, especially in a gagged man, but he seemed to have enough energy for triplets.

He was bound by zip ties and gagged by a scarf. He had up to five people holding him down. What more did he need?

Just die already! Or at least stop moving around!

After my world wrestling smack down, Mr. Money shouted behind his gag, but he moved less. Which made my vertigo settle down from Mach 1 to hangover levels.

I took a deep breath and started to ease my hips in the air. People have died from chest wall hypoventilation, the inability to take a deep breath because they can't expand and contract their lungs. Now that Mr. Money was under control, I could stop acting like the human lap belt.

Alessandro pelted back toward me, screaming. Before Herc swung him behind the wall of men again, Alessandro howled, "Get off him! You're killing him!"

He startled me so much that I almost fell directly onto Mr. Money, but I managed to clench my quads in a squat position. What? I hadn't crushed his chest. He was still moving. He wasn't dead. I hadn't killed him.

Had I?

I yanked myself into full standing position, albeit with one foot straddling either side of his body.

Don't be dead. Forget what I said before.

The airplane dropped far enough that my stomach plunged toward my boots, a woman started praying to Jesus, and I stumbled when Mr. Money thrashed between my legs, whipping his body from side to side like an electrocuted eel.

A woman screamed, "He's bleeding!"

19

W ho was bleeding? Tucker?

I swung my head, peering over my left shoulder. Double vision swelled up again, and I struggled not to vomit as Mr. Money bucked and kicked my ankle, making me drop down on my butt.

No! I'm trying not to kill him this time!

As I fell, I pitched my weight toward his southern end, not his chest. Herc formed a bumper wall, attempting to catch me, so I half-landed on Mr. Money's upper thighs.

"Watch out, Hope! He's bleeding on your pants."

That was Tucker. He was talking, and saying "he," so Tucker wasn't the injured party.

He must mean Mr. Money.

Mr. Money was bleeding under me. I glimpsed bright red blood on the back thigh of my mauve jeans.

Did I get my period for no reason?

No, I took my pill religiously.

How did Mr. Money start bleeding?

Did I break his ribs when I slammed down on him? Maybe I gave him a pneumothorax, popping a hole in his lung?

Oh, my God. I killed a guy. I mean, I've tried to kill murderers before, but this guy was only hitting us and throwing the dog off the plane. He didn't actually kill anyone that I know of.

Chill, Hope. If you gave him a pneumo, then put in a chest tube.

But how can I install a chest tube on an airplane with no equipment?

I heaved myself up with an arm rest. Herc tugged at my elbow to assist me, and I smiled at him in thanks even as I vomited a bit in my mouth. I swallowed it back down. No time to think about that. How and where was Mr. Money bleeding?

Tucker had ripped the guy's shirt upward. It was a button down, fitted black shirt. It didn't want to clear his nipples. I glimpsed a scarlet stain beneath Tucker's fingers. I yelled, "Get some gloves!"

I dug in the pockets of my red fleece jacket as I plunked down in Margaret Thatcher's seat to get myself out of the way. I only had one pair of hospital gloves on me, but I tossed them to Tucker. He was the one doing the bloodiest work, and he already had an open wound. He would need them.

Mr. Money's chest wound looked bigger than anything from a broken rib. The good news was that it meant I was off the hook. My world wrestling move hadn't done that.

Meanwhile, I defaulted to the ABC's. A is for airway. I made my way to the top end of Mr. Money, although this time, I was the one clinging to seat backs to make sure I didn't trip.

"Cut the gag," I told Magda, who hovered around the head end, her hands in the air.

Reluctantly, she struggled with the gag's knots. Gladys must have put some oomph into it, because Magda could barely work her slender fingers between the scarf and the skin, and Mr. Money was gagging.

"Cut it!" I snapped as I used the seat back to maneuver behind her.

Magda gawked at me for a second. I got the feeling that English wasn't her first language before she answered, "I don't have scissors."

"Get a knife," Linda told Pascale.

I squished into some leg room area so Pascale could dash back to first class. The fetch and carry role is not glamorous, but totally necessary in a crisis.

As soon as she cleared the area, Linda and I shot back into the aisle.

"Land the plane," I told her.

"We can't, in this weather," she said. "I can connect you with the flight doctor through the interphone system—"

"What flight doctor?" I brightened up. There were real doctors on the plane?

"Pilots call them on the interphone system. We can't open the cockpit door during a crisis, so I'll have to relay the information between you—"

No way. I didn't have enough spare hands or brain cells to play telephone with Linda, the pilots, and a flight doctor on the ground.

Pascale rushed up behind us with what looked like a butter knife, with slightly sharper teeth, but better than nothing.

Magda immediately backed up so that I could start sawing the scarf with the knife. Although it took forever, I knew Tucker must be doing whatever he could for the bleeding at the chest. I could handle the airway.

I sawed with my right hand and kept tension on the fabric with my left. "Come on, come on," I muttered, and finally, the last filament of cheap polyester gave way. I dragged the ends apart from each other.

Mr. Money's mouth fell open. His chest heaved up and down.

Airway handled for now.

"Breathing?" I called to Tucker, while I checked Mr. Money's carotid pulse. Fast but firm. Good enough.

"I've got a 1 centimetre stab wound in his left anterior axilla and a 2.5 cm one in the left precordial area," he said.

I squinted. My double vision had settled down, but my head still felt like a raw egg being swished around inside a water thermos. It took me a good second to focus on the small incision diagonally below his left nipple. The one in the armpit was even smaller.

Small but deadly.

"That's the box," I said. In trauma, you worry about the heart if the victim got stabbed in the box formed by imaginary lines between the sternal notch on top, the xiphoid on the bottom, and the two nipples on the left and right.

"Yup," said Tucker. Technically, both wounds were slightly lateral to the nipple and therefore just outside the box, but no need to squabble about it. These were potentially dire blows to the heart as well as the lung.

If Mr. Money had been stabbed straight through the left atrium or ventricle, he'd probably have expired within seconds as the blood pumped directly out of his heart. Our timeline had expanded to minutes.

We'd have to put a chest tube in. If that didn't work, we'd have to drain fluid from around the heart.

With no ultrasound. No scalpel. Only one set of gloves. Nothing sterile.

"Give me the stethoscope!" I shouted. Someone shoved it in my hand, and I listened desperately, but all I could hear was the roar of the engine and a few distant barks from Gideon, no matter how hard I pressed it to Mr. Money's waxed chest. "I can't hear any breath sounds!"

His chest pumped up and down, so he was breathing even if I couldn't pick up the noise. I lobbed the stethoscope back to Magda.

His chest might have moved less on the left side. It was hard to tell. The best view is from the feet, the worm's eye view that we used for breast implants in plastic surgery. I wasn't flinging myself at his feet for that.

Tucker tried percussion, placing his right middle finger on the chest and tapping it with his left middle finger, but he couldn't hear anything, either. "Trachea's deviated to the right. Let's decompress the left lung," said Tucker.

"With what?" And then I answered my own question. The fastest thing was a needle decompression. Puncture the chest wall and the lung lining, and all the air would whiz out. "Give me the biggest needle you've got! And a pair of gloves!"

Pascale thumped the entire medical briefcase on the nearest seat. I pawed through it. "All I've got are 23's and 25's to do injections. And what are these, one inches?" Fine needles hurt less, but they'd get clogged up by blood and tissue if I stuck them in the chest. The small calibre isn't a big enough tube to let air out, and an inch long needle might not make it through the average North American chest wall. I did find a pair of blue latex-free gloves, which I slid on.

"Those won't do any good," said Tucker. He was still calm. He might even have been smiling when he raised his eyes to mine. "Let's do a chest tube. We've got a knife."

Yeah, a butter knife. I raised my voice. "Does anyone have a pocket knife?" Probably not allowed, but I could always try.

"Yeah!" Compton dug into his back right pocket and extracted a white plastic fast food knife.

Tucker's hand withered in the air. "Ah, thanks, man. I'll use this one instead."

"Your loss," said Compton, carefully replacing the knife into his pocket. That was one weird dude.

Tucker ignored him, holding up the butter knife to the light. "Brandy. I need alcohol to sterilize everything. Give me the highest alcohol content you've got." Pascale rushed to nab a bottle from first class.

"'I am a knife,'" murmured Topaz, and a woman moaned.

Tucker ignored them. "Get me some oxygen tubing and some oxygen," he told Magda. Brilliant. Oxygen tubing would work for the chest tube, not to mention preoxygenation.

When Magda took off, he said to Linda, "Hanger. A coat hanger."

She bit her lip, but she nodded and headed upstream to find one.

"Give me the Penrose," Tucker said to me.

I hesitated. I knew that was the name of a drain in the OR, but not what it looked like or why he needed one now.

"We need to make a one-way valve. Give me the tourniquet!"

That, I knew. I scanned the medical kit for those blue rubber bands that you tie around someone's arm to make the veins stand out. I handed it to him. He stretched it around the oxygen tubing, but the tourniquet was too big. It flopped around the mouth of the tubing.

Now I understood what he wanted to do. Once, as a medical student, I'd treated a small pneumo with my one and only chest tube. The resident had set it up for me, but I remembered the floppy white rubber bit at the end that acted as a one-way valve. When the air whooshed out of the patient's chest, it fluttered open, but when room air tried to rush back into the patient's thorax, it shut tighter than Gretel closing the oven door on the Hansel-trapping witch. This one-way valve would be even more important on an airplane with precarious cabin pressure.

"I need tape to seal this on. Otherwise, we have to make our own three bottle system!"

Whatever that was, we didn't have time for it. "Tape!" I called, but as the flight attendants scrambled, I told Tucker, "Hang on." I hurried to the front, searching for a little girl wearing a black dress with green trim—and more importantly, the mom with a blue balloon, although there was no sign of it in their laps.

"Excuse me. I need a skinny balloon," I told the mom.

She stared at me.

I tried again, in French. *"J'ai besoin du ballon, s'il vous plaît. C'est urgent."* It always takes twice as long to say something in French, and culturally, it's very rude to run up and start yelling at a francophone, but it couldn't be helped. Tucker was probably taping a Penrose drain to the patient's makeshift chest tube right this very second. *"Et si vous avez un ballon propre, ça serait encore mieux."*

The mom stared at me from under heavy brown bangs. She clutched her daughter to her chest, and they looked identical in their fear and incomprehension. It was quite possible that they spoke a third language. I frantically mimed blowing up a balloon, looking like a puffer fish, and the girl stifled a giggle in her mother's arm.

At long last, the mother reached between them, poked around in her shiny, black purse and handed me a cylindrical blue balloon.

"Merci! Thank you!" I dashed back to Tucker, who said, "You are a

goddess," as I snapped the balloon's mouth onto the end of the oxygen tubing and sawed off the other end.

Since my head was rolling around like a Zodiac on a stormy sea, I didn't feel like a goddess, but I dredged up a smile for him anyway. Tucker would make me feel better on my death bed.

Pascale held a dark bottle that looked expensive. From the look and smell of it, they'd already poured brandy over Tucker's gloved hands, his knife, and the wound, and on the ground, which was gross, but this carpet—this entire plane—would be forensic evidence as soon as we landed anyway. I held out my hands so that Pascale could immerse me in alcohol, too.

Tucker had set the oxygen tubing on Mr. Money's somewhat sterile chest and was trying to hack the other end off it. I pulled on the tube to make it slightly easier to cut and said, "A Foley catheter would be stiffer." Oxygen tubing is pliable, to make it more comfortable to fit around ears and up one's nose, but it would collapse between ribs.

Tucker raised his eyebrows. "You see a Foley anywhere, be my guest."

I glanced at the relatively useless medical kit. "We could ask for a catheter volunteer."

He laughed at my joke. One poor guy on board probably had a Foley catheter draining urine into a leg bag, but you wouldn't stick a contaminated catheter in someone's chest unless you were nuts.

The tubing was now about two feet long and ready to go.

Magda had reappeared with a few white towels. I laid them down, making a keyhole around the base of his sternum. Ideally, we would "prep and drape" Mr. Money, sterilizing the skin and draping the rest of the body to shield it from surrounding microbes, stray vomit, or dog hair.

"This is crazy," a woman muttered.

Topaz's breathy voice answered, "Devaguru says, 'Here's to the crazy ones. The misfits. The rebels ... '"

That was Steve Jobs, but since Tucker and I were both hella crazy misfit rebels, I let it slide.

"I think it'll work as long as I get a trochar," Tucker told me.

Right. If Tucker tried to push oxygen tubing alone inside the guy's chest wall, it would bend all over the place. ("Like a limp dick," a surgeon once pointed out.) Tucker needed metal to keep the tubing rigid as he forced it between the ribs. Hence the coat hanger.

Now my brain was whirling with thoughts of limp dicks and coat hangers. I wanted to puke. Again. I tried to block out Topaz piping, "'... glorify or vilify them. About the only thing you can't do is ignore them ....'" by eyeballing Mr. Money's chest. He was still breathing, but fast and shallow. I took his pulse: same, and at 120. He had his ABC's, but not for long. If this didn't work, he'd die. No pressure.

Come on, coat hanger. What are they, attached to the first class closet or something?

I told Pascale, "Find that coat hanger. And get me another bottle of brandy." She nodded and flew to the front, where Staci Kelly yelled, "What's happening with my husband?"

I told Tucker, "The last pneumo I saw was yours."

His face split into a grin because this time, he was the one doing the saving.

Linda rushed up with a metal coat hanger in her hands. I said, "I'll bend the trochar for you."

"Bend it like Beckham," he said, which is also the name of a movie I love, so that earned him a few more points. I know it sounds weird that we were joking, but this wasn't a TV show like ER where you get to cut out all the boring bits. We had to set up properly before cutting open a man's chest.

I reached for the coat hanger. The wire was a lot stronger than in the dry cleaner ones, which made it even harder to manipulate. I needed pliers.

"I'll do it," said Herc. "What shape do you want?"

I beamed and thrust it at him. "A hockey stick. A straight line with a hook at the end, so it doesn't fall into the patient's chest. Thanks."

One of the onlookers made a horrified face, and I realized that I was used to working in hospitals, where minimal civilians overhear me during a code. I'd have to censor myself. I shut my mouth and settled myself on the patient's right, leaving the wounded side to Tucker.

On the upside, Herc was already bending the coat hanger into a hockey stick. Life hack #2: if you're not born Herc-sized, get one on your team to do the honours. One of the orderlies at St. Joe's jokingly calls himself an ogre. Kindly ogres are essential in times of crisis. In the meantime, I took the brandy back from Pascale and baptized the hockey stick hanger before handing it to Tucker. While I rewashed my gloved hands with alcohol, he threaded our trochar through the oxygen tubing and re-bent the wire so it was the correct length.

He whispered, so that only the two of us could hear, "I'm ready."

20

Tucker picked up the knife. He was left-handed, which made it more awkward to operate on the left hand side of the patient. I itched to grab the blade, but I resisted the impulse.

Let him do it, Hope. Show him you have faith in him.

Gideon barked in response. I'd lost track of him, but he sounded like he was immediately behind Herc.

"Keep the dog away," I warned. The last thing we needed was canine intervention while Tucker had a knife in his hand.

First, Tucker explored the larger wound with his dominant index finger. The wound was almost exactly where we'd make the incision for the chest tube, so it was possible that he could use part of the wound itself for the tube. Not recommended, but neither is a butter knife instead of a scalpel.

"How deep is it?" I burst out.

"Deep, but the wound is at an angle." He wiggled his index finger. "I can't get my finger in. Can't tell how deep it is."

Maybe I could get my finger in the wound. Sometimes small fingers are an advantage, like during a vaginal hysterectomy.

No, Hope. Let him run the show.

Tucker placed the knife less than a centimetre away, at the anterior axillary line. That means the line if you drew straight down from the front fold of the armpit. He was going to cut laterally, away from the midline. That made sense to me. Move away from the sternum, or breast bone. More room to explore.

"Light, please," I snapped. He was casting a shadow on his own work because of the airplane's crappy overhead light. "Does anyone have a flashlight on their phone?"

Three people immediately flashed their LED's, blinding me, but better than fumbling in the shadows. "Thank you," I said, and I leaned forward, resting my hands well away from his work site, but drawing the edges of skin away from each other. By increasing the tension on the skin, I was making it easier to cut with the butter knife. "Try to shine your lights over Dr. Tucker's left shoulder."

More lights beamed over us, kind of like a concert, only much creepier.

Tucker sawed back and forth with the almost-invisible teeth of the butter knife, pressing hard enough to divide the epidermis, the top layer of skin, as well as the dermis, the fatty layer underneath. It was only another two centimetres, but I knew from my limited chest tube experience that you'll need room to explore within the chest cavity, so you can't be squeamish and make too small a hole. Then your finger won't fit, or it gets stuck.

Tucker made a face. "I need a Kelly."

I nodded. It's not safe to stick the knife into the chest wall. He could accidentally go too deep and stab the heart himself. The scalpel is a tool to cut the skin, but you want to stop and separate the muscle fibres with Kelly forceps, or safer yet, your fingers. The first and only time I did a chest tube with the pigtail catheter, I slowly and methodically used the Kelly to separate the three muscle layers of the chest wall until the surgery resident told me, "Go ahead, Hope. You aren't going to hurt anyone."

Now I said to Tucker, "Do you want me to try and find a pair of scissors?" I dreaded the answer, except then I'd be doing something.

He shook his head. "I can do it. Just slowly, that's all."

"I've got one," said Pascale, displaying a small, bronze pair of scissors with a handle made to look like a stork's body. Its beaks formed the two-inch blades. My mom had a pair like that for sewing, but I was astonished to see them on an airplane. Who knew they were allowed by the TSA? It could even have been the weapon used on Mr. Money, although this one already looked clean even before I rinsed it with the last of the brandy.

Pascale held up another brandy bottle for me, anticipating my next question.

I smiled and handed her the knife. The handle still felt warm from Tucker's skin, even through my gloves.

"You want help?" called Compton.

Gideon barked. Every time someone yelled, he barked, adding to the chaos.

"No. Be quiet," I said. Tucker had started the most difficult part, trying to cut through the parietal pleura, the lining inside the chest wall, without piercing the lung or the heart. The scissors were slightly safer than the knife, because he had his thumb on the dull edge of the blade to control it, but he could slip. Some people make a hole and then use their fingers to rip the muscle apart to widen it, but either way, this was risky business.

Mr. Money was still breathing. For now.

I held my own breath and kept the tube in my hands, the hockey stick hook side facing toward me, ready for Tucker's signal.

When Tucker broke through the last layer of the chest wall, it hissed as if he'd opened a pop can.

The air literally blew my hair back from my face like a hair dryer.

My face, neck, and clothes were sprayed with something wet.

I would have sworn, but I didn't want to open my mouth.

I looked at Tucker. He was spattered in blood, too, but he'd commandeered the chest tube out of my hands and was tunnelling it in.

When he paused, I knew what he wanted. I yanked the coat hanger out so he could move the chest tube deeper without fear of impaling the lung or the heart.

A woman screamed. It might have been Mrs. Thatcher.

I was screaming inside, too. Who knew what blood-borne diseases Mr. Money was harbouring under his sleek exterior? I'm more careful than most doctors and nurses when it comes to suiting up. Unlike them, I actually wear the masks with eye protection, even over my glasses, plus a disposable gown, at every code. Another doctor once told me that I looked like I was wearing a condom.

This time, my glasses might've protected me a little, but Tucker's eyes, nose, and mouth were completely naked, and he'd received the full blast with an open wound on his arm.

My man was a hero. Now he could be a dead hero.

It's okay, Hope. HIV is treatable now, and Hep C ... I tried to remember the treatment for Hep C. They've got new antivirals, but my heart cried out. Tucker had barely escaped the OR, and now he might end up back on the treadmill of doctors' visits and blood tests and treatment so harsh that we also use it for chemotherapy.

If Mr. Money hadn't already been almost dead, I would've killed him.

After taking stat samples for baseline HIV and hepatitis testing.

My heart thudded. I gritted my teeth inside my still-closed mouth. We barely had gloves. A plane didn't carry any other personal protective equipment. And Mr. Money hadn't asked us to save his life. Tucker had sailed into the breech because—well, because he lived for that sort of thing. If he wasn't saving lives, he'd be half a man.

The good news was, if this worked, Mr. Money was saved. We could stop right here.

Please work.

Please wake up, you bloody bastard.

21

In the movies, Mr. Money would have stayed still for a crucial beat or two, and then taken a deep breath, opened his eyes, and said something sweet (for a rom com) or salty (for a thriller).

Instead, he lay there, still breathing, but too fast, at about 24 resps per minute. The balloon valve puffed with each breath, so it worked, and I could testify how much air had escaped from the guy's chest based on my new hairdo, but he hadn't improved much. In fact...

"He looks dead," said some guy.

"He's still breathing," I said, annoyed, but I took his pulse.

Gideon growled as I repositioned myself and my fingers.

"Shh, shh," said Gladys, to no avail. Gideon started barking louder than ever, making it hard to concentrate.

I shook my head at the pulse, which was faster and weaker. "About 125," I told Tucker. "No, 130."

I kept my fingers on the pulse. I was afraid we'd lose it at any moment.

"Look at those neck veins," said Tucker, eyeing the right internal jugular.

I repositioned my fingers to try and cast less of a shadow. Even through my concussed eyes, Mr. Money's jugular venous pressure was still through the roof.

We didn't have an ultrasound or cardiac monitor, and I couldn't hear his blood pressure enough to judge a narrow pulse pressure. I nodded anyway and said what we were both thinking: "Tamponade."

Tucker took a deep breath and replied, "Pericardiocentesis."

Doing pericardiocentesis is no big deal on your oral exams. All you have to say is "I stick a needle into the pericardial sac," the examiner replies, "You drain 30 cc of fluid," and you feel like a hero.

In real life, on this airplane, we couldn't confirm the diagnosis before sticking a needle within a few millimetres of this man's heart.

"I'll get a needle. Magda, you put the oxygen on him," I said. This was Mr. Money's last chance. If it didn't work, nothing would. We had to drain the blood that was leaking into the sac around his heart, literally squeezing his heart to death. I told Pascale, "Keep taking his pulse. Tell me as soon as he loses it."

Her eyes bulged. I probably should have said "*If* he loses it." Too late.

I snatched the biggest needle in the kit, but it was still only an inch long. Mr. Money was a stocky guy with a mix of muscle and fat. An inch wasn't going to penetrate his chest wall and pierce the pericardial sac. You have to go through the anterior chest wall at an angle (45 degrees! Toward the left shoulder! Although ER guru Tintinalli suggests you can choose the right shoulder instead!) in order to drain the blood.

"It'll work if I go through the hole," said Tucker. He meant that normally you're penetrating the chest wall with the needle, but since he'd made an incision already, he didn't have to go as deep. He could sink the needle right up to the hub, and it might be long enough.

Or it might not.

We had to try. I attached the needle to the biggest syringe we had, a 20 cc, and said a quick prayer before I offered it to Tucker. Then I poured brandy over the incision as a final attempt at sterility. It would sting if he were conscious, but he wasn't conscious, so booya on that.

I took turns pouring brandy over each of my hands and gave the bottle to Magda, who'd fitted the ridiculous yellow cup-like oxygen mask over his mouth. Pascale licked her lips and dug her fingers harder into Mr. Money's neck. I recognized that movement.

"She's losing the pulse. Try it!" I called at Tucker as he braced his right hand against Mr. Money's chest and turned the business end of the syringe toward the incision.

Mr. Money rolled slightly on his left side.

"Hold him still!" I yelled at the flight attendants, Herc, and Compton. "He can't move, or else we'll stab him."

"Should we be doing this?" a woman squeaked.

Tucker said, "It's his only chance," and the plane quieted down. Even the bing-bing-bings of the alarm and Gideon's barking stilled for a crucial second as Tucker stuck the needle in through the hole.

Mr. Money spasmed.

"Hold still!" I shouted, and three pairs of arms shot out to grab him. We were down a few sets of arms because of the manual phone lights. I said, "The light isn't as important now. Just hold him down so he doesn't move."

"But don't get in my way," said Tucker. "I'm angling the needle toward the left shoulder." We all watched him advance the syringe.

He moved the needle in. Not yet up to the hilt, he advanced in little jabs, half a centimetre a time.

The airplane punted to the left, and the needle sank extra deep. Not terrible, but a few more millimetres for sure.

Tucker froze.

I sucked my breath in through my teeth.

Everyone seemed to gasp. Most of the passengers were too far away to watch the needle, but they'd read our body language.

Medicine is not performance art. My man had testicles of titanium, trying to save Mr. Money's life in front of a planeload of people.

He's dead, I wanted to tell Tucker. That was what a preceptor, Dr. Dupuis, told me when I worried about running my first code. *He's basically dead. If his heart hasn't already stopped, it's going to. We have nothing to lose. This is his last chance. Keep going.*

Tucker might have read it in my eyes or in my body language. He withdrew the plunger on the syringe as he advanced another millimetre. It sounds like a small thing, but it's hard to advance the syringe and pull back on the plunger at the same time unless you use both hands.

I'd been taught to attach an electrode to the needle, to watch for ST heart wave changes on the cardiac monitor, but of course, there was no cardiac monitor and no electrode. Only Tucker's hands.

Even so, I stood by, ready in case he needed me to hold the needle or syringe steady while he drained the pericardial sac.

As he drew up the plunger, a bead of blood followed its path.

I gasped. Holy crap. Tamponade. And we were—he was—draining it.

Pericardiocentesis.

It sounded like a word of prayer now.

Slowly, he withdrew one cc of dark red blood.

You are a god among men.

I laughed in relief, and Tucker's hand twitched.

He kept pulling, but no more blood followed.

One cc of blood wasn't enough to stop the heart, especially one as stubborn as Mr. Money's.

I held my breath.

Pleasepleasepleasepleaseplease.

He adjusted the needle, experimenting with the depth and the angle. A bubble of air entered the blood.

"I'm sorry," Pascale quavered, "but I think—"

"You've lost the pulse?" I should have positioned myself at the head, but now I was at the foot of Mr. Money's body, and I couldn't reach across Tucker's field. "Someone else double check it, but for God's sake, hold him down. I'll do his femoral." I reached for the guy's right groin and mashed two fingers into the fold of his thigh, searching for a pulse.

Linda and Magda both reached for his neck.

"Not at the same time," I shouted. "You'll stimulate the vagal nerve and make him faint."

They gaped at me.

Less information, Hope.

"Forget it. I can't feel a femoral," I told Tucker, and yelled, "Start CPR. Who knows CPR?"

"I do," said Herc, but he was at the leg end, with me, and we needed his strength in case the guy regained spontaneous circulation and tried to rip our heads off.

In the meantime, the three flight attendants had already put up their hands.

Of course they knew CPR. What was I thinking?

"Pascale," I said. She looked the strongest. Magda balked at even touching Mr. Money, and Linda might have to run to the cockpit. "Get in there and do CPR. Magda, get ready to trade off in two minutes."

Pascale linked her fingers together and extended her arms, but she hesitated. "He's there," she said, pointing to Tucker.

"Do it from the top end," I said. "Stay out of his way."

She shied away from the needle and the blood. "I need gloves," she said, and Magda dug in the medical kit for them, while Staci Kelly yelled from the front cabin, "What's happening?" and Mr. Yarborough bellowed back, "Kim?"

"I'm coming out," said Tucker. "Let her try."

A newly-gloved Pascale got on her knees and started CPR after Tucker withdrew the needle. I stayed on the femoral pulse and called, "Good compressions." Pascale looked like a black Audrey Hepburn, slim and elegant, but she knew how to get on her knees, lock her arms, and give what for on her compressions.

"I'll try one last time," said Tucker. "Get me a bowl."

I shoved the empty brandy bottle at him. He squirted the syringe's cc of blood into the opening.

"Ew!" I heard someone say, which I ignored as I entrusted the bottle to Linda, who had donned a pair of gloves and a bland expression as she accepted the bottle.

When I turned back, Tucker had already ordered, "Stop compressions." He began one last pericardiocentesis, faster this time, more certain.

He advanced the needle a few millimetres and barely got a few drops of blood. "I need a longer needle!" he shouted.

"Longer needle!" I barked, in case someone else knew the medical kit better than I did.

Linda's voice came down hard on both of us. "That's the longest one we've got."

Tucker swore as he withdrew the needle.

"Restart CPR!" I called. Magda leapt in this time, also armed with gloves and a pretty good technique.

Mr. Money was dying.

He was dying in front of our eyes. All we'd done was prolong the process.

22

"Fluids!" I shouted. We could compensate temporarily by amping up circulating volume enough to maintain his blood pressure, even if he had too much fluid around his heart.

Tucker said, "I'm on it."

He reached in the medical kit and grabbed an IV needle and a bag of fluid. Soon Magda was holding a bag of saline above the patient, trying to squeeze its contents through a 20-gauge needle.

"Land the plane," said Tucker.

"The weather system won't allow it." Linda's voice was clipped.

"Land the plane *now,*" said Tucker, and I understood. It was his first code since our hostage taking, and we'd failed. All of us had, but it felt like his failure, because he'd done the procedures, even though I was the trauma team leader.

Fluids probably wouldn't help, and they might make things worse by diluting the blood and clotting factors and causing more leakage into the pericardial sac, but I was running out of options. We didn't have packed red blood cells to transfuse him, and our needle hadn't worked.

"Let's run through the H's and T's one last time," I said. We already knew the cause, but you're supposed to follow algorithms and think out loud during codes. "Hypoxia—he has oxygen. Hypothermia—we could get him a blanket, but it's not like he's been out in the ice. Hypovolemia—yes, probably, but we're running normal saline wide open." I left out the fact that the needle was too small. It was the biggest one we had. Tucker could start another IV or two, but the main problem was still the hole in his heart. "Hyper- or hypokalemia—probably not. I can ask his wife if he's a dialysis patient, or on potassium. Hydrogen ions for acidosis—we don't have bicarb."

"T's." Tucker took over, which seemed appropriate because his name started with T. "Tension pneumothorax—he got the chest tube. Pericardial tamponade—we can't fix him with the equipment we've got." He paused a second to seethe. "Thrombosis, either cardiac or pulmonary—he was stabbed, he didn't have a heart attack, or if he did, it was provoked. And toxins, same. It wouldn't be the primary cause."

I shook my head. The chance of survival dropped with every minute. Even if his heart started pumping again, his brain wouldn't recover. At some point, you have to stop. "Tucker, we should call it. He's been down for ... " I checked my watch. "Twenty-three minutes."

His face was frightening. Like a mask. "I'm thinking."

"Okay. Let's switch for CPR. Switch!" The next volunteer was a beefy-looking guy with an artificial tan. He pumped on the chest with so much enthusiasm, it reminded me of a gay male nurse who told me that the way you do CPR mirrors the way you have sex.

Tucker said, slowly and distinctly, "We both think this is tamponade. I can cut a pericardial window."

"Tucker—" I was pretty sure he'd never done one. I'd never done it. Never even seen it. There aren't that many traumas in London, Ontario, where I did my medical school, and the traumas I'd seen in Montreal couldn't be solved like this.

"It's not that hard. And if I open it up, I'll be able to see what I'm doing. I just need to crack the chest." He raised his voice. "I need the knife!"

Pascale and Magda conferred for a second. "We don't have it—"

"I need the knife!"

Linda passed him the butter knife. "Yes, sir. Yes, doctor."

I dropped to my knees and sprayed Mr. Money's chest and the abandoned stork scissors with brandy like I was an arsonist splashing gas on-site. Trauma team leader and trauma nurse rolled into one. If we were going to do this, we needed to do it full bore. No holding back. No doubts.

When actor Carrie Fisher had a heart attack in the air, her family was grateful that the staff on board had managed to bring back spontaneous circulation by the time they hit the gate, and that they got a chance to say goodbye.

Maybe Mr. Money had someone who wanted to say goodbye to him, besides his wife who was calling behind the curtain.

Maybe he'd make a good organ donor.

And even if he didn't, this was my Christmas present to Tucker. I couldn't give him all that he deserved, but I could give him a good code. Or as good as it got on the airplane flight from Hades.

I'd thought our pericardial tap was our Hail Mary, our final attempt, but I was wrong.

Opening the chest was the real Hail Mary pass.

Tucker knelt too, and I whispered to him, "You know this will destroy all forensic evidence." I got my ass handed to me the last time I ran a code on a near-corpse. The coroner had lectured me for an hour when she called me in for an interview.

"Life first," he said simply, and I nodded. That was what I'd told the coroner, too. Saving lives comes before saving forensic evidence. Life first. Live first.

He brandished the knife. I poured brandy on both sides, which cut the smell of blood in the air.

We couldn't land the plane, we didn't have any fully licensed doctors, but we did have brandy.

"Stop CPR," I said. There was no way we could have a knife and CPR going at the same time.

Tucker pressed on the xiphoid process, the small, pinky-tip sized bone hanging on the bottom of the sternum that you're not supposed to break off during CPR. Then he placed the knife beneath the xiphoid and pushed as hard as he could, leaning with his body weight, to puncture it.

I sucked in my breath.

He let up immediately, not wanting to fall through and stab the man, but it might be the most dangerous thing he'd done so far. He could easily lose control and fall through the diaphragm and hit the left lobe of the liver, or slide upwards and jab the heart or lungs.

"Let me!" I shouted, pressing on the skin and pulling it apart to add tension. The first cut was the hardest, as Sheryl Crow and others have sung before us, and he didn't already have an incision made, like he had for the chest tube. My gloves, sticky with drying blood, still slid on his brandy-slick skin. This was a gong show.

Yet somehow, with the tip of the butter knife, and me applying tension, Tucker managed to saw a small, vertical hole, no bigger than half my thumb. "Hope, retract for me!"

I stuck my fingers in the hole and ripped it as wide as I could. That made it easier for him to cut. Also, the bigger the hole, the further my fingers were from his knife. It was a butter knife with laughable teeth, but it had cut through his skin and fat, and I'd already been sprayed by Mr. Money's body fluids. No need to get sliced, too.

I could see black, clotted blood. That was about it, no matter how the people shone their phone lights.

I leaned back to let Tucker get his head in there, because it was his case, but all I could see was blood. And truthfully, I'd never read up on how to do a pericardial window, because I'd never thought I would do one. We don't have that many traumas in Canada, and even in the ER, it's far more likely that the patient will get shunted upstairs to the OR, not get cut open in the ambulance bay.

"Scissors!" called Tucker, and I swiped the stork scissors with a brandy-soaked towel before handing them to him. The brass flashed under the light like the last spark from a star.

"Tweezers!"

I shook my head. "I don't—"

Pascale said, "Oh!" and handed me a pair of tweezers. I had no idea how or where she'd conjured them up, but I cleaned them and passed them on to Tucker.

"I can feel it," said Tucker.

My heart thumped. I wasn't sure what he was feeling. Blood? The heart itself? If he made a big enough incision, we could pull the heart out of the chest and inspect it for a wound posteriorly, like an Aztec sacrifice, only for a good cause.

Instead of asking Tucker and distracting him, I watched his hands. What I could see of his hands looked like they knew what they were doing with those tweezers.

Come on. Come on, I prayed from the bottom of my agnostic little heart.

Blood.

Burgundy blood leaked out of the wound.

Tucker pulled out a quarter-sized clot. Blood poured briskly now, more than 5 cc's. Then he extracted another chunk, undamming a mini river.

I did my best to mop it up with the brandy towels before I called, "Towels! More towels, please."

Was this too much blood? No, because the river's trickle narrowed and stopped, and Pascale said, "His heart ... "

I reached for Mr. Money's femoral pulse. His heart was beating again. The pericardial window worked.

A smile bloomed across Tucker's face. "We did it."

"You did it," I murmured.

"No. *We* did it."

I started to smile too. He couldn't have done it without me, just like I couldn't do it without the nurses and staff who saved my rear end every day. Sure, I wished I'd done the cool procedures myself, but we were a team.

Not a perfect team, but a lifesaving team.

The plane started to applaud. They whistled. A few of them stomped their feet.

"That was *amazing*." Pascale's eyes were still huge.

"Very well done, doctors," said Linda.

Gideon barked, which I took as his version of applause.

Tucker grinned while I tried to take the BP. I couldn't really hear the Korotkoff sounds, which are the actual heart sounds, over the airplane buzz, but the needle twitched when it was beating. "The BP is coming up to 105."

"Yes!" He tossed his hair, and—not going to lie—it was incredible that six weeks ago, he'd been the one on the precipice of death, and now he'd dragged another man back from pericardial tamponade. It made me want to sex him up all over again.

Topaz's little voice climbed above the crowd. "Devaguru says, 'The successful warrior is the average man, with laser-like focus.'"

What the hell? First of all, was she calling my man average when he'd pulled off the most incredible feat I'd ever seen?

And secondly, wasn't that quote by Bruce Lee?

"Now let's reduce the fluid. Just a 100 cc's at a time. I don't want him to bleed any more."

Scary thought. Especially when Tucker was basically operating with almost no lights or equipment, on an airplane, on a man whose family owned a squadron of lawyers.

Pascale looked confused. We didn't have a nurse, and we didn't have an infusion pump. I said, "If you want to be precise about fluid, we can draw it up and push it manually through the IV, 20 cc's at a time."

"No, that's okay. You can just stop squeezing the bag and eyeball how much fluid he's getting."

I glanced at the bag. It looked like it was down a third, so he'd gotten about 300 cc's so far. Not very much, but with a small needle, the fluid travels slowly. It's like trying to empty the world's biggest water balloon whose neck is the diameter of a baby's pores. No matter how much you squeeze it, it ain't gonna go fast. So with no one squeezing, we'd be at a standstill.

Mr. Money had lost a fair amount of blood. On the other hand, infusing too much fluid is dangerous in tamponade. In trauma, we use the technique of permissive hypotension, maintaining the blood pressure only high enough to keep the brain going, not so high that their wounds open up again. So I let Tucker call the shots, but I leaned forward to place my finger on Mr. Money's carotid artery. It's more sensitive than the femoral, and I didn't want to hang around in that guy's groin area any more than I had to. "His pulse is 100 and strong."

"High five," called the guy in the red b-ball cap.

Tucker laughed and waved his bloody, blue-gloved hands. "Maybe later, man." He turned to Linda. "We can land the plane any time." Still, he was smiling, relaxed now. He was in victory dance mode.

She shook her head. "Thank you, doctor. The weather conditions haven't improved, but we're finding an alternative city. Are you able to talk to the flight doctor about what happened?"

Tucker glanced at me.

I nodded. Yes, I would hold the fort over the actual patient while he radioed in, but I was nervous. The pulse had picked up to 110. No, 120. "Heart rate 120."

Tucker frowned and turned back to Mr. Money.

My vision wobbled for a second before it stabilized, and then it seemed to happen again.

The plane dipped. Its lights went out.

I swore.

The only lights left were in people's phones, and that wouldn't last long. The phone lights jigged as if they were swatted mosquitoes coming in for a second landing.

The plane plummeted like a roller coaster ride.

Everyone screamed around us.

"Daddy?" called a little kid.

The baby bawled.

Gideon barked.

But more importantly, I couldn't feel a pulse. I pressed as hard as I could without triggering a vagal reaction. Then I gave up and tried the other side.

"Tucker, I lost his pulse! Start CPR."

"No." He jabbed his hand into the left hand side of the neck, disbelieving.

I threw myself at the chest, arms locked for CPR. "Just tell me if you're coming with the knife, because I can't see anything." Only two people were left with the lights, and the beams were more in our eyes than on the chest, but I didn't care. I was doing compressions. *One-and-two-and-three-and-four-and-five—*

"No! I'll explore his heart! I'll cross-clamp the aorta!"

"Do it," I yelled, trying not to lose count. *And eight-and-nine-and-ten—*

"Get me the scissors! Get me the knife! I'm going in there!"

Magda fumbled for the instruments.

I stopped CPR when the scissors glinted in Tucker's hand.

"If I could just get better light in here. If I could see—"

"Light, please!" I barked, and more phones shone valiantly. The plane lights flickered and came back on, but dimmer than before.

"Over my right shoulder," Tucker said. "No, damn it. More to the right! I can't see anything!"

"Give him light!" I shouted.

They tried their best, but their beams were feeble, and too many heads and shoulders blocked their way as more people crowded the aisle and the surrounding seats, trying to help.

Tucker couldn't see. He couldn't move.

While Tucker dug in the chest, I checked my watch. Mr. Money had been down for 43 minutes. Long enough that we were running out of CPR volunteers, and Tucker was trying to operate in a chest cavity in near-darkness.

No one, not even lay people, thought that Mr. Money was going to make it.

No one except Tucker.

I let him burrow inside him for a while. Eventually, even his movements slowed down.

"Dr. Tucker," I said.

He was crying. His cheeks shone. He ignored that and looked up at me, almost too calm. "I'm going to call it. Time of death, 8:56 p.m., Pacific Time."

23

Magda covered Mr. Money's face and chest with a new, white towel.

I turned my head and took a breath.

The air smelled like iron. The blood was starting to coagulate on my gloves. If I wiggled my fingers, dried blood might peel off and fall to the ground like snowflakes made from fire and brimstone.

Linda spoke in a low voice. "Return to your seats, please. Everybody, we appreciate your help, but you must return to your seats."

A few people whispered. None of them knew what to do, especially with Mr. Money blocking everything from row 14 onward.

Gideon whined and strained to get at Mr. Money's remains. The line of men held him back.

Meanwhile, Tucker's stillness chilled me. I moved closer to him.

He didn't react.

I knew that, for forensic reasons, we should leave Mr. Money in situ, but there was no way we could abandon his remains in the aisle, even without Alessandro silently weeping at Mr. Money's feet, tears running down his handsome face.

Staci Kelly called from first class, "Alessandro, what's going on? Where's Joel?"

"Back to your seats. Please," said Linda, and her voice broke.

I said softly, "Do you want help moving him first?"

Linda's cheeks coloured. "Yes. Of course."

"Where would you like to put ... Joel?" His name clogged up my throat.

She glanced up and down the aisle, and I puzzled over her dilemma. He couldn't go in the cockpit with the pilots. First class would mutiny, especially Mr. Yarborough, who was yelling about going home again. We didn't want Joel in the cheap seats, with the maximum number of people gawking. Taking up a bathroom could cause a problem later on, and the galley kitchen would be gross.

Linda's expression cleared, and she pointed toward the back of the plane.

Of course it would be near row 33. It should be row 666.

"I'll help," said Herc, and I felt a twinge of sadness that I didn't know his real name. He'd been so kind. Everyone had given their ultimate, Tucker most of all.

Tucker stood at Mr. Money—Joel's—feet, watching the blood soak through the new towel on the man's chest. Tucker didn't move aside to let them pick up the body. He did nothing.

This was worse than him pacing like a lion.

"Dr. Tucker," I said. If he'd join in the last task of moving Joel's body, maybe he wouldn't feel so helpless.

He didn't respond.

"Joel?" called Staci Kelly. "You know I don't want to go back there with that dog, but ... are you okay?

Alessandro stood up. "Don't come in."

Staci Kelly's white high heels clicked toward the curtain.

"Staci, don't come in!"

Staci Kelly ignored him, tearing the curtain aside. She stood framed in the doorway, and then she screamed so long and loud that all the hairs on my arms jumped to attention.

The newborn sobbed.

The Portuguese kid cried out in his own language, covering his ears. His mother clamped hers over his, providing makeshift double ear muffs.

And still Staci Kelly screamed.

"Stop it." That scream could provoke a riot. It drilled my eardrums, but I couldn't shield them with my bloodstained hands. I couldn't get through to her because I'd have to climb over Joel J. Firestone's body to shake his widow. I waved at Pascale, exaggerating my mouth movements in case she could lip read. "Get her out of here! I'll see her in front!"

Pascale nodded frantically as the plane roiled.

Staci Kelly fell to her knees, still screaming. Pascale plucked at her arm, but Staci Kelly was larger than she was.

Then Alessandro stepped forward, picking his way over Joel. I stepped into some leg room to give him space. Tucker still didn't move, but Alessandro managed to edge by him so he could wrap Staci Kelly in his arms and lift her to her feet.

Her scream warbled and stopped.

Our ears rang in the sudden silence.

Slowly, Alessandro guided her back to business class. She tottered ahead of him before she seemed to find her feet, almost like a baby giraffe.

Pascale followed them and pulled the business class curtain closed after herself.

And still the crowd didn't speak. They were watching. Waiting.

Only the airplane's engine roared, and Gideon barked.

The people's gaze turned to Tucker, me, and the dead man at our feet. Their eyes felt like a physical weight.

Screw them. I grabbed Tucker's left bloody glove with my right.

He let me, but he didn't meet my eyes. His face was blank. His spirit had flown away.

I shook his hand. "Life first. Remember?"

No answer.

I gripped his fingers, trying to urge sensation back into them, and more importantly, the spark back into his brain and his heart and his soul. "John Tucker. Our job's not done. We have to help the widow now." I couldn't touch the rest of his body, because we were both spackled in blood, and I didn't want to talk when people were watching and probably filming us, so I tried to speak to him wordlessly.

Where are you? Come back to me.

I love you.

I'm not done with you.

Come back.

At last, Tucker turned and stared at me, unspeaking, for a long and terrible second.

Tucker was my "Weebles wobble but don't fall down" guy. Was he losing it in front of my eyes?

. *You can't, Tucker. I need you. The plane needs you.*

I love you.

You are not allowed to lose it.

You hear me?

At last he shook himself, like a dog shaking off water. He squeezed my hand, released it, and reached for Mr. Money's remains.

My mouth opened.

Before I could object, Tucker grasped the scissors and the butter knife in his left hand.

Oh. He was taking the sharps to protect us. It was the first purposeful thing he'd done since declaring the time of death, and it was so like him that I might have cried if my eyes had any tears left.

"You did everything," I told him. More than everything. The College would roast him about going beyond his skill level. He was a first year family medicine resident, not a trauma surgeon. Staci Kelly's lawyers might draw and quarter him as soon as we touched down on the tarmac. Yet I couldn't let him see my doubt. Not when he wavered so close to the precipice. "He couldn't have asked for a better doctor. Let's go take care of Staci Kelly, okay?"

He shook his head from side to side, meaning no. It was so strange, not having him talk. It was almost like he was another man.

Ryan had evolved because of my anti-crime activities, too. He used to go to church every Sunday, unlike my pagan self. That was one reason we broke up in medical school, along with long distance. But 14/11 fractured his faith. Now Ryan was more like me: he didn't know what to believe.

So I'd seen my men change before, in fundamental ways, but Tucker's silence and stillness spooked me.

If he wouldn't come with me, I didn't know what to do.

And then I did. The answer was simple. I would stay with him.

I couldn't abandon him to take care of Staci Kelly while he grieved over Joel's body. I put my hand on his wrist, gently this time. "Never mind. Someone else can help Staci Kelly." Topaz stared at us. Her nostrils pointed at me like an additional set of miniature black eyes, inspiring me. "Topaz can do it. She can quote her guru at her and ... comfort her." Or make Staci Kelly wish she, too, was dead. "We're a team. We'll stick together, okay? I love you."

My heart thudded against my rib cage as he remained mute. Was Tucker so far gone that he wouldn't remember that he loved me any more?

Finally, he spoke. "I love you."

It seemed like I had a few tears after all. He remembered. I watched his face, waiting, because I had no idea what else was going on in his beautiful head. Blood spotted his face, his neck, his hair. Out of the corner of my eye, I noticed someone filming us, but I ignored it. Tucker was all I cared about. His mental and physical survival meant everything to me.

His eyes flicked up and down, cataloguing my equally zombified look, before he gave me a crooked smile. "We'll always stick together. You were awesome." He shook his head, and my heart clutched, but he said, "We'll help her. You'll have to take your gloves off before you go up there, though."

I gazed down at my bloody gloves, and I would have laughed if the entire plane hadn't been studying us.

He grinned, and I mouthed "I love you" before I scanned for a place to dump our gloves. Garbage cans line our resuscitation bays, but where to toss my biohazardous gloves on a plane? Certainly no one would want them in the little brown paper bags hooked on the walls. Only Gideon would have been a fan. "Are we allowed to throw these away, or are they evidence?"

"I have no idea, detective doctor," he said. I smiled. No one had ever looked so good post-resuscitation.

"I'll take them," said Magda. Her nostrils flared. She didn't want to do this. But she held out her own gloved hands, ready to accept our used ones.

I pinched the cuff of the glove on my left wrist. As I peeled it off, I turned it inside out, hiding the bloody surface and all the finger bits on the inside. Then I degloved my right side the same way, turning it into a bag for both gloves, before I placed them in her cupped palms. Tucker did the same.

"Let's clean up," I said. The most important part was decontaminating Tucker's bite, but I also yearned to wash my hands and face. Ideally, I'd take a shower and burn my clothes, but in the meantime, washing up seemed like the right thing to do, both in terms of sanitation and making a mental divide between Joel's death and comforting Staci Kelly.

"Me too," said Tucker, and we hurried to separate bathrooms at the rear of the plane, me on the left, him on the right, while Linda headed in the other direction with what looked like a body bag. She thanked us and passed us each a spare set of gloves, which was perfect, because otherwise, I'd have to scrub my gross face with my bare hands.

By the time we emerged, Joel's body had been moved out of the aisle.

I didn't search for where it had gone. Tucker gestured me ahead of him, his newly-washed hair falling over his forehead, and I stepped over the bloodstains on our way to business class.

24

When I parted the curtain, braced for more screaming, the first thing I heard was Mrs. Yarborough's voice. "Sit down, for heaven's sake!"

"I don't want to sit down!" her husband protested. His grey head rose above the seat and hovered for a moment before she got him buckled up again.

Tucker and I ignored them, zeroing in on Staci Kelly, who was still in the window seat, now wearing a black jacket showcasing her cleavage, a tight black skirt, and stiletto black boots. Her face was puffy, and she was wearing sunglasses again, but otherwise, she'd transformed herself from a caterwauling, white hot mess into a hot widow prepared for the funeral.

En plus, Alessandro had taken Joel's aisle seat. He leaned toward her, murmuring in her ear, although as soon as he noticed us, he straightened away from her. She kept her legs crossed at the thigh, pointing toward Alessandro.

"We're so sorry for your loss," Tucker told her. "We did everything we could. We—I—" He swallowed. I shook my head, but he wanted to claim full responsibility. "—I took out the extra air that collapsed his lung, and removed blood from around his heart, but he was too far gone. I'm sorry."

I nodded and echoed, "Sorry." The movement made my vision heave up and down again.

"Thank you," she said. Her sunglasses slipped down her nose. She handed them to Alessandro, her eyes still locked on me. When I returned her gaze, she stirred in her seat, swaying her breasts forward.

She moved like a sexy python, but I was more interested in how she was breathing, which seemed relatively calm, even though there was still a dog on the plane and she was freshly bereaved.

I have a really bad poker face, so I glanced at Tucker. He raised his eyebrows back at me. The plane quivered.

Meanwhile, Alessandro sat beside her, rubbing her back in a way that didn't seem servant-like. He used the whole flat of his hand, making languorous circles.

I focused on Staci Kelly and reminded myself not to judge, even though I wouldn't have an employee touch me like that. If nothing else, he'd figure out whether or not I was wearing a bra. But in her case, it was almost guaranteed she needed extra support for her mammoth jugs, and maybe she found his touch comforting in her time of loss. On closer inspection, her face was still swollen, and her voice was hoarse when she spoke.

"I know you did your best. I could hear you in there, you know, even with him yelling." She flapped an elegant hand at Mr. Yarborough, who was now saying, "Mommy, I want to go home."

Alessandro nodded. "I told her."

Since this guy had tried to drag me off Joel, he didn't strike me as the best source of information.

I tried to smile. "We did everything we could to bring him back. We did our utmost." *So please be grateful and don't sue us, even though you live in La-la-lawsuit, California.*

"I know. I heard." She thrust a thumb at Alessandro and then at Tucker. "I'm not stupid, you know." Her full lips twisted, and something flashed in her eyes.

I opened my mouth, but Tucker was faster. "Of course. No one said you were stupid."

"Yeah?" She stared at him, a long, slow stare that made me twitch. "Guess you weren't one of the guys on set, then."

Tucker flushed. He's so pale that when he turns red, he almost looks like he's dipped in salsa.

I looked from Staci to Tucker and back again.

Staci Kelly said to me, "You have no idea who I am, do you? But your boyfriend knows."

I started to lick my lips before I remembered their recent history and the fact that airplane water is not clean.

Tucker tossed his head and met my eyes, but I could read the discomfort on his face, even though his blush was starting to ebb, so I turned back to her and said calmly, "I assume you're a porn star."

She bared her teeth at me. "You're a live one, aren't you? I could get all politically correct on your ass, but you just saved my husband's life. Or you tried to, anyway."

I blinked. So did Tucker. She knew exactly where to prod us.

"You know who Joel was, too?" she asked Tucker.

He shook his head, not quite meeting her eyes.

"You heard of Silicone Valley?" It took me a second to realize that she was saying Silicone, not Silicon, and by then she'd already moved on, her glossy red lips relishing her own words. "Pornucopia. San Pornado Valley. That's us. Pounding Flesh Productions. Joel J. Firestone and Staci Kelly. We got in before the money went south." She threw back her head and laughed. "We got some good years out of it. Joel knows how to follow the money."

"What's that?" called Mr. Yarborough.

"Never you mind," his wife answered.

I was still working it through myself. Joel had been a porn magnate, and Staci Kelly had been in her prime when they got together. I'm not good at guessing ages, but she had to be in her 30s now, if not 40s, which is fine with me, but I'm sure porn treats you like you age in dog years. Staci Kelly must have followed the money into the production side too. Certainly they were flying business class and had hired a manservant, and she had an outfit for every occasion.

"Looks like you were doing well." I tried to match her tone. She didn't want effusive condolences or detailed medical explanations. She wanted to talk about herself. I could do that.

She grinned. "We got in a good three years before the amateurs killed everything."

"Those amateurs," called Mr. Yarborough.

Staci Kelly issued a full-throated laugh. There was something fascinating about watching her, even though most of her outer flesh seemed surgically "enhanced." It was like watching a beautiful robot. You wanted to analyze what did and didn't quite look human. Topaz's nose made me uncomfortable, but Staci Kelly had retained an edgy, almost savage kind of beauty.

"Joel and I made plenty of money. And we made plenty of enemies while we were at it. I want you to tell me exactly what happened back there."

"He had a pneumothorax, which means that he had a hole in his lung—" Tucker began.

"Not the medical part!" She throttled down her rage, pasting over it with sweetness. "Someone stabbed him, right? Alessandro told me there was blood."

"He had two cuts on his chest," I said. "We don't know how he got them. We're doctors. We treat the wounds. It's up to the police—"

The airplane bumped. I clung to Alessandro's seat. Tucker automatically reached out to help me, but I gripped the blue fabric and thought, *Don't say it. Don't say it.*

Staci Kelly's scarlet lips formed the words anyway. "Fuck the police. I want to know who did it. You're the detective doctor, right? Joel looked you up before the Wifi died. So here's your next case. I'll hire you. Hell, I'll hire both of you."

I shook my head so hard that my brain started to orbit again. I forced myself to meet her eyes instead. "I understand your frustration. There might be police officers on this flight who could help you." Any officer would have stepped up during our Battle Royale, but maybe she was too upset to realize that. "Then you can file a report as soon as you get home. You need professional investigators, not us."

She snorted. "God knows when we're getting home. We're on our way to a frozen, godforsaken country. We're trapped on this death flight. You two figure out what happened to him right now. I'll pay you."

"It's not the money—"

"For fuck's sake!" She sounded like her husband. "Whoever stabbed him is right here on this plane. If they hated Joel, they're coming after me next. You have to protect me."

She was right. We were jammed on an airplane with a murderer.

We would have to work it out, in self defence, if nothing else.

I shook my head before my brain reminded me not to. All my instincts told me to crawl back into row 33, shake Herc's hand, and sleep on Tucker's lap until we hit Canada.

"This must be very traumatic for you," Tucker was saying. "As Dr. Sze pointed out, we're not the police, and we can't investigate anything professionally—"

I smiled.

"—but we'll contribute however we can."

I glowered at him over my shoulder. My vision telescoped in and out for a second.

He patted my shoulder, although he never broke eye contact with Staci Kelly. "Of course we can't guarantee anything. We can only ask questions. Even though you're grieving right now—"

"Baby, you have no idea how I'm grieving," she said, fitting her oversized sunglasses back on her nose.

"—we can start with questioning you and Alessandro, whenever you're ready."

She pulled her sunglasses down so she could stare at him over the rims. "I was born ready." The words were predictable, but she delivered them with conviction. Then she licked her lips, not in a quick, nervous flick like I did on winter-cracked lips, but a slow swipe that displayed the length of her tongue.

She was so obvious. Even if I played for that team, I would find her displays ridiculous. Still, Tucker's neck flushed, and she smiled before turning triumphant eyes on me. *I could have him if I wanted him.*

I shook my head. *No, you couldn't. He's mine.*

She glanced Tucker up and down, twice. "I do love a man with good hands," she said. "I'd do anything for him."

"Is that how you knew Joel?" I asked, pretending not to notice that Alessandro was massaging her forearm.

"No, sweetie. I got to know him because I was his star pupil," she said, tossing her hair and arching her breasts forward.

"When was that?" I ignored the boobs. She was obviously programmed to a) Say something sexy, b) Do something sexy, c) Watch men react, d) Laugh, e) Repeat.

"In 2002. But then, I was underage. All men like that sort of thing. That's why they're into Asians, right?"

I paused. Her husband had called me prepubescent, too. Should I ignore her barb or lob something back at her? Unprofessional, but so tempting.

Tucker cut in. "I try to treat people like individuals. So you met him in 2002. How long had he been in the business?"

She pouted, nestled against Alessandro for a moment to reactivate him—he kissed her cheek—before she fluttered her eyelashes at Tucker. "Don't you want to know how old I was?"

"Sure, but it sounds like Joel was more established in the business already. Were you in the San Fernando Valley?"

She issued a low, throaty laugh. "Yes. I was deep down in the Valley. And so was he."

He'd probably been ten years older than her. If she'd been 17, he would have been 27 like me and Tucker, which is not old, except in Hollywood. "I bet he'd been there about five years, and he was scrambling, but he wasn't making much headway. Am I right?"

I'd managed to startle her more than her husband's death. "Yeah, that sounds about right. How did you know?"

Alessandro spoke. "She must have looked him up on the Internet."

"I'd never heard of him before now, and I've kind of had my hands full, trying to save his life—"

Tucker rubbed my shoulder, silently asking me to simmer down, but I was calm compared to Alessandro.

The Italian man climbed to his feet. "Everybody's heard of Joel J. Firestone. He's famous. He worked with all the biggest people. People who wouldn't want to be named!"

That reminded me of evil wizards. I nearly smiled.

"Shhh." Staci Kelly patted his knee absently, like he was a cat, and Alessandro dropped back in his seat, resentful, as she said, "Sex is natural and beautiful and powerful. All we do is harness that energy, but most people don't understand that, even if they consume our products every day and night."

Strange. She was preaching, much like Topaz had done, but while Topaz worshipped some self-proclaimed guru, Staci Kelly worshipped money and power, which was the USA's god of choice, so she fit right in. Sex was the Occam's Razor delivering Staci that power through money. She might like sex, or put on a good show about it, but her real love was power. Now that Joel was dead, she was probably four times as rich, and she didn't have to put up with him any more. No wonder she wasn't in mourning.

But she couldn't have killed him. She'd stayed behind the business class curtain the entire time. She had an alibi.

"Are there people here who would have resented Joel?" Tucker said.

She laughed. Two types of female laughs are classically sexy: the high pitched, childish cheerleader giggle, or the low and throaty, Mississippi Delta down and dirty. Guess which one she offered Tucker. "Probably one hundred percent of the people on this plane hated his guts."

Including you? I wondered, but I held back. I wanted to see what else she'd reveal.

Even Alessandro settled back into his seat, distancing himself from her, but she tossed her hair again and blew her nose. "Just telling the truth, like I always do." She had trouble maintaining her magnetism behind a tissue.

"What exactly did he do? How did he make his money?" I said. Officer Visser once told me, *Always follow the money.*

"He's—he was a director and a producer."

I was fuzzy on what directors and producers actually did, but Tucker nodded.

"He was very professional. He wouldn't do amateur work. Everyone got paid according to industry standards. That's more and more rare these days. All the amateurs are taking over the industry."

Even the porn star producers felt broke. And clearly, in her mind, the guy had been a hero instead of an arrogant prick. Yet if I forgot all that and followed the money, from the way she talked, his expenses were too high. He should have *lost* money. How could I ask her tactfully?

She sniffed and tossed her used tissue on the floor. Alessandro scooped it up as she said, "It's not what you think. Everyone comes here with the same dream, and we let them live it out. We film them. We pay them, and pay them well. The directing, the staging, the script, the makeup, the lighting, it's all professional. It may not be what they thought they'd be doing, but they're still acting. Film is film."

And yet my family would implode if Hollywood live-streamed my sex life with strangers. Even if Joel provided better lighting.

She jabbed a neon red nail at me. I stared at it, hypnotized by the ring of crystals embedded in it, as she said, "You're a doctor. You should be supporting us. We use *condoms,* even though it limits our overseas market!"

Alessandro nodded. "We've used condoms since 2014."

"Yes, and we do it voluntarily. We have to in L.A., but there's no law for San Fernando Valley. We do it of our own volition, because Pounding Flesh cares about its performers—"

Tucker snapped his fingers. "Right, since that guy who got HIV and killed himself."

Both Staci Kelly and Alessandro looked taken aback. Tucker

explained to me, "That case was in the newspapers because he was from Montreal. Holden West, uh, contracted HIV because, uh, one of the other performers, uh ... "

Staci Kelly raised an eyebrow behind her sunglasses.

Alessandro said flatly, "He did double anal."

Double anal. Did that mean ...

"Two black cocks up his ass at the same time," said Staci, watching the expressions play across my face. "It can be pleasurable if done right."

I couldn't imagine how, but I tried to appear impassive.

"We use a lot of lubricant, and the performers know how to work together to maximize both their pleasure and optimal viewing. We're professionals."

She used the word "professional" a lot. Strangely enough, doctors do, too. My head ached. I tried to drag the conversation back on track. "Is that how you made your money? By making ... edgy adult movies?"

Staci issued a hard, bright laugh. "That's not edgy. You should see the last one I co-produced, *The Vampire Diarrhea.*"

My brain couldn't even compute that.

She laughed and tossed her mass of hair. "Scat porn is a thing. Vampires are another thing. It did *very* well."

Ugh. I had to swallow down another sudden surge of vomit. It tasted like acid, and this time I felt chunks. I took a few deep breaths and thought of blue skies. No, not blue skies. After this flight, skies were no longer calming. I pictured myself as a whale swimming with my mate. Just the two of us, swimming and singing our whale song, peaceful and beautiful.

When I tuned back in, she was still laughing at me. "You're not a virgin, are you?"

My face contorted. Why did people keep asking me that? Tucker's hand tightened on my shoulder. He didn't like the implication either. I told her, "It's none of your business."

"I only want to know if Jane the Virgin can handle everything she finds out about me and my husband in this investigation. I could tell you so much shit about everyone on this plane."

My heart gave a double thump. "Like what?" I said, ignoring the swearing.

Her scarlet upper lip curled, but I could tell she was tempted. "You really want me to do that? You want me to out all the porn stars and porn watchers on this flight?"

Of course I did. I didn't, but I did.

This was going to get ugly.

25

"Let's start with my section," she said, smiling a little. "You see the old couple at the very front?"

I nodded, puzzled. "You mean the Yarboroughs." No one could miss them. He'd started pounding on his tray table, from the sounds of it. Pascale had gone to try and calm him down.

"The woman made millions of dollars from her underwear."

I was confused. Not even the richest celebrity makes millions from selling her underwear. Not from literally selling her used panties, and not even from an advertising campaign.

Alessandro explained, "She made ShapeR."

Oh. ShapeR Shapewear. Now I knew what Mrs. Yarborough had been calling China about, and how she could afford business class. Even before the Santa girl and my mom, I knew ShapeR. My friends cursed it as they struggled into it, or out of it—it's not meant for public display, and if you've had a few drinks, it's hard to fight your way free. I don't wear it, but I'm small-built in all respects, and after my mother forced me into a few options, I swore, like Scarlett O'Hara, that I would never again be squooshed into torture devices masquerading as clothes.

However, I represented the one percent of the global female

population holding out against the modern reinvention of the corset. The rest of the world loved ShapeR, which billed itself as the more comfortable, more sleek, 2.0 version of shapewear.

"What does that have to do with ... your industry?" said Tucker.

Staci Kelly snorted. "She should call it ShaperXXX. I'm sure she got the idea from staring at naked bodies all day, trying to make them as perfect as possible."

I shook my head. "She was a porn star? Back in ... " I was trying to figure out Mrs. Yarborough's age. Did they have porn fifty years ago? But then I remembered a picture of a smutty black and white post-card from the cowboy days. Yes, they would have had porn. And yes, Mrs. Yarborough could have starred in it.

Staci Kelly laughed. "No, that old horse face wasn't a porn star. As if." She gave a little shudder. "She did makeup. There used to be good money in makeup. Like, $1200 or $1500 a day."

Damn. Canadian doctors want to make that much, and we don't get paid in American dollars. That's serious coin. A makeup artist wouldn't have to put out on camera, and could work for decades. Mrs. Yarborough was smart.

"Before the Internet ruined everything, of course."

Ah, yes, the evil Internet. But if you went from $1200 a day to $200 a day, that would seem Satanic.

"I gotta hand it to her, though." Staci Kelly snorted at her own joke, probably because hands are key both in porn and in makeup. "Making that kind of money, most of 'em would've stuck with that. But she didn't want to spend her whole life fixing girls' mascara. She left and made a shit ton of money. More than my husband, and doing what? Making bras and underwear? That's nothin'."

"I'm sure she worked at it. It's a different industry," said Tucker.

"Yeah. I should be in that *industry*."

"Well, maybe you could talk to her. You're on the same flight," I said.

"Are you nuts?" She stared at me. "Yeah, you're nuts. Either that or stupid. Get it together, or you'll never figure out who killed my husband."

I thought she was the stupid one. If I were sitting near a million-aire and wanted to work with her, I would say hi. But that wasn't my problem right now. "Can you tell us who else you recognize?"

"It's more like who don't I recognize." She grinned. She enjoyed having secrets and didn't want to give them up too easily. "That stewardess."

Tucker and I were stunned. "Pascale?" I said, when I unlocked my lips. She was so elegant and reserved, but I'm sure guys would throw down the cash to see her lose control.

"I don't know her name. The old one."

"You mean ... Linda?" I said. The head flight attendant, who looked like she wouldn't know which end of the dildo was up? Man!

"She's not in the industry, but she comes to sex clubs sometimes. I know who she is."

It was hard not to let my jaw drop. I'm pretty sure my eyes bulged more than a British bulldog.

Staci smirked. "It's the pilot she hooked up with. Kinky guy."

I like gossip as much as the next bored bystander, but this was too much. It was like I'd said, *Sure, let me peek behind this curtain,* and stumbled upon a full-blown orgy.

"When you get to the top—or the bottom—L.A. is a small town. We all know each other." Staci Kelly held up her thumb. "You prob-ably noticed the whale in business class. He likes golden showers." Oh, dear.

She'd moved on to her index finger. "Trina, the synth pop singer, used to do some work for us under a different name. You might have noticed her." She used her chin to indicate the mixed race woman sitting across from Alessandro, hiding behind a pair of sunglasses. "She's hung over or strung out or both."

Third finger. "Darren Adam, the accountant, took the exit row in cattle class. That guy loves money more than his own dick. He's richer than me and Joel put together, but he wouldn't spring for first class even if he knew he was gonna die tomorrow."

Fourth finger. "The girl with the 32F's beside Darren tried out for us a few times."

Fifth finger. "One of the guys who used to do work for us is here too, but I won't out him because he left the industry. You want me to keep going?"

I rubbed my temples. The plane bumped again, which didn't help. "That's too many suspects. You're only in the first few rows of the plane, and all these people knew him and could have hated him."

"And they could have helped hold him down," said Tucker, his lips thin. "I didn't pay attention to where everyone was. Did you?"

I shook my head, and instantly regretted it. "I was backwards half the time, remember?" I was doing reverse cowgirl on his lower half while someone was stabbing Joel. Tucker would have had a better view, but he'd probably been watching me, especially after Joel punched me.

In a way, it was good that Joel had punched me, because if Staci Kelly sued us, I'd sue her right back. Her husband had whacked me hard enough to give me my first concussion. A doctor's brain is her primary asset.

"Ask around," said Staci, waving her talons. "You can do that right now. Go on. I can pay you whatever you need."

She was trying to get rid of us. The whole thing stank worse than an abandoned cargo hold of fish guts.

Time to jump ship. I said to Staci Kelly, "This definitely sounds complicated. I wouldn't blame you for hiring a professional."

"You two," she said. "That's your job. Find out what happened to my husband. Please. I'm a widow now. I have nothing left."

Yeah, right. She still had a production company, the rights to *The Vampire Diarrhea*, Alessandro slobbering over her, and the best plastic surgery that money could buy. We should run, not walk, away from her. "You have my condolences."

"And mine as well." Tucker interlaced his fingers with mine. "We'll do everything we can to help you."

I shook my head at him. "Dr. Tucker—"

"Everything," he repeated, clasping my hand.

26

Who's we? I detached my fingers and walked away while Tucker was still talking to Staci Kelly. He touched my shoulder, but let me go. In other words, our teamwork snapped as soon as the code ended.

"Excuse me," said the woman on my right, the one across from Alessandro's original seat. Her musical voice arrested me in my tracks.

"Hi," I said. Even I knew that this was Trina, the singer with the most downloaded synth song of all time.

"Could I speak to you in private?" Trina rose to her feet in one smooth movement. I'd never paid much attention to her music, because I'm not much into processed sound, but she was physically striking even before she removed her sunglasses, revealing the most beautiful face I'd ever seen. Everything else, including the plane's crazed vibrations, became irrelevant.

Somehow, I was mesmerized by her liquid brown eyes, the sweep of her eyelashes, the height of her cheekbones, and the point of her chin. She was so thin that she probably weighed less than me, even though she was about a foot taller. To make things even more unfair, she still had slender but real-looking curves. Yet I wasn't truly jealous.

What would be the point? She was so extraordinary, it would be like resenting a galaxy. The galaxy doesn't care. It simply is.

"Sure! Let's talk." Tucker zipped behind me and beamed over my shoulder at her.

"Hey!" squawked Staci Kelly, starting to rise from her seat.

"I'm Katrina Masserman." The richness of her voice heightened her allure.

"Hi!" Tucker chirped.

Most people fall somewhere on the bell curve of good looks, ranging from ugh to meh to pleasant. This was the kind of woman who seized every eye. She made Staci Kelly, with her masses of blonde hair and her giant white teeth, look like a plastic, oversexed Barbie. No wonder Trina masked herself with sunglasses and nondescript clothes. She still couldn't hide her gloriousness.

"Nice to meet you, Katrina." I tried to concentrate on her actual words. I never knew her full name. It sounded Jewish, which was kind of cool. I've gotten to know Jewish culture a bit more since living in Montreal. Katrina reminded me of Hurricane Katrina, though.

Trina glanced at the front of the cabin, where Pascale was trying to placate Mr. Yarborough with a bottle of water, and then at Staci Kelly and Alessandro, who were watching us. We were all hemmed so close together that Alessandro could have grabbed both cheeks of Tucker's bum with one hand and Staci Kelly's with the other.

"Maybe we could head toward the back?" Trina asked. Even her smell made me want to lean closer. It wasn't only perfume, although there was a hint of vanilla.

"Sure," said Tucker again.

I couldn't blame him. Still, I hoped he remembered who had just fucked his brains out. Twice.

"You don't have anything to say." Staci Kelly tried to step over Alessandro. "You were here the whole time, with me. What do you want to tell them that you can't say in front of me?"

"We're having a private conversation," said Trina.

"They already know that you used to be one of Joel's sluts. You think you're too good for us because of your music? I remember when you couldn't make rent because of your music, darling. I remember exactly what you did. You remember that too, hmmm?"

I recoiled at her viciousness. I'd only spent a few seconds with Trina, but she seemed intensely private. Even shaking her hand would be a violation. Her self-contained beauty probably spurred on whoever starred in those films with her. I got that flash again, that same feeling of kinship with Alessandro, only stronger. This time, I knew what it was.

I wanted to protect Trina.

What? I shoved the thought away. She was richer than me, more powerful than me, and more beautiful than me. Why did she need me to protect her?

Plus, shielding people was the exact wrong attitude for the detective doctor. Everyone here was a suspect. I couldn't forget that.

They do studies on how we react to looks, and good-looking people earn more, get married more easily, become elected President, and even elicit more reaction from babies. That's right, life is sweeter from the cradle onward.

It only made sense that beauty would get away with murder.

I shook myself. My vision wobbled, and I ignored it. Trina had been sitting in business class the entire time, same as Staci Kelly. I needed to stick to the facts. Beauty was irrelevant.

Tucker laid his hand on the back of my neck gently, as if he sensed my concussion. He said to Trina, "Maybe we can borrow the galley. Let's go."

"You don't need to go anywhere. I told you. What about me? I'm his wife! You should be talking to me!" Staci Kelly scrambled over Alessandro, shoving her way into the aisle.

Tucker quickly backed up before her breasts hit his chest.

I darted to the curtain, beside Trina.

Staci Kelly started humming a tune, and after few seconds, I realized it was "Weathervane," Trina's breakout song, but too high, and twisted.

Trina started before she caught herself. "Stop it," she said, her hands forming fists at her sides.

"That's enough," I said. Not only was she making fun of Trina, it felt like she was satirizing me singing "Give Peace a Chance."

Staci Kelly placed her hands on her hips. "Hell, no. These two work for me. Leave them alone, you Fluorescent Seaweed Kokeshi Doll!" Staci Kelly mashed up Trina's song titles, goading her, before she drew herself up to her full height, clasped her fingers around an imaginary microphone, and began singing about luminescent seaweed.

Mr. Yarborough tried to join in from the front of the plane.

"We're not working for you," I said, cutting through their ululations. We were poor, but we weren't Staci Kelly's slaves. There is dignity in not taking money from someone. "Come on."

I grabbed Tucker's hand. Staci Kelly couldn't stop us from exiting her section, even if she was a horrendous singer and even worse person. Time to go.

"Oh, no, you don't!" Staci Kelly snapped.

"Hey!"

That was Tucker, so I whipped around. Staci Kelly had snatched his 42 shirt from behind.

She twisted her hand, winching the material around his armpits. Trina and I glimpsed his scarred abdomen before he spun around to detach her talons.

More images flashed into my head:

Tucker yelling through the smoke on 14/11.

The police hauling me away from him when I thought he was dead.

Mr. Money's shirt yanked up to his armpits.

The flash of stork scissors in Tucker's hand.

Tucker pulling blood clots out of Mr. Money's chest.

"You're not getting away from me. I own you!" screamed Staci Kelly, hauling me back to the present, and to my own body.

I ran at her with my fists raised. "Get away from him!"

If I'd had a weapon in my hand, I would have killed her. Hell, if I'd had the stork scissors, I would have driven them into her eyeball.

But it was Alessandro who tackled her around the waist.

27

"What the fuck?" Staci spat.

Alessandro didn't answer. He concentrated on acting like a human handcuff for her arms and torso as he tried to drag her backwards a foot or two, into Joel's seat.

We followed in case she managed to break away. Tucker was in the lead and wouldn't let me cut past him. Over Tucker's shoulder, I saw Staci Kelly's face turn puce with wrath.

Alessandro looked agonized. He strained to walk backwards down an unstable airplane aisle while carting a hellion.

"Let *go* of me!" Staci Kelly tried to wrench her arms free from her sides, but the disadvantage of her Scarlett O'Hara waist was that Alessandro could easily encircle her. She hadn't expected an attack from him.

"Excuse me," said Pascale, hurrying down the aisle from the front of the plane. "Mrs. Kelly? Would you ... could I interest you in ... " She floundered.

"More zip ties," I said, "The medical kit. And get help."

Staci Kelly wouldn't take Benadryl by mouth, that was for sure, but maybe there was something else I'd missed earlier.

Pascale pounded up the aisle, already calling for help.

Mr. Yarborough swiped at Pascale as she passed him. "Hey, missy!"

We all ignored him. Staci Kelly was far more dangerous.

She kicked Alessandro with one spiky heel.

He grunted, absorbing the impact.

"You like that, you little pussy?" Staci Kelly cackled with glee before she jabbed her toe at Tucker.

He stepped out of range.

That enraged her enough to plant both feet on the ground, press against Alessandro, and rear up to kick at Tucker with both feet at the same time. "Fuck off! I own you! I own all of you!"

Mr. and Mrs. Money. Hobbies: flaunting cash, beating up bystanders, recreating the good olde days when slavery was legal ...

"You're fired, Alex!"

Alessandro's mouth worked. He didn't answer.

"You'll never work again. Not in this town, not anywhere in America. Hell, I'll follow you to Italy and curse anyone who tries to help you. As for your art—"

Even half-hidden behind her, I saw him recoil.

She felt it, too. Her red lips stretched into a Joker-like smirk. "Ah, yes. Your *art.* Your *oil painting.* Also known as the *stupidest thing in the world.*"

"Leonardo da Vinci and Monet would beg to differ," said Tucker.

She whipped her head to glare at him. The whites showed around her irises, and her pupils were enormous. "They're dead. They can't beg."

Her body relaxed visibly. It cheered her up, contemplating those dead men, and Alessandro lifted his chin.

"Don't let go of her!" I told him.

Fury twisted the cords in her neck. "What do you know about it?"

"Not much," I admitted. I was willing to entertain her as long as it took for them to come back with more zip ties—*please don't have run out of zip ties*—and if she was yapping, Tucker wouldn't tangle with her, and I wouldn't have to jump all three of them. "Mostly I work at the hospital. No time for anything else."

"If you did buy art, would you buy an *oil painting?*" Contempt treacled out of her voice, slow and dangerously sweet.

"Maybe," I said, before honesty forced me to add, "Probably not. But I'm a student renting—"

"See? Why would you paint giant murals with oil when no one gives a shit about any kind of painting, let alone oil painting, let alone *portraits* of *poor people. Everyone* hates *poor* people!"

Something clicked in my head. Staci Kelly must've grown up poor. "Not everyone," I said.

"Really." She focused on me again. "You remember that Syrian refugee kid who drowned?"

I nodded. Who could forget the three-year-old boy who had washed up on shore, face down in the sand, in his red T-shirt, blue shorts, and tiny shoes?

"Alan Kurdi," said Tucker. "His brother and mother drowned, too."

"This idiot painted him! He painted a picture of him alive! He said it was important to remember him in life!"

Tucker shot back, "It *is* important. The Human Rights Watch worker who shared his photo has asked people to take it down now, to let him rest."

"Well, then, let him rest! Don't make *oil paintings* of him! Who the fuck is going to hang that on his wall?"

"I might know someone," said Trina, who had remained silent at the curtain until now. She moved behind the last row of seats, speaking directly to Alessandro. "We should talk."

His eyes widened. His mouth opened, but no words came out.

And in that unguarded moment, Staci Kelly head butted Alessandro.

Crunch.

Blood gushed out of his nose. He choked, his hands reaching to staunch it before he remembered to clamp down on Staci Kelly, but she'd already flown straight at Tucker.

"I got 42 problems—" she howled at him.

He stepped back and let her momentum carry her forward as he guided the back of her shoulder to her right. She plowed into Trina's empty seat, caught herself on the seat cushion, and started to lever herself back up, still howling.

Tucker backed up, shielding me from her and urging me away by using his back and butt. "Get out of here, Hope."

"I'm not leaving you with that monster!"

"Alessandro—" he said.

"No!" I shouted. The Italian guy was mopping up his nose. We couldn't count on him. Granted, Tucker had just performed some fight move that I didn't fully understand and couldn't duplicate. I still wouldn't go. "I'm not leaving you. I'm *never* leaving you."

He smiled. His cheeks bunched up from behind. I ran forward, because Staci Kelly specialized in ganking guys who were distracted by happy thoughts.

Staci Kelly swung her arms in the air like she was going to strangle him, but when he raised his own arm to block her, her heel shot up to nail him in the belly. Just like her horrible husband.

I snatched him around the waist first. "Get down!"

I was trying to yank him away from her, but he was heavier than me, and he wouldn't move.

Her heel bashed me in the forearms.

I gasped, but I didn't let go. It was like the legend of Tam Lin, where he gets kidnapped by the faery queen for centuries, and in order to save him, the heroine has to hold on to him no matter what. When he gets transformed into a slashing bear and then a red hot piece of iron, she hangs on.

Staci Kelly guffawed at the tears in my eyes. "Did that hurt? I hope I broke your wrist. I hope you'll never be a doctor again, you stupid slag."

Alessandro lunged at her from behind.

She spotted him at the last second and drew her hands into fists, but it was too late. He winched each arm behind her, and Magda finally bolted out of economy class with a zip tie.

28

"I'm going to sue you," said Staci Kelly. She sounded almost calm now, with her wrists bound behind her and her ankles loosely bound.

No one spoke. *Don't feed the trolls.*

The airplane shook. Tucker twitched in front of me. He was ready for her to stop, drop, and fight, but I worried about her poisonous tongue. Like another fairy tale, she spewed toads and vipers every time she spoke.

"I'm going to take you for everything you've got. Which isn't a lot. I'm guessing you've got about 42 cents."

Tucker probably had negative money. I smiled anyway. The Wicked Witch of the West had been contained.

"We tried to save your husband's life, and you attacked us," said Tucker. "Would you like something to help you calm down?"

"I'm not taking anything from you, Dr. Frankenstein."

Oh, good. She knew Victor Frankenstein was the bad guy, even though the movies blamed his "monster."

"I'm going to sit here," she continued, "in my chair, which I paid for, and contact my lawyer." Technically, she was in Joel's seat, but what the heck. It all came from the same porny bank account.

"We're going to find you a different place," said Linda, in a sweet voice. She'd rushed after Magda so fast that she'd left the curtain open to economy class. Over a hundred witnesses feasted their eyes on us.

"What are you talking about? This here is my place. I paid for it. Hell, we paid for both seats, me and Joel's. I'll hang out here as long as I want. We could've bought this whole plane. You owe me!"

None of that followed, but I no longer expected it to. She was either on drugs, or had a serious personality disorder, or most likely, both. Time for us to go and tend to our latest wounds.

Alessandro kept touching his nose, even though it meant daubing blood on his own hands. My wrists, shoulders, and arms ached, especially if I made fists or tensed my arms, in addition to my concussion and back ache. I suspected Tucker didn't feel great after my bear hug and Joel's bite/stomach kick combo.

Only Trina had slipped back into her seat and was ignoring us. I wondered what she'd wanted to tell us before, but we could always ask her later.

"We can't have any disturbance in this area," said Linda. She was a master at doublespeak. She should become a politician after this. Tucker could cut open Joel's chest in the cheap seats, but God forbid that Staci Kelly break a man's nose in executive class. She would have to be expelled. Where, I had no idea, since the flight was sold out.

Then Linda turned to us. "Doctors, would you permit me to exchange your seats? You could both stay here, and Ms. Kelly could move to row 33."

A smile bloomed across Tucker's face. "I should like nothing better."

"Pascale will bring you your things, when time permits," she said.

"Perfect." Tucker looked like he was already sipping port and enjoying the complimentary slippers.

What about Herc? I pressed my lips together before I said, "The other man in 33A might not want—"

"I'll ask his permission as well," she said smoothly. "Come on, now, Ms. Kelly."

"I'm wearing high heels!"

"I can take those off, if you're having difficulty ambulating," said Linda. We all moved out of her way. There was enough room for me and Tucker to hide behind the last seat and let them pass.

"Are you joking? These are Louboutins! They cost more than you'd make in a week!"

"Then you can walk in them," said Linda.

I wasn't sure how Staci Kelly could walk with ankle ties and high heels, while the airplane did the hokey pokey, but if anyone could manage, she would. With extra ass twitching.

Staci Kelly stood up. She loomed over Tucker and Linda in her heeled boots. The only person who matched her height was Trina, who'd replaced her sunglasses and her headphones, and who wasn't offering a seat swap.

"That's it," said Magda, in her gravelly voice. "Come this way, Mrs. Kelly." She and Linda beckoned Staci forward while Pascale stood behind. "We'll guide you to your new seat."

Staci inched into the aisle, testing her feet and how much she could move the ankle ties. It looked like only a few centimetres. She would take ten years to walk to the back of the plane.

"Maybe you could use a walker," I said. "Do you have the kind you can sit on? Or even a wheelchair?"

"Hell, no." Staci Kelly dropped like a dead weight.

Magda cried out and stretched to catch her, too late.

Linda shied out of the way.

Staci Kelly sat her butt on the floor, feet planted. "I paid for business class, and I ain't going anywhere."

"You're creating a disturbance," said Linda, between her teeth. She grasped Staci Kelly's ankles.

"Hell, yeah, I am, Linda. A disturbance. Is that what you call it when your boyfriend spanks you at SN8k?"

Linda flushed. This was the first time I'd seen full-on slut-shaming. Doctors are too overworked to become slatterns. Some would call me one, because of my two boyfriends, but the actual amount of time I can get it on with either one of them? Way limited.

"That's neither here nor there," I said, adopting a crisp enunciation for more authority as Linda pressed her lips together and vanished behind the curtain.

"So what's here or there, Jane the Virgin?"

Sigh. Women couldn't win. Either we were virgin-shamed, slut-shamed, or in my case, both. I wished we could gag her too.

"That's enough insulting people," said Tucker. "We can't have this kind of talk on an airplane when everyone is already upset. I'm sure you need some counselling, but—"

"I don't want *counselling*. I want you all in jail!"

"You want vengeance," Tucker said. "You want us to suffer because you lost your husband. I understand that. Some people cry. Others get angry. It's normal. It's okay."

"It's not okay. What are you, some sort of head shrinker? I'm going to sue you until your *balls* shrink up like Raisinettes! I could buy and sell you with my lunch money!"

They say that a crisis makes you more of who you are. She was the ugliest person I'd ever known. Even her husband, bellowing and bashing everyone in a two foot radius—you knew he was constantly radioactive and could deal accordingly. Staci Kelly played Beauty and the Breasts, luring you in with compliments until she could splinter your nose and shatter your dreams.

I wanted to pin this murder on her.

I wanted it so badly that I could envision her hair ratted and reeking of cigarettes, her body swathed in orange coveralls, her teeth loose in her gums.

I had the terrible feeling that I was staring at the killer, but I would never catch her.

I passed my hand over my face. I said to Staci, "That's enough."

She stopped. The look on her face seared me for an instant before I steeled myself. I'd faced much nastier people than her, and I'd lived every time so far. I said, "Who cares about money? Money doesn't mean quality. It just means money."

She cackled, and I wondered how I'd ever found her attractive. "That's what poor people say."

"They're right," I told her. "Dr. Tucker and I are poor. We're students. But we would have saved your husband's life. That's worth more than money. Isn't it?"

"He died anyway," she shot at us.

It didn't hurt as much the second time. "But we tried. We got his heart beating again. We did our utmost for him."

Linda reappeared with three hefty white men from economy class. I was relieved not to see Herc dragged into this, although I wondered how he was doing. Linda said, "I'll need one of you on her legs and—"

"They're not touching me," said Staci Kelly.

"—one of you on her arms—"

"Not one of you is touching me. You have to pay to touch me!"

"—one of you to act as backup, in case she incapacitates one of us."

"No problem," said one of the men, with a French accent.

Staci Kelly immediately cursed him out, thrashing and kicking, but the Frenchman grabbed her ankles and hauled her closer to the curtain, where they had more room to maneuver. No matter how she wriggled, her screams grew fainter as he and a second man with enormous biceps carted her to the back of the plane. The third man tipped an imaginary cap at us.

Tucker and I raised our eyebrows at each other and slid into our new seats. My heart batted like a rabbit's.

The only problem was, I'd landed in Staci Kelly's seat. The cushion was still warm from her skin. I didn't want anything from her.

And not that I'm superstitious, but Tucker had taken over the chair of a dead man.

29

"You okay?" I murmured. I nuzzled the blond fuzz on Tucker's earlobe with my nose. I wanted to lick it, but not after we'd both been baptized in Joel J's blood.

"Yeah. You?"

"Surviving this death flight." I was glad I'd climbed on board, though. What if Tucker had flown by himself? He would have managed, but two doctors were better than one.

Tucker cased the cabin, lingering on Alessandro in the seat behind him, before he whispered in my ear, "It's funny that she picked that term. They used death flights to make people 'disappear' during The Dirty War in Argentina."

I paused. "She didn't make 'death flight' up?"

"No. Well, if she did, it was a coincidence."

I hated coincidences. It reminded me of Ian Fleming's line, "Once is happenstance. Twice is coincidence. Three times is enemy action."

Still, the chances of Staci Kelly being involved in Argentina's Dirty War were remote. Wasn't that during the '70s? She wouldn't have been born yet. Just because I was paranoid didn't mean everything was enemy action.

Only most things.

I'd only heard of people "disappearing" in Chile, but no doubt dictators shared villainous tips. Come to think of it, Joel J and Staci Kelly would have egged on each others' immorality. It would only have been a matter of time before Alessandro was corrupted, if he hadn't been already. I felt him staring at us from between the crack in the seats. There was more leg room in business class, but your neighbours' eyes could still bore into your shoulder blades.

"It happened to my friend's great uncle," said Tucker. "They told prisoners they were releasing them. Sometimes, they made them dance for joy. 'Look. You're going to be free. Dance!' They told their families the prisoners were going away. Then they loaded them up in a plane, said they were sedating them for the flight, and injected them with Pentothal. Once they were up in the air, over the ocean, they dropped the prisoners out of the plane."

To their death. Death flights. "But ... why?"

Tucker tucked my head against his chest. "Sometimes there is no why."

I breathed him in, closing my eyes. Even that made my brain spin a few times before it stabilized. I linked my arms around him, surreptitiously checking my wrists, which seemed bruised but not broken.

I heard the iPhone camera shutter sound and lifted my head. I couldn't keep my eyes closed while someone was taking a picture of us. Too vulnerable. Too much in the spotlight, like that lion pacing in a Costa Rican zoo, unable to shield itself from our relentless eyes.

Then I realized it wasn't a picture of us. Alessandro was taking pictures of his own nose.

Alessandro met my eyes in the crack between our seats. "Thanks."

"You're welcome." He was out of a job, and both Joel and Staci Kelly had smacked him, but his brain, heart, and lungs were intact, he got to stay in business class, and Trina had asked about his art. Definitely a step up.

"Do you want me to try and fix your nose?" I asked him.

Tucker loosened his embrace, although he kept an arm draped around me.

Alessandro touched his nose and frowned. "What would you do? Break it again, like in a cowboy movie?"

"Only if it's crooked. If it's already in the centre, then just like any other fracture, we let it heal in place." Sometimes we put a splint on it, which looks really funny.

He lifted his hand away so I could examine him. I unbuckled my belt so I could stand up and look down on it. Tucker shifted out of the way when I crouched to get the "worm's eye" view of him from below, between the seats, while the plane cast me from side to side. Then I said, "It's a bit off to the left."

"She's right handed." He grimaced and touched the blood starting to trickle from his left nostril again. "Maybe her head hits that way too."

I smiled, more to try and bond than because it was actually funny. "It hurts to put it back in, though. It's better if we inject freezing. Sometimes we put you to sleep."

"And then what?"

"Well." I tried to remember the time I watched a plastic surgeon do it. Tucker leaned forward, desperate to put in his twenty cents' worth, but he managed to hold back while I said, "I could stick the blade of a scalpel up your nose to reduce the septum along with the outer bones." It makes a huge crunch. "We should pre-pack both your nostrils with cotton because it bleeds so much afterward."

He shuddered. He definitely wasn't a blood and guts kind of guy. "If you don't do it now, am I going to have a crooked nose for the rest of my life?"

I laughed. "Of course not. Sometimes we leave it for ten days anyway, to let the swelling go down, and then we move it back into place." That sounded nicer than "break it all over again." "I'm sure there are thousands of doctors in L.A. who'd be happy to do it for you."

"They'd charge me for it, too," he muttered.

Money. The root of all evil, or at minimum, a fair amount of heartache. "Well, we're landing in Montreal. You could always come see me at the hospital, and I could do it for you then, with proper anaesthesia."

"It's a deal," he said, giving me a crooked smile.

I liked him a lot better now that he was on his own. "How did you end up working for them, anyway?"

His cheeks reddened, and he looked away. "They recruited me."

"Okay." I wasn't sure what he meant, but I wouldn't press him.

He sighed and lowered his voice. Tucker and I leaned forward in tandem as he explained, "I had my own YouTube channel in Italy. I was popular enough, but I wanted more. I wanted to be a big star, go to Hollywood. They said they'd help me. When I arrived, though, I had no credits and no connections, and ... "

"Yeah." How many young, beautiful people get sucked into that dream?

"I said I would act in a film for them. Just one! But once they got me in that one ... "

I shook my head. Tucker's body pressed tight against mine.

"I'm not from Rome or Milan. Small town Italy is very conservative, because of the Vatican. You may have heard of the gay men who were exiled under Mussolini, or the ban against same sex marriage until 2016."

I hadn't heard of any of those things, but Tucker nodded as he slid his hand under my hair to touch my neck. I leaned into him and imagined muzzling any hint of affection for fear of beating, exile, or worse.

Alessandro continued, "After those movies came out, I couldn't go back to Italy. People sent the links to my grandmother! I was a dead man. All I had was my painting, because I didn't own my face or my body any more."

I understood what he meant. Since I've become notorious as the "detective doctor" who was kidnapped, people construct strange ideas about me. My face was even made into a meme that my own brother told me not to look up. How much worse would it be for a porn star?

"No one would hire me except *them.*" His voice lifted on the last word, and I knew he loathed them. Anger and sadness bristled out of him.

But did he kill Joel?

Although my scrambled brain couldn't piece together all of the fight, I distinctly remembered Alessandro hauling me around the waist, much like he'd grabbed Staci Kelly, come to think of it. *"He'll come after you, he'll hurt you, you have no idea ... "*

Now I had some idea of what Joel J and Staci Kelly had done to him.

"I'm sorry," I said, and I meant it. People are such hypocrites. Sex is smeared over our ads, our music, our shows, and probably even our breakfast cereal, but heaven forfend the gorgeous actors who carried out the acts for our amusement. They were our modern day gladiators in the ring, but as in the days of Rome, they weren't allowed outside the ring.

Stay on the screen or die. Or disappear.

We who are about to fuck, salute you.

I leaned against Tucker the way Roxy the Rottweiler leaned against me, for silent comfort, before she nudged my hand with her cold nose and licked me. I wished Ryan were here, too. And I tried to find the right words. "They're terrible people. They enjoyed ... creating illusions on screen and sowing misery in real life."

Alessandro's hands fisted. He assessed Tucker and me, pressed against each other, and now that I knew he was an artist, I understood the depth of his gaze. His eyes were his instruments. He used them to weigh the world and reinterpret it. I felt more kinship with him than with Staci Kelly or, frankly, most people on this plane.

Or on this planet.

Our world teaches us how to kill or be killed. Cut those trees, snatch those fish out of the ocean. Burn everything left standing.

Almost no one honours the quiet people, the ones trying to hold everything together, the ones who invite the whole class to birthday parties, the ones silently tending to their gardens, reading their books, or watching the moon glow.

But I do, when I have time. And I could tell Alessandro was one of those people. Someone who hadn't achieved commercial success, but probably had more talent in his dandruff than Joel had accumulated in the past fifty years.

Yet Joel was the one who'd scored the money and the glory while Alessandro died inside.

So I had to say, "Someone stabbed Joel."

"It wasn't me," Alessandro returned. "I'm their body guard."

I hadn't known that was his official role. Tucker twitched, eager to cut in, but I pressed a hand on his thigh to shut him up. "Great. You must have been watching him. Did you see anyone with a knife?"

"No. How would anyone bring a knife on a plane?"

Compton carried a plastic knife. Pascale whipped out stork scissors. Even post-9/11, there were ways of getting sharp objects on a plane. "It didn't have to be a knife. Some sort of blade near his chest. Did you see that?"

"No," he said. "The flight attendants were in the way. I had to pull them aside to get at you." His cheeks reddened. It embarrassed him, to talk about this, but we had to do it.

"What did you see? How did you move the flight attendants out of the way?"

"I don't remember. It's kind of a blur. I don't think I hurt them. I probably tunnelled right through them—" His face screwed up for a second. "Wait. I did see something. That crazy guy with a plastic knife."

Compton. But how could he have gotten past Herc? And it was only a plastic knife. You probably could stab someone if you used enough force, but you'd have to be out of your gourd to shank them, clean the knife off, and then offer it up again to the doctor trying to rescue the victim.

Although it would be a clever way to explain, afterward, why it was covered in the victim's blood. And it would be easy to carry multiple plastic knives.

I rolled the idea around in my addled brain one more time.

No, I still didn't think Compton had the time, the motive, or really, the correct weapon to kill Joel. But if the real weapon was the stork scissors, the forensic team would be hard-pressed to prove it after Tucker had sunk them into the guy's chest.

"Anything else?" I knew I shouldn't lead him, but I couldn't resist saying, "There were scissors too."

"I didn't see the scissors. I didn't see anything. Everyone pushed me out of there, even though I was only trying to do my job."

"He was trying to throw a dog off a plane," I pointed out. "He hit you. And—"

Alessandro shrugged.

"It wasn't the first time, was it?" Tucker said.

He shrugged again. After a minute, he said, "I could take it. It wasn't the worst thing he could do to me."

Eesh. Did he mean something sexual? I nodded sympathetically and left that one alone. "Do you think he hurt Staci Kelly—"

He almost laughed. "That one can take care of herself."

"Do you think she killed him?" The words leaped out of my mouth. No filter.

But he didn't seem offended. He sat in silence. At long last, he shrugged. "How could she? She was in a different part of the plane."

There it was again. How could she?

30

Alessandro lapsed into silence. I asked Pascale to bring him some ice for his nose and whispered to Tucker, "We should interview everyone who held down Mr. Money. That's how we'll figure out what happened."

"You mean Joel, right?"

"Right." My cheeks burned. I was so in my own head that I'd forgotten to call him by his real name.

Tucker didn't seem to care. "Good timing. She seems to have stopped screaming."

I attuned my ears. I'd blocked out Staci Kelly's yowls, but they did seem to have died down. So to speak.

When Pascale offered us water, I gulped down mine, plus a refill, with profuse thanks. I'd face Staci Kelly better with some rehydration.

The curtain twitched aside. I turned, expecting Linda with a request to talk to the flight doctor, but Compton shambled toward us, his pants still at risk of falling off his bony hips. He didn't make eye contact. "Hi."

Tucker glanced at me and spoke for both of us. "Hi there. What's your name?"

"Cody."

Well, that was a C name, which made it easier for me to remember.

He pointed to the shirt. "Cody Compton."

Ah. So the shirt wasn't only a retro cool thing for him. His name was technically Compton. That made it even easier for me to remember.

"Thanks for helping us out back there," said Tucker.

"Yeah. I'm a giver."

I choked back an inappropriate laugh.

"Yeah, that's awesome," said Tucker. He sounded like he meant it. I'll never be as good an actor as him.

Compton rubbed under his left nostril with the top of his index finger. He repeated the action slowly. I was afraid he was going to start picking it, but after a long moment, he wiped his finger on his pants and said to Alessandro, "Hey, man, you got something there."

Alessandro paused. None of us had expected that one. I suspected that his handsome Italian pride smarted. "Thank you."

Compton nodded. "Just helping a brother out. That's what I do. I'm a giver." This time, he gave an odd emphasis to the last word.

"What are you giving?" I asked, interrupting their bro-man-dude moment.

"Help," he said, as if I were particularly dense. "Whenever and wherever there's a need. You'll find me."

Was he quoting Batman?

"Daddy!" called a little kid's voice from behind the curtain.

"I felt bad about holding his leg, though," said Compton, ignoring the child's voice. "That was too much. I came here to tell you, you shouldn't have cut him open."

I tensed, but Tucker simply asked, "Why?"

"There was too much blood."

Was it okay to cut someone open, as long as there wasn't much blood? I expected Tucker to pursue that. Instead, he watched Compton's body language. Compton had shoved his hands into his front pockets. His hands twitched under the fabric, almost like he was snapping his fingers.

Did he have tardive dyskinesia? It isn't common, but it's a side effect from antipsychotic medication. I stared at him, trying to match his activity to YouTube videos I'd seen. No, it didn't look like the same rhythmic movement.

I couldn't pin down a diagnosis. Tucker, the would-be psychiatrist, would know better.

"You don't like blood, huh?" Tucker said finally.

"Sometimes it does have to be spilled, though."

My body jolted against my seat back before I could control myself. Tucker placed a hand on my arm. I struggled to slow my breathing, my heart rate, and my brain.

Compton's vague eyes locked directly on mine. "You know that 'without the shedding of blood, there is no forgiveness.'" It sounded like a quote.

"I've heard that," said Tucker calmly. "Could you remind me where?"

"Hebrew 9:22."

The Bible. I gave Compton another once over. *Quotes the Bible, carries around a plastic knife* ... this did not auger well for me, the infidel. I was running straight up into a lot of different belief systems today, and I didn't trust any of them.

Compton scratched his head. "'And almost all things are by the law purged with blood; and without shedding of blood is no remission.' That's the King James 2000 version."

My heart thumped. I tried to console it with logic. *He was behind Herc. He couldn't have reached around to stab Mr. Money.*

My heart didn't care. Goose bumps prickled my arms.

I am a knife.

Topaz had said that, not Compton—I recognized it as a snippet from Roxane Gay, because our friend Tori had me read her book, *Difficult Women*, which may not have been a compliment—but it made me think of something else. The killer could have been someone's knife, someone's instrument. Not killing for him or herself, but for a higher power, or a mission of some kind.

That was the only thing that made sense to me. Otherwise, why would you take the risk of stabbing someone on an airplane, in front of over a hundred potential witnesses?

It didn't narrow down the suspects, but it did give me an idea of the killer's determination.

"Blood has been shed," said Tucker.

Compton nodded.

"Is there forgiveness?"

Compton shrugged. "It's not for me to say." He glanced up at the ceiling as if a higher power might be visible through it. Then he stared at Alessandro who, true enough, seemed like the one who'd have to forgive both Joel J and Staci Kelly.

Alessandro stared back at him like Compton was a fly on its back, buzzing itself around in a circle before it died.

Tucker leaned into the aisle, breaking contact with me. I tried not to reach for him again as he spoke, keeping his voice casual. "Did you make sure that blood was shed?"

"Huh?" Compton turned his large, brown eyes on him.

"He had cuts in his side. Do know where that came from?"

"Do I know where that came from," said Compton, not like he was offended, but more like he was testing the shape of the words in his mouth.

"Hooooooooooo!" Mr. Yarborough yelled.

My hands fisted.

"Quiet, Harold!" his wife shushed him, none too gently.

"Yes," said Tucker, keeping his eyes on Compton. "Did you cut him in his side?"

"Like Jesus?" said Compton.

"Excuse me?" The words burst out of my throat. I was so taken aback.

Compton smiled and crouched over me. I could see orange crumbs clinging to the fine hairs around his lips, as if he'd forgotten to wipe his mouth after scarfing down the Cheetos. "That's what happened to Jesus. It was one of His five holy wounds. The first two were in His hands or wrists. The second two were in His feet. For the crucifixion, you know." He stared at Tucker, then me, as if he could transmit his thoughts through his eyes. His breath smelled like sweet tea. "The fifth wound was in His side. A soldier stuck Him with a spear, to see if he was dead. Blood and water poured out of His wound, according to the Gospel of John."

Was he trying to educate us, or confess?

I realized I'd unconsciously pressed myself against the wall before I caught myself. I had to be ready in case he attacked Tucker.

I peeled myself off the cool plastic, confused. In my head, Joel was a bad guy. No one, not even his own wife, seemed to like him. But here was Compton, comparing him to Jesus and smiling like he'd laid some serious wisdom on us.

Tucker brought us back on point. "Cody," he said softly, as the guy turned his trusting orbs on him, "did you give this man a holy wound?"

Compton nodded solemnly.

Even Mr. Yarborough fell quiet for a moment.

"Really?" I said.

"Oh, yes," Compton answered.

Tucker and I exchanged glances. "Do you know what you're saying?" I said.

Compton nodded. "For sure. I gave him a holy wound in his left side. I had to, you know."

"You stabbed him?" said a man's deep voice on our left.

I looked up. It was "the whale," the man who'd taken up two seats, now blocking the aisle. He had a red face and a beard, but what drew my eyes were his massive hands. If he ever decided to strangle someone ...

"He confessed," I said. I highly doubted Compton had done it. And even if he had done it, had he known what he was doing? He hadn't even tied his own shoes. The laces trailed on the ground. How did he get the wherewithal to kill a grown man?

"Let's put him somewhere safe, then."

It seemed natural to fall in line with the vast man with the basso profundo voice.

I resisted. "Hang on. Let me ask a few more questions."

"You can ask questions when we have him squared away. There are women and children on this plane, including yourself, miss."

The "miss" disarmed me a little, even though it shouldn't have. "Where are you going to put him?"

"I'm not going to hurt him. I'm just going to sit with him. I've got a seat next to me that he might be able to squeeze into. You want a bump into business class, buddy?"

"Oh, yeah!"

"Cody," I said, but it was too late. Basso Profundo was leading Compton to his row.

Compton said, "I've never sat here before. This should be cool. I heard you get free drinks and everything. And in Montreal, they have an exhibit on Miles Davis. Did you know that he revolutionized jazz five times?"

"No," said Basso Profundo kindly, gesturing at Pascale to bring him yet more zip ties. "I had no idea."

Tucker and I looked at each other. This was the first time I'd felt terrible about someone's confession. Every other killer had been— well, one or two of them had been viciously intelligent. All of them had something upstairs. Compton almost seemed like a child, or schizophrenic.

I wanted justice, and this didn't feel right. "We can't let him take the blame without evidence that he did anything wrong. I probably hurt Joel worse than he did by sitting on his chest."

Tucker twisted in his seat to grasp my upper arm. "What are you talking about?"

"He kicked you. He was getting away, so I jumped on his chest, and it turned out he'd been stabbed. He wouldn't have been able to breathe with me compressing his chest. I—"

"Don't say it, Hope." His fingers clenched so hard that each fingertip would probably bruise my arm, and I didn't care. I deserved it.

Tucker bounded out of his seat, towing me to the curtain before he finally released my arm. "Now." Tucker turned on me. "What are you doing, Hope?"

"Oh, Tucker." Exhaustion slammed me. I sagged where we stood. "You know what I'm talking about. I sat on top of Mr. Money. That's how I got blood on my pants. He already had a pneumo and tamponade, plus I gave him compressive hypoventilation. If you're going to zip tie Compton, you'd have to put me away, too."

"Don't be ridiculous. You got off him the second that we saw blood."

"But he'd still have chest hypoventilation—"

"We didn't do anything to Compton. He offered information. The police and the courts will handle it. If they declare him incompetent —and I think they will—he'll be tried as not criminally responsible, or the U.S. equivalent. I'm saying it again, Hope. What are you doing?"

"I'm confessing." I bit my lip before I remembered that was a bad idea. "He can't take the whole blame. He hardly knows what he's doing. I contributed, too."

"Shut up, Hope."

His words stopped me like a slap. That, plus his eyes hooded with fury. He said, "I love you. I'm not going to let you self-destruct because you feel guilty after *someone else* stabbed a man on a plane. I know you have PTSD, but you can't throw yourself in jail to escape."

"I'm not doing that!" Doubt flickered in the back of my mind. I did hate torturing him and Ryan. Was I so far gone that this was my solution: escape through a criminal conviction? "But I will have to tell the authorities—"

"You have a fucking concussion, on top of everything else. You have trouble seeing, and you have a headache. Right?"

I nodded, which made me wince. "But it's not like—"

"You have PTSD, and now you have a head injury. You are not thinking straight, and I'm telling you, you sitting on his chest for one second did not make a difference."

"It was longer—"

"It was not. I was there. I was watching you. I watch you more than anyone else, and I will swear on a stack of Bibles that I was the only medical doctor on board in full possession of my faculties, and that you did nothing to harm him. *Nothing."*

More doubt sprouted in my chest. He did watch me. He loved me. If Armageddon sprung up on this plane, he would rocket through the air to protect me. But that meant he was biased. It meant he would lie in court. He would lie right to my face, if he thought it was best for me.

Ryan wouldn't lie. Even though he'd stepped away from his church, the core of him still held out for a higher power.

Tucker's eyes blazed, and I knew he didn't have any higher power than me.

It scared me. I didn't feel worthy. Of the billions of people in the world, I didn't deserve that kind of love. But he was giving it anyway.

"I love you," I said, because I didn't know what else to say, and that much was true.

"I love you." He folded me into his chest. His arms viced their way around me. My nose got squashed, but it didn't matter. I breathed and tried to believe what he was saying, while the plane shook and voices spun in my head.

I was only on there for a second.

It sure felt like longer than a second.

I could ask other people who witnessed it.

Who?

Maybe someone filmed it.

"Filmed it," I said out loud.

Tucker's arms stiffened.

"We have to review any footage of the—subjugation," I said. "We asked for witnesses, but we should have been asking for video."

Tucker eyeballed me. He knew why I was searching for footage. I didn't believe his testimony 100 percent, the way he thought he would have believed mine.

My hands twitched, but I said, "You know it's true, Tucker. People can lie." I recoiled at my own words. It was like I was still accusing him.

Tucker despised it. He despised everything I was implying. He ground out, "We could leave that to the police. We've got a confession. That's more than anyone else would have gotten."

I knotted my hands together. "We can't use him like that. He would be, like, the sacrificial lamb."

Tucker changed the subject. "You shouldn't be watching videos anyway, with a concussion."

That made me laugh, and his mouth yanked up in a crooked smile. How many times had I told a patient, "No movies, no texting, no nothing after a concussion"? You're only allowed to lie still, in a dark room, for 24 hours. And here I was, gallivanting up and down a plane, trying to solve a murder.

Before Tucker could cut in with an excuse, though, I raised my voice. "Let Linda make an announcement. Anyone who filmed the ... altercation can step forward. We're not going to force people. We won't harm any concrete evidence if we're looking at footage."

"Unless we delete it by accident," said Tucker.

I'd never seen him so stubborn and so unwilling to investigate. "Computer forensics would get it back, unless you're a real hacker, which you're not." That was more Ryan's specialty. "So let's get some volunteers."

Tucker hesitated, and that was when the depth of his resistance finally hit me. He'd dropped his figurative magnifying glass because he was worried we'd find something incriminating about me.

Despite his protests, he worried that I was guilty too.

Fuck.

I closed my eyes. When I opened them, I had to blink more than usual, and my voice trembled, but I said, "The truth will out. And I'd rather be forewarned. If I accidentally—if I get charged with manslaughter or accessory to murder—"

"Don't say that. Don't fucking say that." He held me so tightly that I couldn't breathe for a second. Tucker was my whalebone corset. "I need you. I just got you. I'm not giving you up like that."

"It won't change anything, unless you're going to zip tie me in the back with Staci Kelly," I said.

He shook his head. "I'd zip tie us together first. I'm serious, Hope. You can't get rid of me. I'm here forever."

Ryan wobbled through my mind. He was less vocal than Tucker, but equally stubborn. I'd picked two guys who would never back down.

I did worry about losing both of them, but it had never occurred to me that our love story might end with me in prison. Do they even allow you two different conjugal visitors? Or was I so paranoid post-concussion that I should follow my doctor's orders and just shut up?

Tucker moved his hand to my face. He pressed his fingers against my cheek, still too tightly, although I didn't protest. If we were going to be ripped apart, I wanted him to mark me. It would be all I had.

He stared into my eyes. "I wish it had been me. If he hadn't kicked me in the stomach—"

"My parents would hire a really good lawyer. Don't worry." But my stomach dropped. My parents would hire the best lawyer and bankrupt themselves if they had to, leaving themselves and my brother Kevin with nothing.

Don't panic, Hope.

Breeeeeathe.

The curtain twitched aside.

I stifled a cry. Tucker held my head against his chest and only slowly released me. I could still feel his heart hammering, as if it had etched itself on my ribcage.

"Excuse me," said the female senior citizen with smooth, brown skin, greying dreadlocks, and glasses, who was watching us from the economy class side.

She didn't look like an ax murderer. In fact, she managed to impart an air of gravitas, like a judge, even though she was wearing jeans. "I was walking up the aisle and couldn't help overhearing your conversation. I did film the altercation on my phone, and I can show you the video."

Tucker's hands clutched my back. Neither of us spoke for a microsecond before he slowly let go.

31

Then woman drew the curtain behind her and pressed play on her phone.

I swayed on my feet. I wanted to blame it on the rocky airplane, but Tucker didn't stir, except to bolster me up. "You sure you want to do this?" he whispered.

"Sure." I spoke through my teeth. Fortunately, I'd remembered not to nod.

The screen was so dark that at first, I could hardly tell the video was playing. Either the woman's phone didn't have a flash, or she hadn't activated it.

She'd also shot from the rear of the plane, filming the backs of people's heads as they stood up, blocking the aisle.

I released my breath and straightened up in my seat. I could make out a head here or a hand there. That was all.

Good news: this video probably wouldn't incriminate me.

Bad news: it looked next to useless.

The audio was okay, but punctuated by people swearing and saying, "Get him!" and "The dog—!" Staci Kelly shouted, "I can't breathe."

Then Joel J kicked Tucker off-screen.

Tucker oofed.

"No!" a female yelled. Maybe me.

I swore under my breath. If only this camerawoman had filmed Joel J's direct attack on Tucker, that would have been useful.

She did manage to capture my retaliatory kick, although I had my head down, and the video was so pixellated that I hardly recognized myself.

Joel J's arm swung. My face toppled backward, off-screen.

Tucker sucked his breath through his teeth, and I remembered the look on his face as he pulled the clots out of Joel's chest.

Please have done everything right, Tucker. Even if he was a hellhole of a human being. There will be an autopsy when we land.

Herc yanked Joel's leg in the video.

The screen wobbled when Joel hit the ground. People screamed and jostled the camera.

Soon I landed on Joel's chest, but it was hard to see. Too many other people in the way. Thank God.

Another flurry of movement. Shouting. When the camera bobbed forward again, Tucker was yelling for chest tube equipment.

Her video taught us exactly nothing about the murderer, and I was grateful.

"I don't know how useful it is, but my name is Elizabeth Rodriguez y Calderón. Here's my card." She handed me a bright blue card with white script on it.

I glanced down at it. She was an attorney for family law.

Here was an intelligent woman whose very presence seemed ... peaceful. I trusted her instinctively. She took incompetent videos that didn't incriminate me. And it never hurt to be friends with a lawyer. "Thank you very much, ah, Ms. Rodriguez y Calderón." I imitated her accent as best I could.

She chuckled. "Elizabeth. Please. I can identify some other people with videos more helpful than mine. Would you like me to do so?"

I gulped.

Tucker's eyebrows drew together across his forehead in a clear *Hell, no.*

But it felt like it was out of our hands now. After umpteen threats, a lawyer had finally materialized.

I'll be judge, I'll be jury.

I closed my eyes and nodded. My head throbbed.

"Ladies and gentlemen, may I have your attention, please. This is your captain speaking."

I caught Tucker's hand. Captain James Mesaglio had repossessed the microphone. With our luck, the plane had been hit by lightning.

"Because of the weather patterns and the unusual conditions on the airplane, we're proceeding to Chicago's O'Hare International Airport. Our estimated time of arrival in Chicago is 12:19 a.m. Central Time, which is two hours ahead of Pacific Time. The weather forecast there is cloudy with a temperature of 8 degrees Celsius or 18 Fahrenheit."

Less than 30 minutes away from landing.

Oy oy oy oy oy, to quote one of my Jewish patients.

Passengers cheered so loudly that I hardly made out what he said next, something about ground agents finding alternate transportation solutions for us.

Oh, right. We'd been jetting toward family, friends, and fun in time for Christmas. Now our only priority was survival, as in, *Land this plane as fast as possible.*

Basically, everyone on board had PTSD paranoia. I fit right in.

Linda materialized at our seats. "Doctors, could I ask you to speak to the flight doctor?"

"Of course." I'd rather do that than review more potentially incriminating videos. But when we stood up, Mrs. Yarborough called, in her thin voice, "Help! Help me, please!"

No. There couldn't be yet another emergency on this plane.

Tucker dashed toward her anyway, and I pelted after him.

Tucker called over his shoulder, "He's seizing."

FML.

I tried to shove past Mrs. Yarborough, who stood in front of the aisle seat, saying, "He started shaking. There was so much going on, I didn't want to bother you. I thought he was shaking in his sleep, and maybe he was cold, but he shook so hard that his blanket fell off ... "

"What time did it start?" I snapped.

Harold sure looked like he was seizing. He was gazing off into space, diagonally to the right, while both arms trembled. I haven't seen a ton of seizures, and I've seen more obvious seizures, but this looked like a seizure. Of course, we didn't have much to treat it with. "Glucose," I said, while Mrs. Yarborough abandoned her bag on her seat and retreated to the aisle, giving us more room.

"I'm on it." Tucker had scooped up Harold's Accucheck and test strips—maybe his wife had left it on her seat, along with her bag— and was now pricking Harold's index finger.

Harold didn't react. Another sign that he was down for the count.

"Could I have some orange juice?" I called. If in doubt, give sugar. Hyperglycemia won't kill you the way that hypoglycemia will.

"I have apple juice," said Pascale.

"Perfect. Now, please!" I told her. She skirted by us to grab it from the little kitchen, and I asked Mrs. Yarborough again, "What time did this start?"

"Oh, I don't know. He's been bad for more than five minutes—"

Five minutes is worrisome. The new guidelines are to treat seizures aggressively if they're still seizing in the ER.

"—but there was so much going on. And I wasn't sure before that. Maybe half an hour?"

"Half an hour? That's status epilepticus!" Definitive brain damage time. Holy crap.

Meanwhile, Tucker said, "His sugar is 60."

"What's that in our measurement?"

He thumbed up his app. "It's, uh, 3.3."

It was low normal, not seizure low, but we had so few choices. "Let's give the juice anyway." Pascale was holding a little plastic cup over my shoulder. I grabbed it, spilling a bit of the apple juice. She yelped, which I ignored. "Get me some gloves."

She handed me a pair. Thank God she'd anticipated that. I dipped my gloved index finger in the juice and moved to smear some inside his cheek when his teeth clamped down together.

Ugh. I prefer not to go near anyone's mouth when they're seizing, but I couldn't pour it down his nose without drowning him. I plucked his cheek, like I was an auntie giving a kid a good cheek pinch, and pulled it away from his teeth. Harold swiped at me, but Tucker caught his arms first.

"Sorry, sir! Just trying to help you," I said. I wasn't sure he could hear me. It was a good sign that he'd felt the pinch. Maybe he was coming out of his seizure; it can be hard to tell.

I dipped my index finger in the juice. I swiped the juice on the inside of the cheek to avoid his incisors.

His teeth rattled, and I realized that I'd hit his dentures. Good. They'd be less of a weapon than real teeth. I pulled them out and handed them to his wife, who made a face.

"You can do this yourself," I told her, but she shook her head. I slathered more juice inside his cheek pouch. Go big or go home, like we say in the ER. Better one good juice swipe than a few tentative attempts, with him biting down on me for each one.

I didn't want to fondle his orifice too long. There's something intimate about feeling someone else's mucous membranes, even through gloves.

I yanked my hand back out. His mouth slopped shut again.

I hoped I gave him enough juice. A nurse would have done a better job. More experience. I'm always jonesing for the intubation or central line, but not as good at the practical details.

Tucker smiled at me while he pulled equipment out of the medical kit Magda had magicked up behind us. Soon he was inserting his second IV of the hour with dextrose. I felt my shoulders relax below my ears. Before Mr. Money, Tucker and I had only run one other code together before. Now we were pros.

"I think he's opening his eyes!" said Mrs. Yarborough.

I held my breath. Was this it? Just hypoglycemia? I'd never seen anyone seize from a sugar of 3.3, but hypoglycemia's effects are legion. Your brain needs glucose in order to function. Bizarre things happen when neurons don't fire, not only confusion and weakness, but even temporary paralysis and, in very rare cases, blindness.

Mr. Yarborough's face twitched, including both eyelids. His mouth smacked.

And then both his arms jerked.

I said, "Damn it. We can't fool around with status epilepticus. Give me a list of his medications. Is he on Ativan or Valium or Dilantin? I need those."

Mrs. Yarborough shook her head.

To Tucker, I said, "ABC's."

"He's got an airway for now," said Tucker. "I could intubate him, but then one of us will have to bag him."

"No, don't do that!" said Mrs. Yarborough.

Tucker nodded. "Let's try and stop the seizures first. Do you have oxygen?" he asked Pascale.

. She nodded and did something to an overhead compartment to open it. An oxygen bottle came out, along with its yellow cup mask.

While she straightened the tubing, I said, "Fair enough. D is dextrose, and we're giving it. If that works ... " My voice trailed off. It would be so nice if it worked, but we couldn't wait. "E—exposure. I guess we could take his clothes off."

Mrs. Yarborough paused in the middle of searching through her bag on the seat. "Absolutely not."

"Sure. There's no cardiac monitor anyway." No cardiac monitor, no blood pressure cuff, no oxygen saturation probe. We did have Pascale fitting the oxygen mask over his nose and mouth, kind of like a fake pig snout.

Tucker said, "Let's start with some more metabolic causes. I use the mnemonic SICK DRIFTER."

I'd never heard that one, so I shut my mouth and listened to Tucker.

"S is for substrates, like sugar or oxygen. We've got both of those covered right now. I is Isoniazid overdose. Is he being treated for tuberculosis?"

Everyone circled around him shuddered. The last thing we needed on this airplane was TB.

Mrs. Yarborough shook her head and licked her lips, which were trembling. Poor thing. We usually let family members go to a quiet room, if they don't want to see us shoving tubes and medications in their loved ones. I wanted to tell her to keep looking for his meds list, but Tucker was on a roll.

"Any other infectious diseases, while we're at it?" he asked her.

"He had prostate cancer."

"Good to know. Was he on medications for it?"

She shook her head. "He had surgery, but they were worried about his bladder. He went for a test on Monday."

"A cystoscopy, which is a camera? Or a scan?"

"I don't know." She played with the rings on her fingers. She seemed to have shrunk and aged about 20 years.

"Okay, it doesn't matter. Did anyone find the list of medications?"

Mrs. Yarborough said, "It's on his phone, and I don't have his password. He's—paranoid, I'm afraid."

Join the club. Out loud, I said, "Let's lie him down in case he's anoxic." Even in first class, the seats don't lean all the way back, and we needed as much oxygenated blood as possible flowing to his poor brain. Since we hardly had any room, Tucker and I tried to lie him down sideways, using his wife's aisle seat as a pillow. The purse on the seat made a plasticky and rattly sound that I recognized over the rumble of the engine.

"Hey! You've got his medications in there," I said.

Mrs. Yarborough stared at me.

"In your purse. You thought you packed them. I heard some pills in there. I know it sounds funny, but I've got good ears." I reached for the purse.

She picked it up first, unzipped it, and lifted out a white plastic bag. "I was sure I packed them."

Maybe she was losing her memory, too. I stayed cheery. "Good thing you brought 'em. A list is better, but we can catalogue these." It would be a lot faster than quizzing her about his prostate cancer history.

Linda said, "I'll make the list. Could I have the bag?" She grabbed it in one hand and slipped out her phone with the other, ready to make notes.

I hesitated. I'm a control freak. I wanted to go over those medications myself. On the other hand, it was a relatively unskilled task. I had to focus my brain cells on stopping his seizures.

Tucker waved his hands to get my attention. "Cations next. Sodium, calcium, magnesium."

We both paused to contemplate that. I said, "That could be it. But how are we supposed to test that on an airplane?" I turned to Linda and Pascale. "Can we do a blood test on him?"

"You want a blood sugar monitor? We have one," said Linda.

"No, not his blood sugar. We already did that. I want his sodium, ionized calcium, and magnesium levels. Can you ask the flight doctor?"

Linda wavered. "I'll ask. Pascale, can you make the medication list with the doctor?"

"Yes, ma'am." Pascale accepted the white plastic bag. This was a messy code. That was the problem with not enough skilled people. At a hospital, I yell, "I need a meds list!" and someone gets one, either locating a pharmacy slip in the wallet, calling a drugstore, or requesting a fax from the government. Similarly, I say, "CBC, lytes, BUN, creatinine ... " and someone is obtaining them before I close my mouth.

Right now, we were on an airplane with nothing. Just me and Tucker, one dead man, one seizing man, and a killer lurking among us.

32

The white plastic bag crunched as Pascale pulled a full bottle out of it, oblivious to my frustration. "This is—Tradjenta?"

"Right. It's a diabetic medication." It was better to have a task to ground me. Maybe I was a working dog, too. I took the bottle and wrote the name down in a little notebook that Pascale had handed me, along with a pen. The Americans seemed to have added an extra d to Trajenta, but it was recognizable. "Five milligrams. Okay. Let's separate the ones we've already done." I pushed the Tradjenta in the closest seat pocket.

Pascale stared at the next bottle for a blank second. I passed the notebook over to her and said, "Look. I'll call out the names, and you write, okay? You probably have better handwriting than me."

While I grouped the medication bottles together by type, Tucker said, "D. Drugs. I've got another mnemonic for that. CRAP. Cocaine, Rum—or some other alcohol—Amphetamines, PCP."

"Where can I get some of those?" called a man's voice. I smiled as I clumped together Mr. Yarborough's drugs for diabetes, angina, high blood pressure, high cholesterol, reflux, depression, dementia, all filled two days ago, and—pay dirt on the last bottle. "Tucker, he's on Apixaban."

Tucker stopped in the middle of his monologue. "Two point five mill?"

"No, five." I frowned at my own words. He was on the higher dose, and at a higher risk of bleeding, especially if his kidneys crumped.

"What is it?" said Pascale.

"He may be bleeding in his head, and that's why he's seizing. This is a blood thinner." I turned to Mrs. Yarborough. "Did he fall and hit his head?"

She shook her head. "I don't think so, unless he hit it in the bathroom without me."

This was not helpful. I raised my eyes to Tucker. "We can't reverse the anticoagulation right now."

"No? No Andexxa or PCC on board?" he said, which was a joke, but I couldn't laugh. We couldn't check Mr. Yarborough's calcium. We couldn't drain a brain bleed. We couldn't correct an ischemic stroke. I felt so helpless. I always secretly worried that I'd be useless in a zombie apocalypse, with precious few antibiotics and no imaging, and that was exactly our situation now. My shoulders slumped. "Does anyone have Ativan or Valium?" I called.

Linda returned from the cockpit, already shaking her head. "We don't allow other passengers to share their items."

"Even though it's an emergency?" I said.

She shook her head again, but she looked troubled. "I'll have to get permission from Avian Air."

"Status epilepticus causes brain damage! Neurons die, he could choke, he could have a heart attack—" I said.

Mrs. Yarborough moaned from the aisle. She'd been pushed so far back behind the flight attendants, she was close to Trina, who leaned away from the aisle.

"I'm sorry. I'll have to ask first," said Linda. "I just wanted to tell you that the flight doctor said we can't test for anything except glucose on board. Everything else, we must land the plane."

"And when is that?" said Tucker.

"About 30 minutes," she said.

The pilot had estimated half an hour about fifteen minutes ago. It felt like we'd never get off. I tamped down my panic.

"These are for you," said Linda, showing me two bottles. "I accidentally walked away with them when I started cataloguing the medication."

"Hey! Those are Seroquel and Clonazepam." The latter is in the same family as Ativan, although it has a longer half-life. As in, it would take twice as long to clear Clonazepam out of his system compared to Ativan. That would be dangerous if we overdosed him and he stopped breathing.

On the upside, he'd also stop seizing, and we could intubate him to protect his airway. It wouldn't stop the electric activity in his brain, but it would make me feel better.

I popped open the bottle and counted ten Clonazepam pills.

"He might be having a withdrawal seizure from the Clonazepam," Tucker pointed out.

"All the more reason to give it to him. Now." I eyeballed Mr. Yarborough, who was still shaking and rattling, although not rolling, and still mostly sitting up. "I usually give it IV." Clearly, the blue pill was not an intravenous form. We could crush it and try to dissolve it in something, but would probably end up giving him Streptococcus instead if we tried to inject it.

Tucker shook his head, and I bit my lip. "We could try under the tongue."

Ativan is great under the tongue. It's one of the only drugs we give SL, or sublingual (along with nitroglycerine, which was another one of his bottles). But Clonazepam looked pretty small, and he only had the 0.5 mg tablets. According to the bottle label, he took these twice a day. He might choke on it. Even if we crushed it, he might choke on the spit. Maybe if we mixed it in applesauce and painted it on the inside of his cheek again?

"I can push it rectally," said Tucker.

"Thanks, man."

Tucker raised his eyebrows in a *You owe me* way, but I smiled and said, "Everyone, please stand back and give Dr. Tucker some privacy."

I might even have said *priv*-a-cy, with a short i, the way the British do, to give him extra decorum.

"What are you doing?" said Mrs. Yarborough.

"I need access," I huffed. Even in business class, there's not much leg room to roll over a sizeable old man who's convulsing on a swooping airplane.

"Stop!" She thundered toward us.

"We're giving medication to stop the seizures. Please, Mrs. Yarborough," said Tucker in his most charming way.

"Stop touching him!" She grabbed Tucker's arm.

I had only barely started to unbuckle his leather belt. "It's because he might choke on the pill, even if we crush it. This way is safe."

"No! He—wouldn't want this! He's DNR!"

I hesitated. "Mrs. Yarborough, that means no heroic measures. But this isn't a heroic measure. We're only putting a pill or two up his back end. It won't hurt." Especially if we found some lube.

"I said NO," she hollered, flinging her arms wide open, nearly clipping me in the head.

I ducked. "Someone take her out of here. Pascale!" We've done mock codes before where someone pretends to be an obstructing mother. It's impossible to run a code that way. You have to get someone to take charge of the mom and yank her out of your way.

Pascale tried to tug Mrs. Yarborough behind the seats, but she stood her ground. "No! You're assaulting him! I'm the one who speaks for him! You can't strip him naked in front of an airplane! He would rather die!"

Tucker and I both paused. Consent was a tricky issue. Mr. Yarborough was unconscious, so his wife had to speak for him. "Do you have your DNR papers?" asked Tucker.

"Of course." She rummaged in her black bag and lifted out her iPad. "I hope it works. If not, I have it on my phone. I can text it to you."

The tablet screen worked, displaying a neon pink form different from the one we had in Canada, but easy to understand. She had ticked off both the boxes "Do not attempt resuscitation" and "Comfort-focused treatment."

I let go of Mr. Yarborough's pants.

She was calmer now that we'd backed off of his buttocks. "And doesn't he have his bracelet?"

"What bracelet?" I had a bad feeling about this.

"His DNR/POLST bracelet."

I understood DNR, for Do Not Resuscitate, but not the second one. She said, "POLST. The Physician's Order for Life Sustaining Treatment. That's the form I showed you."

Sure enough, when I glanced at her screen, the heading was POLST. Although the name suggested it meant you had to sustain life at all cost, or that's the way my emergency-trained mind worked, she had signed not to do that.

"There's no bracelet," said Tucker, who had pushed up both of Harold's sleeves.

"Well, that's strange. It's not supposed to fall off," she said. "Maybe he pulled it off at some point."

I was more concerned with the fact that he was still staring into space and tweaking his arms, with an occasional leg twitch. "How long has he been down? Forty-five minutes?"

She looked at her watch, and Basso Profundo said, "That's what she estimated."

"You want me to time him?" asked Compton, who was squashed beside him, but looked reasonably happy.

"Yes, please, Compton. You'll be our time keeper." I turned to Mrs. Yarborough. "Are you telling me that you refuse rectal medication, but you'd accept oral? Even if he chokes on it and gets pneumonia?" I said, enunciating and looking her in the eye as I spoke. "Pneumonia is treatable, if we—*when* we manage to land. But status epilepticus—"

She bit her lip. "I don't know what to think." She crossed her arms. "I don't want him to suffer."

"Then let us help him!" Could I give him medication without her consent? Otherwise, I had nothing for Mr. Yarborough. Unlike Meredith Grey, I wasn't about to drill a hole in his skull. I couldn't reverse any bleeding or usher more blood flow through his cerebral arteries. But we had medication right in our hands that could help him.

"We could also try to give saline," said Tucker. "If he's hyponatremic, maybe it'll bring him back up to normal, and uremia can cause seizures."

I eyeballed the DNR sheet. Mrs. Yarborough hadn't ticked off the middle box for IV. "Can we still give IV fluids?" I asked her.

She covered her mouth. Probably she could feel everyone's eyes boring into us, the way I did. "I don't know what to think."

Think fast, I thought. It was what my classmates used to say, usually before whipping a ball at my head.

"It's hard, eh?" said Tucker. "You love him. You don't want him to suffer. But I assure you that an intravenous isn't suffering. He won't choke on an IV. And if he wakes up a little, we can try the Clonazepam."

After a long moment, she nodded.

"I'll start a second IV." Tucker was careful and respectful as he tightened a tourniquet around Harold's left arm and swabbed the inside of his left elbow, looking for a second vein.

I smiled as I held the arm in place. It's more common to put IV's in the hand, because people want to bend their arms, but Tucker was thinking like an ER doctor: put as big a needle as close to the heart as possible, so we could get the drugs in ASAP. The only disadvantage was that Mr. Yarborough might dislodge the needle, but that was true of anyone anywhere.

When Tucker got a flash of blood up the angiocatheter, I grabbed the normal saline. The smooth bag was heavy in my hands. If we thought hyponatremia was causing his seizures, we should be using hypertonic saline instead. But we had no idea of his sodium level.

"What about CPM?" I whispered to Tucker as he attached the saline. If you correct the sodium too fast, you can end up with Central Pontine Myelinolysis. They might look fine at first, but then end up confused and unable to walk a few days later. You need your pons. You need your whole brainstem.

"We'll go slowly," he said.

Not reassuring. Tucker had cut open another man's chest an hour ago. His determination to save Mr. Yarborough's life might make him even more reckless. I'd have to keep an eye on the fluids. And how were we ever going to solve the stabbing?

It's Ooooooooh. Kay, Hope, I told myself. *You can't solve everything. It's not your fault people are killing each other and going into status epilepticus.*

One at a time. That's what nurses tell me in the ER when I feel defeated by the stack of charts.

Tucker was ready to hook up the saline IV now, so we did.

Mr. Yarborough seemed to slow down his movements for a second. I shot Tucker a look: Is that possible? Maybe because of vagal stimulation from the IV?

He shrugged. My guess was as good as his.

Then Harold started seizing again, and everyone sighed.

"I'll crush the Clonazepam," I said. "Could I have a spoon? Maybe two spoons." Nurses do most of the crushing, so I was improvising, but it sounded right to me. Pascale handed them to me post haste. I grabbed two little blue pills and used the spoons to crush them together.

My hands shook. Not cool, but having people stare at me made them shake even more.

"We could put them in applesauce and put them in his cheek pouch," said Tucker.

"We don't have any applesauce," said Pascale.

Sure. Why would you? It's not a high demand item. An airplane isn't a day care. I tried to think of something else pureed that they might carry. "Do you have really thick Clamato juice?"

Tucker laughed. "Try some yogurt. Or honey."

"Right. Sure."

Linda spun off to grab some.

Please work. Please stop these seizures so we save this guy's brain and figure out who the killer is.

"We might be able to stick a wad between his gums and his lips," said Tucker.

He had a lot of good ideas. I loved how creative he was as I tried to scrape all the pill bits together in the middle of the spoon. "How is that different from a cheek pouch?"

"Easier to administer. Not as many blood vessels, but maybe he'd be less likely to choke on it."

"Maybe." I felt more helpless than with Mr. Money. I'd rather crack open a chest than argue with a near-widow about whether or not we were allowed to give a medication that might choke him.

Fortunately, Linda slapped a packet of honey in Tucker's hands. He tore off the foil, and I dumped the pill powder in the middle before he swirled it around with a spoon. "Ready?"

"Ready. You want to try the gum-lips method?" he said.

"Whatever works. And doesn't get us bitten."

"Done!" said Tucker, and I scooped up some honey on an index finger while Tucker pulled Harold's lower lip out. Harold clamped his gums together, so it was much easier to honey up the inside of his lower lip than reach inside the cavern of his mouth. The honey was sticky, though, with a particular love for my glove, so that took longer than I wanted. I ended up using a spoon to scrape off the honey into his gum-lip crevice while the plane tried out "the floss" dance moves.

"It'll help for hypoglycemia, too," said Tucker, and I nodded.

He squeezed the IV bag. "We've done everything we can," he said, more quietly, and I understood his pain. We were at our limit. If this didn't work, we'd have to roll Mr. Yarborough into recovery position and wait for the plane to land.

The hardest part of a code is standing and waiting with no direction and no clear idea if anything is going to work.

"Now what?" said Mrs. Yarborough. "What's going on? Harold?"

"Now, we wait," said Tucker.

She grabbed her husband's face. "Harold. Oh, Harold!"

"Nguh," he seemed to say, his head twitching in her hands.

She laid his head back on the seat, gently enough, before she wrung her hands. "I can't believe it!"

"Give the medication a few minutes to work, and then we can try the rectal option," I said. I swear, people think drugs are like magic wands, because TV doesn't show Procainamide infusing over an hour.

"No," she said, but with less force than before.

"Seizures are a sign that the brain's not working properly," said Tucker. "The electrical system has short-circuited. Over time, brain cells die, and people stop breathing—"

"So breathe for him!"

"We can," said Tucker, "but that means putting a tube down his throat, and you showed us a paper that you don't want that."

Her fingers tangled in her own hair, and she started yanking so hard that it distorted her eyes. "I don't know what to do!"

"Let us give the rectal medication," said Tucker. "If he gets too much and falls asleep, we can always support his breathing. We can treat his pneumonia once we land and get him to a hospital. But right now, he's seizing, and it's hurting him."

She started crying. "This is so horrible. It's not right, making me think like this when he's so sick. I want you to leave him alone. I want you to go away."

"But Mrs. Yarborough—"

"I said go away!" She stood up and shouted so hard that her face turned red and her veins throbbed. "Get out of here! Don't touch him. He wanted comfort measures, not you pulling down his pants or shoving things in this mouth. He said no tube! No tube! No tube!"

33

"I hear you," Tucker spoke to Mrs. Yarborough in his low, measured voice. "No tube. You don't want any further treatment."

"That's right!"

"You want us to stop touching him, so we'll take a step away from him for the moment."

I glared at Tucker. I didn't want to leave Mr. Yarborough. We might be able to argue that his wife wasn't competent and we had to make decisions for an unconscious patient.

Tucker used his chin to indicate Mr. Yarborough's body, which gave a twitch and fell still.

His wife cried out.

Tucker gazed at Mr. Yarborough. "It's okay. He's still breathing."

His wife covered her mouth with her hand.

We waited to see if he'd seize again. He lay quiet.

"I'm sorry," said Mrs. Yarborough. "I don't know what I'm saying any more."

"It's fine. Maybe the saline's having some effect," said Tucker. "We can only hope. What a terrible ordeal for you."

She nodded. Luckily, she wasn't screaming. Inside an airplane, post-concussion, post-PTSD, post-Staci Kelly, that would make me want to yank off my own ears.

"We can't predict anything one hundred percent. Health care isn't straightforward like business."

Mrs. Yarborough nodded in soundless agreement.

"I've always admired your success. ShapeR seems like such an innovative product."

Huh? I assumed Tucker had a plan, though, so I nodded along.

"Best shapewear on the market." Her answer was like a reflex. She gazed at her husband, who was breathing peacefully for the first time since I'd met him.

"Didn't you win an award for it recently?"

She smiled. "Which one?"

"Businesswoman of the Millennium," said Tucker.

That didn't make any sense. The millennium had barely begun.

"Yes, the ceremony was incredible."

"It was all over social media, those pictures of you and Kenneth Vaughn Reid."

I had no idea who Kenneth Vaughn Reid was, but her eyes flashed with recognition.

Tucker laughed. "Businessman and Businesswoman of the Millennium. It's like Ken and Barbie, only better, because you're entrepreneurs."

She started to smile before she caught herself. "I already have a husband."

"Yes, you do," said Tucker. "Tell me about him. How did you meet?"

"Online. Harold posted a wonderful ad. I found out later that Kim wrote it for him, but I liked his sense of humour, and he was of sound mind and reasonably sound body." Her hazel eyes cut into mine.

I blushed. Tucker had the mind, and it felt like everyone in a two-mile radius could tell that I was recently acquainted with his body.

"He proposed immediately. I put him off for a year before I gave in. Within five years, he had gone from forgetting his car keys to forgetting his children's names." She paused.

I glanced at Tucker. *Please don't forget our non-existent children's names.*

He pressed my hand. *I won't.* To her, he said, "What a shame. Were you working on ShapeR at the same time? It seemed to explode on the market two years ago."

"Yes, it was a very hectic time."

Mr. Yarborough's shoulders tweaked, but settled back down. We all sighed.

"Excuse me," said Pascale softly, in her French accent. "Maybe this could help?"

We spun around to look at her.

She bit the corner of her lip. The ends of her red scarf trembled as she extended a piece of paper toward me. "I found a list of medications stuck in the corner of the plastic bag."

I didn't really need the list now that we'd compiled the pill bottles, but I uncrumpled the paper and scanned it. Then I snapped to attention.

"Desmopressin," I said aloud.

"DDAVP." Tucker stared back at me, and then at Mrs. Yarborough.

We use DDAVP for incontinence, which is common in dementia. This medication makes you retain water so that you don't pee in bed, or all over the plane. The problem is that when you take in more water than sodium—like when you keep glugging out of your favourite water bottle—your sodium drops into your boots, and you can't stop seizing.

I whirled on Mrs. Yarborough, who had backed against the cockpit door.

"Why didn't you tell me he was taking DDAVP?" I said.

She lifted her shoulders. "I gave you a bag with his medications."

Not until he lay down on them. "You didn't include the DDAVP. Where is it?"

She clasped her hands. Her posture would rival the Queen's. "I have no idea. Perhaps it fell out during the ... incident at the airport."

"I didn't see anything," I said.

Tucker opened his mouth, but she rode over him. "Well, then, when we were boarding the plane the first or second time. How would I know? You can call to complain to the airline about it." She sniffed.

I checked at her meticulous makeup, her suspiciously smooth neck, and her bland expression. "You said you took 'wonderful' care of him. 'All his bills and all his pills.'"

She barely blinked. She would be a tough negotiator. "I do."

And yet she'd claimed to have checked his medications in his main bag, had supposedly forgotten about the bottles in her purse when she was taking her iPad in and out of it, and couldn't keep track of one of the most deadly pills. Her story kept changing. For the Businesswoman of the Millennium, she sure didn't keep an eye on her husband.

California splits its property 50-50 when you divorce. It would be much cheaper to kill your husband than to divorce him before you take up with the Businessman of the Millennium.

She regarded me coldly. "Dr. Sze, I don't care for your tone. You have no proof of wrongdoing, and you can't search me. You're not a police officer."

"No." I snatched her purse from her seat. "But I can hold onto this for them while you head to the back of the plane."

Her facade cracked. "With the—"

"The remains of Joel J. Firestone and his widow, yes. That's a good place to recollect where you might have misplaced his DDAVP."

"I absolutely will not. I'm calling my lawyer. How dare you."

The plane pitched to the right. We all grabbed hold of the seats— she pushed on the wall—and I said, "You can call all you like. There's no reception, the last time I checked."

At last, she patted herself down, reached under her billowy black outfit, and said, "There's no need to be unpleasant. I might have forgotten this." She handed me a translucent orange bottle.

I read the label. *Desmopressin 0.1 mg at bedtime.* I held it up to the light to see how many tablets were inside. "How come you only have ten of these and the Clonazepam, but the other pill bottles are full?"

"I must have forgotten to refill—"

I twisted the bottle to read the label. She'd refilled it two days ago.

She noticed me noticing. "My hands are shaky. Maybe they fell out."

Into his mouth. I turned to Tucker, who shook his head at me. I was too angry to care.

Mr. Yarborough wasn't seizing, but he hadn't woken up, either. It's normal to be out of it after a seizure, with a post-ictal period, but we'd have to do a full neurological exam and scan him for brain damage, especially with his blood thinner.

Her mouth snapped shut. "I want my lawyer."

34

There it was again. Lawyers flung in our face. It's like when you're a little kid, and you have to watch out for the bogeyman. I was sick of it.

"Guess what? There's a lawyer right here. She does family law. Let me get her." I stood up, still carrying the DDAVP. I'd have to put it in a safe place.

Tucker grabbed my arm. "What Dr. Sze means to say is—"

I handed Elizabeth's card to Pascale. "Could you call her, please? She's in economy class. She asked us to notify her any time we need her services."

Pascale looked confused, but I beamed, *Trust me, I'm a doctor* at her, and she moved down the aisle.

"—we don't want to imply anything," said Tucker.

I opened my mouth. I wasn't implying anything. I'd say it straight out.

Mrs. Yarborough told him, "You seem like a gentleman, Dr. Tucker, but your ... partner does not."

Like that was going to stop me.

"I have considerable resources. It's a shame that both of you don't seem to be aware of all the things we could do together."

Oh. She's moving on to bribery.

"You mentioned you'd recently had surgery at the Healing Hospital. I know one of the board members. I'm sure he'd be happy to take your ... heroic efforts into consideration when tabulating your account."

I felt my face flush. With one call, she could remove the black cloud of debt plaguing him.

"In fact, it would be my greatest pleasure to compensate you for your commendable care with such limited resources on board a plane."

She'd discovered my weakness. She, too, knew that she could accomplish more with honey than with bitterness.

She'd silenced both of us by the time Pascale returned with Elizabeth Rodriguez y Calderón, who was holding an electronic tablet. "Dr. Sze and Dr. Tucker, I'm so glad you called me. I've got something you need to see."

Not even the Sze/see juxtaposition seemed funny now. I turned dead eyes on her. I didn't want to be the kind of person who'd sell out an old man for a few thousand dollars, and yet, if it would save Tucker from years of compounding debt ... I tried not to look at Mr. Yarborough, who had started to snore.

"It's okay, Hope," said Tucker. He turned to Mrs. Yarborough and said gently, "This is the lawyer Dr. Sze was telling you about, if you need her services."

"I do not." Haughtiness crept back into her voice. "I have the best lawyer in Los Angeles at my disposal."

"He's not here. Elizabeth is."

Elizabeth nodded. "I'm happy to discuss—"

"No one asked for your opinion," said Mrs. Yarborough, staring at Elizabeth. "You crawl back to your *practice* now."

Why was she so rude? Only one answer made sense: fear. Elizabeth must be triggering her. No matter how much Mrs. Yarborough invoked lawyers, she didn't want to meet one in the flesh right now.

We might be able to use this, if Elizabeth could handle the attitude.

Fortunately, Elizabeth appeared far calmer than I did. "Dr. Sze and Dr. Tucker called me, and I do need to discuss something with them."

"Right now? Right when my husband is unconscious?"

"I can wait," said Elizabeth.

"I don't know what the world is coming to, when we can't count on common courtesy," Mrs. Yarborough said. The irony of her own words? Lost.

We made sure Mr. Yarborough was in the recovery position, lying on the floor on his side so that his tongue fell anteriorly, before I faced his wife. "The world must seem like an improvement in some ways, Mrs. Yarborough. After all, you started a business empire. It must have been so difficult when your husband was losing his memory at the same time. Thank you for offering to ... help Dr. Tucker." I was running out of euphemisms. "The bigger question for me is, when we land, what are you planning to do with your husband?"

"He'll have to go to the nearest hospital, of course."

"Such a shame that you'll spend your Christmas in hospital," Elizabeth murmured.

"I don't mind. As long as he gets the care he needs. He'll be there for a while, I imagine." She fluffed her white bob.

Tucker stepped in. "Depending on his complications, I'd estimate he'll need a week or even two before you take him home."

Her hands stopped fluffing. "I'm not taking him anywhere. He needs to be with his family."

"Your husband will adapt best in a familiar environment," he said.

She pressed her lips together "He needs his daughter, Kim."

Mr. Yarborough's mouth worked for a second. I wondered if he'd recognized Kim's name.

"Both of you would be the best. In sickness and in health," Tucker said.

"Blood is thicker than water," she countered.

It was certainly thicker than her marriage certificate. However, now I knew why she'd hatched this plot, and Elizabeth's electronic tablet gave me an idea. The courts have made their first convictions based on cell phone evidence. Your phones show you where you were, who you called, and everything you've texted. "Speaking of blood, why don't you contact Kim and let her know what's happening, if the Wifi is up?"

Mrs. Yarborough's eyes sharpened. She didn't reach for her phone.

I leaned closer and tried to look trustworthy. "She'll be worried about him, don't you think?"

She nodded. "I'll call her as soon as we land."

"I could help you with that. I know you were having trouble with your tablet earlier. I'm pretty good with electronics." Nothing like Ryan, of course, but with any luck, she'd see my Asian face and assume I was symbiotic with all silicon chips. "If you want me to contact her, I'd be happy to. We know more of the medical details. She might have a lot of questions."

She arched one razor brow at me. "You want me to give you my phone and tablet."

"Right." My heart double-thumped. "Often doctors talk to family members to update them."

"But you want to talk on my phone."

"I'd be happy to." If I kept chirping, it might start to sound normal to her.

"So would I," said Tucker. "Kim might not answer a strange number calling her, but she could trust your number. It makes sense to use your phone."

"You could use *his* phone," she said, pointing to her husband.

"That's true." I wasn't sure if he had the wherewithal to use search engines properly, but what the heck. I'd take it.

"Why would I trust you with my phone?" she said. "It has my business, my schedule, and personal information on it."

"You trusted us with your husband's life," Tucker pointed out.

Boom. With one sentence, he'd revealed that she cared more about her phone than about her husband. And she had no answer for Tucker except to gape at him. Eventually, she managed to say, "Well, of course he's more precious than anything." But she clamped her electronics in her beringed hands.

Tucker held out his palm.

Slowly, reluctantly, she placed her phone in it.

"I can take your tablet," I said, going for the full Monty, but she shook her head.

I wondered what was on it. It must be incriminating. *We needs ze tablet.*

Tucker took her phone, shook his head, and gave it back to her. "You'll have to unlock it."

Flashback to Tucker and me mounting in the family bathroom. I stared at the phone screen, trying to push that memory away, when I spotted a text.

You do it yet?

There was more, but she grabbed the phone back before I could read it. "You don't need to see that. I'll call Kim's number, even though the Wifi seems to be down."

"Thank you," said Tucker, but from the look on his face, I knew he'd glimpsed more than me.

There was evidence on that phone, if we could get it away from her.

She pressed the buttons and brought the phone to her face, then shrugged. "Can't connect. Too bad."

Elizabeth pointed to the name on the phone screen. "I thought her name was Kim. That's Tim."

"Oh. How silly of me. Getting old. You know how it is," she added, with a poisonous look.

Elizabeth smiled. "I can help you."

"Absolutely not." This time, she really did dial Kim Yarborough. "No signal. Too bad. Well, as soon as we land, we'll go to a hospital, and I'll contact her from there. I do hope your Canadian health care system is as good as she says it is."

That clicked. "Kim said we have a good health care system?" Quebec health care is so underfunded that the media constantly reports on how emergency departments are at 150 percent capacity or that the wait time hit 15 hours.

"Oh, yes. The social safety net is so much better in your country. Old, young, you take care of them. A much more evolved society, wouldn't you say? With wonderful doctors like you."

She was back to flattery, but the skin prickled on the back of my neck.

Elizabeth said, "Of course, no social safety net can take the place of a family."

Couldn't have worked better if we'd cued her. Tucker agreed, "Yes, it's terrible when families don't take care of their own."

"*What* are you implying?" Mrs. Yarborough's lips drew back from her teeth.

I snapped my fingers. "Granny dumping. That's what they call it. Or grandpa dumping, I suppose."

"*Granny* dumping? *Grandpa* dumping?"

The more she said it, the more it conjured up the image of an old man on the toilet. But the reality is much more sinister. "One Nova Scotia family abandoned their demented granny in the ER while they took a trip to Florida. They wanted free babysitting."

"How *dare* you!"

"How dare *you* overdose him on DDAVP and water so you could hook up with the Businessman of the Millennium—"

She lashed out at me. I swooped away before a ruby scratched my eyeball.

Tucker sprang past me and pinned her arms to her sides.

"I started out with *nothing*," Mrs. Yarborough shouted. "I came from the south side of Chicago and dragged myself from rags to riches. He was lucky to have me. Every day he had with me, he should have gotten down on his knees and thanked God that I was looking after him instead of putting him in an institution with someone like you. You little bitch!"

"That's enough," Tucker said, but she rode right over him, still machine gunning her words at me.

"You wouldn't know anything about it! You've never been

shackled to an invalid and had to change his diapers in an airport bathroom!" Spit shot out of her mouth. "I hope you *die*. I hope you end up covered in shit and vomit and raped by a thousand cocks. That's what you deserve, you little cunt prick!"

Someone gasped.

Tucker shouted, "That's enough!"

Otherwise, utter silence reigned in business class, apart from my heart pounding in my ears.

None of it made sense (cunt prick?), but every one of us understood the hatred and the violence seething in her.

I glanced into a sea of faces, some of them shaking their heads. Most avoided my eyes, although Compton stared back at me, blank.

Pascale stood still, her mouth agape.

Movement caught my eye. The little Portuguese boy had wandered into the cabin with an iPad. He was filming her outburst.

Slowly, the blood returned to my face. She'd just confessed to hating her demented husband. Not as good as a full confession, but more than enough to strike a death blow on social media.

Mrs. Yarborough followed my gaze toward the Portuguese boy and said, "Oh, no, you don't. Delete it. Delete it immediately! You little shit on a stick. Give me that. I'll pay you a thousand dollars if you delete it right now. You can have my wedding ring. Come here. Give me your iPad!"

Oh, boy. Literally. The Internet trolls might secretly cheer and/or try to join in raping me with a thousand cocks, but none of them would condone yelling at a cute little kid with huge brown eyes.

"You think you're going to get me to confess to murdering my husband? Well, I'm not! I want a lawyer, you little shits. Fuck you, and fuck this entire airplane with a whale dick!"

Now she sounded insane. Or demented. Or possibly like a Shakespearean swear word app. They sure knew how to curse in Pornucopia.

In the back, Gideon barked frantically. He could tell that she was a madwoman.

"Be quiet," said Basso Profundo.

He unfolded his bulk from beside Compton. He unsnapped his seat belt and stood up. He rose and rose into the air, seeming to double the height and weight of anyone else in the area.

He loomed over her. He didn't speak.

I hovered. I couldn't let him beat up an old lady. He wasn't quick, but he had sheer mass on his side, and her bones were more fragile than her words.

"You are a vile woman. Now be quiet and stop shouting," said Basso Profundo. He may or may not have liked golden showers, but I knew three facts about him: he could afford business class, he could calm down Compton, and he wasn't afraid of the ShapeR millionaire.

Amazingly, Mrs. Yarborough fell silent too. The Portuguese boy filmed it all, including the flight attendants descending on her with zip ties.

Once she'd been secured, with Trina offering to switch places with her, we made our way to our seats. Tucker hugged me and whispered in my ear, "Sorry, Hope. I should have shut her down."

"No, I wanted her to confess to plotting against her husband." I buckled my seat belt. "She didn't quite. I don't know if it'll hold up in court. She'll claim she was coerced, or on medication, or something."

"ShapeR has become a shapeless mess, though," said Tucker, his mouth quirking. She'd torpedoed her own company. Sure, some of her fans would stick with her, but of all the shapewear companies, why buy from the one who screams "cunt prick" at a doctor who helped save her husband's life?

The Businessman of the Millennium would ban her too. Socially and financially, she was already toast.

There was a rough justice to that. I smiled at Tucker.

35

Now that Mrs. Yarborough was semi-controlled, Elizabeth stood beside our seats and indicated the tablet. "You have to see this."

It seemed like we couldn't have one minute of rest. On the other hand, all this crap was like a band aid. Better to rip it off.

Tucker took the tablet and pressed play.

Someone had filmed the brawl with Joel J. We could see more on a bigger screen, although it was still mostly the top of people's heads. The perspective had changed, though, and when the cameraperson deviated to the left and showed the seated passengers' faces, including a startled Margaret Thatcher, I realized that this one was filmed from the front of economy class.

Joel kicked Tucker on-screen. I felt him tense beside me as he watched it.

Then Joel slugged me on camera, which made real-time Tucker's hands clench on the tablet and his breath whoosh out of his nose.

On-screen me fell out of sight. On-screen Tucker dropped down to tend to me, also out of sight.

The cameraperson focused on Joel, on the ground.

Off to the side, barely within the frame, Margaret Thatcher

ventured out of her seat and bent down. Her hand grasped some-thing off-screen, but she clearly jabbed his side before she rose.

Then Gladys's bulk eclipsed the rest of the show.

Tucker replayed the video.

I hit replay the third time.

We stared at each other.

At the very least, we had to speak to Margaret Thatcher.

At best, the camera had caught the killer.

"I'll come with you," said Elizabeth, and we nodded. Her presence should help.

As I pushed myself up out of the chair, my arms and legs ached, and my head seemed to swing on my shoulders. I was confronting someone against my will.

Margaret Thatcher seemed like such a *nice* woman. Why couldn't we pin this on Staci Kelly?

Before I spoke to Margaret Thatcher, I glanced down the aisle at row 33.

Herc met my eyes from the aisle seat, 33C. In the middle seat was a lump covered by a navy blue blanket, presumably the remains of Joel J, and in the window seat, glaring back at me, was Staci Kelly.

She was awake. She wasn't screaming. She was biding her time, which was even more eerie given her seat mate.

Death flight.

In contrast, Mrs. Thatcher appeared to be the ideal passenger in row 17. She'd been reading while swathed in a navy blanket. When she caught our feet in her peripheral vision, she turned off the e-reader and folded the case over the screen before she placed it in the seat pocket in front of her.

"You know why we're here," said Tucker. He and I blocked the aisle to the front. Elizabeth had preceded him and stood behind Margaret's seat, sealing off her egress to the rear, but Margaret Thatcher didn't attempt to flee.

She simply looked at Tucker and shook her head.

"Would you like to talk here or in the front?" he asked her.

Mrs. Yarborough yelled from business class, " ... and your little dog, too!"

Margaret Thatcher didn't stir. "I assume it's not about the dog." We'd passed Gideon and Gladys on the way. Gideon had watched us while Gladys rubbed his fur ruff and murmured to him. They weren't causing a disturbance, and no one was complaining about allergies.

I leaned around Tucker to get a better look at Mrs. Thatcher's body language and to lip read, since her measured voice was difficult to hear over the engine noise.

"Would you like to come with me?" Tucker asked. He was giving her the chance to minimize witnesses. I stepped backwards to give them room to walk up the aisle.

"I would not," said Margaret. She surveyed Tucker from behind her glasses. She glanced over her shoulder at Elizabeth, nodded at her, and met my eyes directly. Here was a woman who'd been consistently ignored and underestimated. She was twenty times more dangerous than the sound and fury of Staci Kelly.

I no longer assumed she was a nice woman.

Tucker gazed down at her. "Then can you explain what happened with Mr. Joel J. Firestone?"

She shook her head. "He was a madman. Who can explain him?"

Tucker exhaled.

I had to unclench my teeth. My head ached, my vision swam, and I was in no mood for word games. "Look. You know what we're asking. We have a lawyer here if you need her."

"I haven't been retained," said Elizabeth.

"Right. But you could be. We're trying to make this easier for you," I told Mrs. Thatcher. "You can wait for the police, and for your own lawyer, but someone saw you at Joel's left side—"

"Eyewitness testimony is notoriously unreliable," said Mrs. Thatcher.

Tucker shook his head. "This eyewitness is reliable."

As long as it doesn't get deleted.

"Then why do you need me, if you've already convicted me in your mind?"

"Right now, everyone on this plane is terrified that we're stuck at 35,000 feet with a murderer." As I spoke, my lips felt numb. I hadn't had a chance to dwell on it, but if I'd been trapped in my seat, I would have armed myself with anything at hand—a paper clip, the tab off a soft drink—if I thought it might keep the airplane killer at bay.

She folded her arms neatly. "Do you expect me to confess, as they do at the end of every detective novel?"

"That would be nice," Tucker shot back. He kept a stiff hand on my shoulder. "Let's start at the beginning. What's your name?"

Margaret Thatcher shook her head.

"You won't even give your name, rank, and serial number?" I said. It seemed positively unneighbourly.

She raised an eyebrow. "'It is better to remain silent at the risk of being thought a fool, than to talk and remove all doubt of it.'"

It sounded like yet another quote. I ignored it. "No one here thinks you're a fool."

"'Silence is the language of God. All else is poor translation.'"

"Are you going to be like the witch in *A Wrinkle in Time* who spent all her time quoting other people?" I'd loved that book, but I'd never considered how annoying that would be in real life.

"Mrs. Who," Tucker murmured. He's Mr. Trivial Pursuit.

She inclined her head, as if she were accepting that as a title.

"You want us to call you Mrs. Who?" No way.

"I prefer to be called nothing at all. I prefer to dwell in silence."

I tried to gauge her based on direct observation instead of forcing her to talk. She looked ordinary. Fuzzy dyed-red hair, a slightly prominent nose, good teeth, a beige shirt and khaki slacks with walkable brown shoes. Maybe she was younger than the sixties I'd assumed, but she was someone you'd pass over in a crowd, like those deliberately neutral FBI agents.

She'd been sitting in the exit row, which is hard to get unless you're either rich, charming, or an advance planner. I'd bet on the last one.

I gave up. I couldn't read her. I'd have to force her to talk. "You were seen beside his torso, picking something up from the ground." I didn't tell her what object it was, or how she'd been seen. Maybe I could trap her.

Tucker shifted beside me. He wanted to talk. He was the would-be psychiatrist, the people person. I was the concussed wild woman. I should leave this to him, and yet, I couldn't. Not yet.

I said, "We spoke to the flight attendants. You haven't gone to the bathroom since the—incident, so you didn't have a chance to flush any weapon."

Her impassive face remained composed. She wasn't scared of me.

I'd have to force her hand some other way. "Either it's on your person, or you hid it somewhere around you. It should be a fairly simple matter to search every passenger, take apart everyone's baggage, and rip apart every seat. We'll end up sitting on the tarmac for twelve hours once we land, but that's life, right? Merry Christmas to all of us."

"Hell, no," a short, square, fiftyish woman burst out from row 20. Her cartoon voice reminded me of Cartman on South Park. "I got grandbabies to see."

"If this lady would tell us what she did, and where she hid any weapon, we could all disembark more quickly," I said.

"Weapon. You saying she's the one who stabbed that guy?" said the South Park woman.

"She must be," chipped in the man beside her.

The rest of economy class erupted into whispers and not-so-whispers.

"How do they know that?"

"I thought so."

"What are you talking about?"

"She looks shifty."

"What are we waiting for? Just search her."

" ... SUE YOU!" shouted Mrs. Yarborough from the front.

The guy in the red ball cap cracked his knuckles, one by one.

A very tall black guy stood up in his window seat. He almost had to bend himself in half so he didn't bash into the overhead compartment, but he, too, was fixed on Mrs. Thatcher.

Her eyes widened.

Ah. Here was another clue. She was scared of big, black men. Interesting, because I knew of one other one whom I could call from row 33 if I had to, although it would leave Staci Kelly guarded by only her dead husband.

It was a delicate operation, leveraging the air rage on the plane, but my job was to make her uncomfortable. I'm pretty good at that.

"There was one case where people were stuck on the tarmac for fourteen hours, in Ottawa," I said. "They didn't get any water or food. The air conditioning broke. Someone started vomiting. The toilets got backed up. Parents ran out of diapers. The airline refused to let them off the plane." I couldn't recall every detail, but the point wasn't historical accuracy. The point was to paint a story. I could do that. "They were trapped. Just like we're going to be trapped with this murderer. I bet it'll take longer than fourteen hours. We've got a dead man. We have a killer. We have to find that weapon. You know how the cops always say, 'Don't leave town'? We're not leaving this plane."

It must have been my imagination, but I felt like I could smell Joel's body as I spoke, adding to the pressure.

"Show us the knife," called the man in the baseball cap.

"You can't keep us on here," said the businesswoman, her voice lifted in fear.

Oh no. There must be people with mental illness on the plane, and I was exploiting them. Ruthlessly.

I kept my face stern. "We're at the mercy of the large northern weather system in the air, and then we'll be at the mercy of the police when we land, all because one person wants to get away with murder."

"I have anxiety," Gladys singsonged from her row. She'd crouched over her dog while he lay on the ground.

Gideon got up on all fours. At first, I thought he was trying to shake her off, but he didn't move his shoulders much. He had a weary look in his eyes as his hind legs settled into a squat that brought his rear end closest to the ground.

"I think he's going to—" I called.

The smell of dog feces assaulted our nostrils.

We gasped. Someone started praying.

I held my breath and breathed through my mouth. I've smelled pilonidal abscesses (butt pus) and melena (stool with digested blood), which smelled worse, but I hadn't been locked in the belly of a plane with either of those. My stomach roiled.

Don't let me throw up. I can't puke now.

"Oh, Giddy," said Gladys, "did you have to go? I'm sorry. Mommy's sorry." She made no move to scoop the poop.

Gideon continued to crap, even as Magda squeaked and ran at them from the galley with a newspaper. Elizabeth moved out of her way, holding her nose.

The South Park woman shouted, "I can't take it!"

She unbuckled her seat belt and bounced out of her seat.

I thought she wanted Gideon, but she headed straight for Mrs. Thatcher's seat. "Did you stab him? Yes or no?"

Mrs. Thatcher didn't answer, but her lips, chin and hands trembled.

"Show of force," I muttered to Tucker. He and I and South Park surrounded Mrs. Thatcher.

We didn't have to speak. We didn't have to threaten. We didn't need a gun. But we did need a mob.

Tucker waved his hand, beckoning the rest of the plane, and people detached themselves from their seat belts and stood up.

"Sit down," called Linda, from the curtain. She was clutching something in her hand.

No one sat.

"I'm getting off this plane," said the businesswoman, holding her nose.

"Not if I get off first."

"They can't hold us here!"

"They can do whatever they want."

"Come here and tell her what we need," said Tucker.

"All we need is the knife," I said, never looking away from Mrs.

Thatcher. "That's all. One knife, the one that was used to stab Joel J. Firestone, and then we can all get off the plane when we land."

The businesswoman squared her shoulders.

The Portuguese father stood up, even though his wife pleaded with him.

People clogged the aisles in a silent, staring mass.

I could hear the people breathing. Breathing in the foul air, which made all of us even angrier.

One white guy at the back of the plane flexed his hands. He had a scar from the corner of his left eye down to his mouth, and tattoos on both arms and his neck. I couldn't have picked a more threatening figure if I were casting a movie.

Mrs. Thatcher sat the epicentre of a very ugly, very determined mob.

If she didn't start talking, the mob—infuriated by the weather, the delays, and cramped seats, then scared out of their minds by the death of one of their own, and goaded to the limit by dog shit—they might take it all out on Mrs. Thatcher.

Mobs have done terrible things. They have poured hot tar on people and rolled them in feathers. They have set them in arenas with hungry lions. They have castrated men and hung them from trees. They have immobilized them with tires and set them on fire. They have attached people's limbs to four different vehicles and driven away, tearing each limb from the torso.

I could feel their rage. They were ready.

The man with the red baseball cap swore under his breath.

The scarred, white man glared.

The tall, thin black man towered over all of them.

"Show us the knife," said Tucker.

Mrs. Thatcher's lips trembled before she pointed to her seat cushion.

36

"Don't touch it," I warned Tucker. "It's evidence. And you don't want your fingerprints on it."

"I have to make sure it's there, though," he said. "She could be lying to us. Linda, do you have one more pair of gloves?"

"Don't touch it, John Tucker." My voice escalated. I was terrified I was going to lose him. I didn't care that Linda was steering Margaret Thatcher into the aisle. The mob wasn't laying its hands on her yet.

Tucker snapped on a pair of too-small blue gloves. The airplane must be running out of equipment, or Linda had grabbed the wrong size.

"Let me do it!" I said, but he was already reaching for the seat cushion, starting with the edge near the window.

His back tensed. "I see it. There's something metal here. Does someone have a flashlight?"

I hit the flashlight on my phone, although my fingers were trembling.

Magda dug up a proper flashlight that we could have used during the pericardial window. She angled it over his shoulder. "I can see it too," she said.

"Looks like there's blood on the blade," said Tucker. "Okay. I'll leave it in situ, Dr. Sze."

Tears gathered in the corners of my eyes.

When we turned around, the very tall black man and Linda were zip tying Mrs. Thatcher in the aisle. She didn't fight them. She met my eyes. "You're not a mother. If you were a mother, you'd understand."

Her words slammed into me before my tired brain worked out the implications.

"He hurt her daughter," I whispered. "Or her son." That kind of ferocity, to stab a man while he was already being subdued—that flared when someone defenceless was hurt or killed. "One of the movies Joel did—"

He nodded. "Probably."

"Come on," said the black man, not unkindly.

Mrs. Thatcher nodded, but as she turned her back to us with her hands bound behind her, she twisted her right hand and tucked her thumb over her pinky so that her right index, middle, and ring fingers made a spiky shape in the air. Like three tines of a pitchfork.

Or a W.

"I'm sorry, Mrs. West!" I shouted to her back.

Her shoulders stiffened. She dropped the W. Otherwise, she didn't acknowledge me. She carried on her procession to the back of the plane.

I stared up at Tucker in mute agony. Pornographers like Joel J and Staci Kelly—they made all the money and squatted in first class, while the rest of us, the people who slaved away for minimum wage, the permanent students—we were the ones getting raped up the ass. Yet only Mrs. Thatcher would go to jail, or even get the death penalty. "It's not *right*."

He folded me in his arms. We stood like wooden markers over a land mine, although in our case, we were human markers clotting up the aisle over the knife seat. I didn't want to cry. I hated the tears that spewed out of my ducts anyway.

I've encountered more killers than I care to count. But when I take them down, there's a sense of justice to it. They killed someone. They go to jail. We can live happily ever after.

Not today. "Her son was Holden West, the Montreal man who killed himself after he got HIV. It makes sense because we're flying to Montreal. Maybe Mrs. West was following Joel the whole time, trying to get close to him." My throat ached.

Tucker nodded. "Could be. I wonder how she got the knife. That looked like a metal blade, not plastic. She shouldn't have been able to get that through security. How did she—"

I sniffed hard. "People can bring guns through security. They only have to check them in their luggage and store them in a proper case. It wouldn't be hard to sneak it back out of your check-in items."

Tucker shook his head. I could feel his chin moving on top of my hair. "It still doesn't make sense. You did carry-on only, so you probably didn't notice, but as soon as you check your luggage, you put it on the weight scale, and they tag it and put it on a conveyor belt. You don't get to dig back through your checked luggage for your knife or gun."

"The police will figure it out," I said. "Her fingerprints will be on the blade, along with anyone else's."

"Excuse me," said a little voice.

Tucker stiffened, although his voice sounded as friendly as usual. "Hi, buddy."

Oh. The Portuguese kid with the iPad. "Yes?" I said, although I didn't detach myself from Tucker. We deserved a hug right now.

"I didn't get to show you my video."

I drooped. The last thing I needed was yet another video, especially after we'd already lived through Mrs. Yarborough calling down a thousand cocks on me, but Tucker said, "I'll watch it, buddy. Why don't you fire it up? Dr. Sze is a little tired."

"I'm okay," I said, and turned my head, still in Tucker's arms. It'll be a sad day when I'm too exhausted to open my eyes and take in a video, even though I'm not supposed to watch them with my concussion. I stared at it with half-lidded eyes.

Once again, the kid showed us a video of the Joel J takedown.

This one was also from the front, which made sense because they were in row 14. The only difference was that the kid was lower down, more around waist and knee height. The adults had tried to get higher, standing on their toes or even on seats, in order to get a better angle, but it also meant that everything was filmed further away and darker.

This kid had gotten right down to the ground and shot through people's knees.

That was why he got the only clear shot of a woman with the knife in her hand.

The woman who wasn't Mrs. Thatcher.

37

I swore aloud. We hadn't exactly convicted Mrs. Thatcher, but we'd almost set a mob on her.

When all along, it had been Gladys.

Gladys, creeping up to Joel's side, struggling to hold on to the knife.

Gladys, her hand slashing at his armpit.

Gladys, her hand shaking so much that she—

She dropped the knife.

Mrs. Thatcher scooped it up.

Immediately afterward, the kid must have dropped his iPad. The screen blacked out.

My heart was still pounding. I could hardly talk.

I felt sick at the near-miss. I wasn't 100 percent sure that Mrs. Thatcher had stabbed Mr. Money, but she might have delivered the bigger wound off-camera. At the very least, she deserved to be zip tied at the back of the plane and properly interrogated. She was the last person with the knife, and the knife was at her seat. She was at minimum an accessory to murder.

But Gladys. Gladys had stabbed him first. And she'd gotten him in the armpit, which was a pretty good way to kill someone.

We had more than one murderer.

"Gladys," I said softly.

Her head snapped up from row 16. "He was trying to kill Giddy," she said right away. "I can't let him do that. I told you. I'd die without him."

I stopped for a second. She had said that. And yet, dogs die before their owners all the time. Does that mean she'd planned to commit suicide when he died? It was possible. People can die of heartbreak, and she loved him as much as some people love their spouses.

I don't judge love. I can't. Even so ...

"You can't stab people," I said softly. "We were stopping him already."

"Oh, no, you didn't. You think you were going to stop him?" She looked me up and down, and even though I was two inches taller than her, I obviously didn't measure up. "He kicked your boyfriend. He almost knocked you out. I had to take care of it."

Strange. We'd considered her feeble, but to Gladys, we were the incompetent ones.

Tucker zeroed in on the weapon. "How did you get the knife, Gladys?"

She flapped her hand at him. "From the guy."

"What guy?"

"The—I don't know his name. The one with the bags."

I frowned, but Tucker was ahead of me. "The baggage handler?"

My heart dropped. "The baggage handler who died? Mr. García?"

She shrugged. "I told you. I don't know his name."

"But how did you get his knife? You took a bus to the gate. The bus driver isn't a baggage handler." Post-concussion, I had trouble remembering all the details, and I needed her to tell us anyway.

She frowned. "I had Gideon, so they took me early. The bus driver was really mean. He got mad and started yelling at us about how ESA's shouldn't be allowed on flights. But I have anxiety—"

The whole fucking world knows you have anxiety, Gladys.

"—and he upset me so much that I had trouble holding on to Giddy and my bags ... "

I flashed back to her trundling on our plane with her dog. Yes, she wouldn't have been able to manage.

"So I dropped his leash, and he started running away. He's a dog. He needs to be free."

I caught a whiff of dog feces again and wished he were free some place else. "And then?"

"They all started chasing him and scaring him! That bus driver was the worst! He kicked the other guy out of one of those baggage carts. He started chasing Gideon with the baggage cart. I thought he was going to kill him!"

That did sound horrible. *But the knife, Gladys. Where did the knife come in?* "So what did you do?" I asked, trying to sound sympathetic.

"One of those guys dropped a knife. I picked it up. The bus driver jumped out of the buggy, yelling at one of the other guys to take it, and I cut the seat belt. You're not allowed to drive without a seat belt. If he couldn't drive, he couldn't hurt Giddy."

I saw the scene in my head: the corpulent bus driver trying to mow down a panicky dog. Gladys, too out of shape to run, so weak that no one would hear her scream. But she could pick up a knife. And she could sabotage the vehicle.

"They didn't see me," she went on. "They were too busy yelling at each other and talking to their radios. I was trying to tell them that I could get Gideon back to me in no time. He loves his liver treats."

Yes. No wonder his shit stank. And it was telling that he'd come back for the treats, if not his owner.

"One of the other guys jumped in the buggy, even though the seat belt was broken! I told him it was against the rules, but I don't know if he even spoke English." She shook her head in judgment. The eternal anglophone lament. "He started to run down Giddy. I was terrified. He went much faster than the bus driver."

It must have been the baggage handler, who actually knew how to drive the cart, unlike the bus driver.

"He scared Giddy so much that he ran back to me. I held tight to his leash. And later, I gave him a liver treat. So everything was fine."

"You held on to the knife," said Tucker.

"Well, of course I did. How else was I supposed to defend myself against these crazies! They tried to run over my dog on the ground, and then another one tried to throw him out the window on the plane! Good thing I had my knife!"

"Gladys," I said softly, "the baggage handler died. He was thrown out of his cart without a seat belt."

Gladys frowned. "He shouldn't have driven so fast, then. I knew he was a fast driver. You should have seen him trying to run over Gideon!"

"Gladys." I controlled my anger. "He was driving fast because he was trying to make up time after you let your dog loose on the runway."

Gladys's scowl deepened. "There's never an excuse for driving dangerously. That's what a police officer told me last year, and he was right."

I wanted to shake her. "Gladys, did you see him die?"

"No, I didn't see anyone die. I was on the plane, and I didn't see anything."

"Gladys, you made him drive fast with no seat belt. He was thrown out of his cart. He probably died of head injuries. Didn't you notice all the ambulances and police cars closing down that part of the airport when they took you back off the plane?"

As I spoke, she curled around her dog. At last, she muttered, "No one would help me with my bags."

"Because a man died!"

Tucker put his hand on my arm. I tried to breathe more slowly and regroup. Gladys didn't understand. She would probably never understand. Yelling at her was as useful as screaming in outer space. But I had to add, "You kept the knife and stabbed Joel J."

"He was trying to throw my dog off the plane. He would have opened the door and killed us all! Sucked us into outer space!"

Slowly, reluctantly, pity flooded my body.

Gladys was messed up.

So was I.

She was defending the one she loved.

So did I.

If Joel had tried to kill Tucker, I would have executed him without a second glance, consequences be damned. And since he was a pornographer, I can't say I'd cry too hard.

Still, the saddest part was when they went to zip tie Gladys, and she said, "Can I bring my dog? I have anxiety."

38

We escaped to business class. I didn't want to hear Gladys crying, and the fecal smell was slightly better on the other side of the curtain. I needed to drink water and snooze until we landed, which the pilot assured us would happen in the next 35 minutes. Sure, sure.

Mr. Yarborough had opened his eyes. He wasn't speaking yet, but he could sit up. That was an improvement.

Pascale brought me orange juice, which was sour, but I needed the calories, so I downed it, plus a refill. Tucker sipped his apple juice more slowly. I couldn't help worrying about his post-operative stomach. Before I could ask him about it, Trina hovered by our seats.

"Sorry to bother you, but I heard Staci Kelly tell you that everything was always aboveboard on their productions. It's not true. They violated lots of safety codes."

I craned my neck up at her. Her skin seemed to be filled with light. It was irrational, but her beauty lifted my spirits. "You mean ... "

Trina turned away, not meeting my eyes. "We might not win a case against their production company. I didn't work for them recently. I don't know what's going on now."

I hardly dared to breathe, the moment was so delicate. Tucker silently set down his apple juice.

"I worked for them a long time ago. I figured they might have gotten better, and I didn't want to mess with them," she said.

That made sense. Trina was the world's biggest synth star. Why would she volunteer that she used to work in the sex industry, which would erase her entire conservative fan base, plus risk a libel lawsuit by the Terrible Two?

"The rules have gotten more strict, especially after Holden West died. Things should have improved." She paused. "Then I heard rumours that the opposite was true. They were getting more desperate for cash and cutting more corners."

That made sense. But rumours wouldn't prove anything, especially on someone as lawyered-up as Staci Kelly.

"So I looked into it," Trina murmured. "In 2014, Staci Kelly got in touch with Holden by telling everyone they wanted to help him with his new diagnosis, but once they got a hold of him, they told him he was disgusting, no one would ever touch him on-screen or off, his life was over ... "

I closed my eyes. I could hear them screaming in my head.

"He hanged himself," Trina finished.

That poor man. HIV is treatable. There was no reason for him to die like that, alone and scared, climbing up on a chair with a noose around his neck.

Tucker's voice was hoarse. "If we can't prove anything—"

"They filmed it. The whole thing. Them harassing him, them giving him drugs and liquor. Even the rope to hang himself."

Tucker's hand clenched in mine. I clamped down on it, tight.

"I haven't seen it myself, but one of my people got a hold of it. I hadn't decided what to do with it." She looked directly at me. "Until this flight."

I nodded. Death flight took on a different meaning now. Joel J and Staci Kelly had spent their post-Holden years flying away from death with every tool imaginable: wealth, surgery, drugs, drinking, vacations, movies.

In the end, death still won. Death always won.

"You'll turn it in to the police?" said Tucker, in the same gentle tone he'd used with Gideon.

"Yes. I was going to anyway." She stopped and swallowed.

Thank God. I don't believe in you, but thank God anyway.

"I don't know why they'd film it," I said, almost to myself.

Trina's eyelids sprang open. Her brown irises burned into mine. She said two words. "Snuff film."

"Don't—" said Tucker, but it was too late. I already knew that those were films showing an actual murder. Staci Kelly's voice tunnelled directly into my brain.

Snuff porn is a thing.

Killing people is another thing.

It did very *well.*

"They didn't release it," said Trina.

I breathed a little more easily. At least they hadn't profited directly from his death. At least they hadn't disseminated the images around the world. At this very moment, no one was laughing or jerking off as Holden West died over and over and over.

Trina turned her head away. "I think it was because it wasn't gory enough."

39

I crept back to Compton's former seat to talk to Mrs. West. She was in the middle seat, flanked by the guy in the red baseball cap and the tall, thin black man.

"So she'll go to prison for killing Holden?" said Mrs. West.

"I hope so," I said. I Hope so. I Hope Sze. As the words came out of my mouth, I realized it was, in my own way, a promise. *I, Hope Sze, will do everything in my power to ensure Staci Kelly goes to prison.*

Behind me, Tucker nodded. He was promising too.

"Good," she said. She glanced toward the bloodstained carpet, and I knew she was thinking of Joel J. Firestone. He was dead. His wife would be incarcerated. Their deaths wouldn't bring back her son, but she'd rid the earth of one of them, and the other would rather be dead than in prison.

"I'm so sorry for your loss." My voice dipped and broke.

Tucker placed one hand on each of my shoulders, supporting me, trying to absorb some of my pain.

Mrs. West stared at me from behind her glasses without blinking. "Thank you. My son is at peace now." After a moment, she added, "I think you and your young man are very good doctors."

I turned my head away. I couldn't speak.

I stumbled back to our seats.

When Tucker folded me into his embrace, I sobbed into his shirt. "The good people are going to jail."

Tucker stroked my hair. "She doesn't care about jail. She doesn't care what happens to her. As far as she's concerned, she avenged her son. That's all that matters."

I understood Mrs. West in my bones. I would be a mother like that, if I ever crossed that threshold. Right now, I couldn't imagine bringing a child into this world. After 14/11, every one of us seemed like a hostage to fortune. I couldn't afford to have my heart pulverized if and when something happened to my baby.

Tucker nuzzled my cheek and kissed my ear. "Hope, I love you. It's going to be all right. You remember me telling you about *tikkun olam?* The world isn't perfect, but our job isn't to make it perfect. You just have to repair one little piece at a time. We did that today."

Did we? I cried until my head ached even worse, and then I slept fitfully, leaning against him, as the engines rumbled. Subconsciously, I felt the change in pressure in my ears.

I woke up when I heard the pilot speaking. "Ladies and gentlemen, this is Captain James Mesaglio. Thank you for your patience during this ... unusual flight. Because of the large northern weather system, we were stuck in a holding pattern above Chicago before we elected to continue on course. We anticipate landing shortly at Montreal's Trudeau International Airport. Please return to your seats, buckle your seat belts, and prepare for landing."

The plane erupted into applause. Business class, economy class, it didn't matter. We whooped and whistled. Even Gideon's barking seemed like part of the chorus.

We'd survived one man's death, another man's seizure, and not one, not two, but three would-be murderers. We didn't need any more drama before we made it home.

Ninety-nine percent of the time, we were enthralled by the minutia of our own lives. *Should I have sushi or sashimi? Should I swipe left or right?* Or, in Tucker and my case, *Have you memorized the latest studies? Did Dr. Callendar hammer you because you couldn't regurgitate the normal range for the oral glucose tolerance test in pregnancy?*

Me too. When we'd boarded, I'd fretted about Tucker vs. Ryan. Right now, all I could feel was profound gratitude that all three of us were alive. We'd work the rest of it out.

Alessandro buckled up behind us. Trina listened to music on her headphones, maybe mentally composing a new song. Basso Profundo tried to wedge his legs behind the seat in front of him.

I made sure my steel water bottle was tucked inside the seat pocket in front of me, focused on one thing: *get me off this plane.*

I grabbed Tucker's hand and amended my prayer.

Get us off this plane safely. Along with everyone else. If you have to take anyone, take out the ones with zip ties. Amen.

I was breathing too fast. I started to slow it down. I closed my eyes.

Something dinged. When I opened my eyes, the seat belt light blinked at me.

"Ladies and gentlemen, the seat belt sign is illuminated," said Linda overhead. "Please return to your seat and fasten your seat belt. I repeat, return to your seat and keep your seat fastened until the plane has come to a full stop."

Take your seat, idiot. What is wrong with you?

My nose twitched. I could smell something. It wasn't dog, dog feces, or human sweat. It was acrid.

"Do you smell smoke?" I whispered to Tucker.

He nodded slowly and, disobeying Linda's orders, unbuckled his seat belt.

I laid a hand on his thigh. "Hang on. Tell Linda." I pressed the button for the flight attendant. With any luck, we both had oversensitive noses.

"The matches," I murmured. "The ones you had at, uh, LAX." I was blushing again. "Did you—where are the matches?"

"I left them with Marina," he said. "She's the one who gave them to me, along with the candle."

God bless perky little Marina. It meant no one could have stolen Tucker's matches and lit the plane on fire.

"It could be something electrical. We can't just sit here," he said.

"You can't go running around screaming 'Fire' either."

Pascale answered the call bell. "May I help you?" She offered us a wilted smile. I couldn't blame her.

"I smell smoke," I whispered.

"So do I," said Tucker, louder than I would have liked. "I'm happy to help you look for a source."

"No, don't do that!" she said. "Let me tell Linda." She rushed to the front of the plane.

"See?" I hissed at Tucker. "You don't go strolling around the plane with a fire extinguisher in your hand. Follow the protocol."

"Forget protocol. We have to put out the fire."

"Give them a minute." The smell seemed to grow stronger. "Okay, don't make them panic. Get up quietly, and just ... sniff around."

Tucker hurried toward economy class and pulled back the curtain. The smell billowed into our cabin, stronger now. The air looked hazy too.

I swore up and down and back again, but no one heard me. Someone shouted, "Fire!"

"Is it the engine?"

"Are you serious?"

"Can't you smell it?"

"Oh, my God."

The Portuguese dad dashed toward us.

Why was he abandoning his family? My heart clenched, but the dad pounded past us, up the aisle, and launched himself at Compton, leaning over Basso Profundo in order to yell directly into his face, while Pascale tried to split them apart.

"I didn't do it!" said Compton.

"You were asking for a lighter!" Pascale said, her hair slipping out of her bun.

"Yeah, for later! The 420's legal here!"

Compton must be talking about marijuana. It seemed ridiculous to fly all the way to Montreal to get it. They grow it in California, and isn't it legal in some states, too? But if you're rich enough, maybe it's worth flying across the continent to get a new buzz.

The Portuguese dad switched over to his native language in order to curse more effectively, ignoring Pascale, who was telling him, "Go back to your seat!"

"I know you can't smoke on a plane. I'm not some foreigner who smokes all over the place," said Compton.

The dad reached for Compton's throat.

Compton raised his ziptied wrists defensively before Basso Profundo knocked the dad's hands away. "That's enough!"

"We've got to get to the fire," said Tucker in my ear.

I hesitated. What if these guys strangled each other?

"The big guy will stop them. The fire might kill all of us. Let's go!"

We sprinted back to economy class, where the smoke was definitely worse now. You couldn't even smell feces anymore, although Gideon was barking away, making his presence known.

The air had turned greyish. I could see Tucker's face, but it was hazy.

People were coughing. Some of them were wheezing. The baby was coughing a tiny, helpless baby cough.

"Get me off this plane!"

"We're going to die."

Topaz yelled, "Don't worry! My guru said I'm not going to die on a plane!"

I gritted my teeth, and someone slung back, "Shut up about your guru."

"Girl, if he ain't here, I ain't listenin' to him."

Mrs. Yarborough started screaming from the front, her trademark scream that perforated your ears and rattled your spine.

I clamped my hands over my ears. No wonder Tucker had rushed to help her at the airport. She was the human equivalent of a five-alarm fire.

"Attention everyone, this is your captain speaking. Given the situation, we are going to do our best to land this plane. Please remain in your seats and remain calm as we prepare for landing."

As if to punctuate his words, the plane juddered and thumped. A red light strobed overhead, and a real fire alarm spiked our ear drums. We could barely hear the pilot say, "Flight attendants, please prepare for landing."

Prepare for landing? When there was a *fire?*

"Sit down," said Tucker. "I'll take care of the fire."

I snatched his arm. "You will not."

He tried to shake free. "Hope, I've got to do it."

"You know nothing about fires. You stay with me. You are *mine."*

He hesitated. He'd told me that himself before, and now I flung it in his face. "If you try to play the hero, I will throw myself across you. You can't drag me across the plane. You're not allowed to lift anything, let alone a full-grown woman."

"Hope—"

"Absolutely fucking not, Tucker." I held his arm so tightly that I indented the skin.

He blinked. I knew I was hurting him. I didn't care.

He said, "No one else is going to do it, Hope."

He was right.

"I'm not letting you go. You are not a fireman." I was the heroine in Tam Lin, maniacal in my determination, despite the screaming and the shouting and the high-pitched praying swirling around us. He was my line in the sand.

"Hope."

That wasn't Tucker. The voice was deeper and further away.

I peered through the haze. Herc's face emerged from the chaos at the back of the plane. He said, "I'll do it."

"Stay in your seat, sir!" cried Linda, who stood between us, holding a fire extinguisher in one hand and shooing him back to row 33 with the other. "This is a case for airline personnel."

"I'm an airline mechanic," he said, reaching for the fire extinguisher. "Give me that."

"Are you an Avian Air employee?" she said, but she handed it to him anyway.

He strolled back to the bathroom on the right and pushed open the folding door. Black smoke billowed into the hall.

I threw myself on the ground, covering my nose with my shirt. So did Tucker.

People were hacking, especially the baby.

Do we have any Ventolin? Do we have pediatric aerochambers? I'm going to have to get that kid breathing again.

More ghastly noise from the ShapeR ScreameR in the front.

A man's voice rose above the fray, also from business class. "'The time has come.'"

"Sit down, sir," called Pascale.

"'So there was hail, and fire flashing continually in the midst of the hail, very severe, such as had not been in all the land of Egypt since it became a nation.'"

Hail. The snow storm, or "northern weather system," was playing into Compton's mind.

Even through my T-shirt, I could smell something new, not precisely smoke, but something dark and off and wrong.

The baby shrieked. This time, it sounded like a condemnation.

The plane shuddered. We plunged in the air.

Someone gasped. Someone else started retching.

My stomach quailed.

I had faced death before. I'd worried about my imminent survival, as well as Tucker's or Ryan's. But this was the first time that I might die en masse. Somehow, this was more terrifying, feeling the panic rise in the plane like a palpable force, from people who would claw and kick and kill.

If we were going to die now or in two seconds, every single one of us would take the extra two seconds. I thought of the claw marks on the walls of the gas chambers.

Mobs are never pretty, and this time, we were trapped in a container in the air with three murderers and a fire.

A woman in front of us began to pray loudly. "Help me, Jesus."

"'Then the LORD rained on Sodom and Gomorrah brimstone and fire from the LORD out of heaven.'"

A hissing noise broke through the cabin. It sounded like something was leaking. I prayed that it was the fire extinguisher, but what if the plane had broken a crucial piece?

A chemical smell permeated the cabin.

My heart nosedived, along with the airplane. I had to swallow to make my ears recalibrate.

Linda stumbled over us to get to the cockpit while a woman yelled, "What is happening!"

The smoke seemed to thicken.

"'As they were walking along and talking together, suddenly a chariot of fire and horses of fire appeared and separated the two of them!'"

An abrupt scream cut toward us. Not Mrs. Yarborough, because this one shot from the back of the plane.

I struggled to see through the smoke. That scream meant danger.

"'For six days, work is to be done, but the seventh day shall be your holy day, a Sabbath of rest to the LORD. Whoever does any work on it must be put to death.'"

My mind shot toward Joel J, giving "one hundred percent" to his work. He had been put to death.

"Everyone needs to take their seats and put on their seat belts," said Magda. Her low voice trembled.

That silenced Compton for a moment. I dared to take a tiny breath of smoky air before he yelled, "'Again the devil took him to a very high mountain and showed him all the kingdoms of the world and their splendour!'"

An answering scream arose from the back of the plane, like a cougar sounding a warning.

Topaz piped up. "My guru says that the splendour of the world shouldn't distract you from your higher purpose."

We were going to die. We were going to crash to our doom with a planeload of idiots.

The plane tilted, pitching me and Tucker toward the cockpit. Why, oh why hadn't we stuck to our seats with our seat belts?

I relinquished Tucker with one hand so that I could grasp part of a seat and stop the slide. He did the same.

We still gripped our other hands together, even though the plane plunged at such an angle, we were like children poised to roll down a hill, if the hill were airborne and on fire.

"'And the LORD saith unto us—'"

The airplane's engines roared. I could feel their vibrations through the floor.

"'—Do not suppose that I have come to bring peace to the earth—'"

The engines howled.

Something snapped outside the window. I cringed. Pieces of the plane breaking off?

Tucker's chest started to heave. He didn't smoke or have asthma, but since 14/11, he'd had more trouble with his lungs.

"'I did not come to bring peace, but a sword!'"

Compton's voice grew closer. I lifted my head from the smelly blue carpet to gauge his position. Would he shiv us with his plastic knife while we lay on the bloody carpet like Joel J?

The wheels bumped on the ground so hard that we bounced back up into the air before we hit the ground again.

I managed to partially cushion my head with my arm. Still, my vision pinwheeled.

Did we—

Are we—

The pilot hit the brakes. The air outside the plane shrieked as he drew to a slow, careful stop.

We landed.

Alive.

40

"Ladies and gentlemen, welcome to Montreal's Trudeau International Airport. If you want to adjust your watch, it is 3:05 a.m. local time."

Captain James Mesaglio was drowned out by whoops and tears. The baby alone made enough noise for triplets, and Gideon tried to win the award for World's Loudest Dog.

Tucker offered me a hand. I took it as I stood up, my knees and head only somewhat wobbly.

The cheering rose another decibel. I smiled and winced at the same time.

"The weather in Montreal is overcast, and the temperature is 14 degrees Fahrenheit, or minus ten degrees Celsius."

Tucker breathed more easily. The smoke had cleared, and we'd get off this plane soon. Or in ten hours, if they held us for a forensic investigation. Whatever. We were alive.

"Thank you for your patience during the most ... demanding flight I've ever seen. On behalf of all our crew, thank you for choosing Avian Air as your airline this holiday season."

The bathroom door folded open as Herc carefully made his way out. "All clear," he said.

The cheering grew delirious, overriding Mrs. Yarborough at the front of the aircraft.

Herc held up his enormous palm for silence. When he got it, he said, "Someone set a bunch of paper towels on fire in the sink, the wastebasket, and behind the toilet."

Magda gasped. "A fire is the worst thing—"

Topaz spoke over her. "No, fire is for purification."

A few people shouted in disbelief, but most of us gawked silently as she continued, "My guru talks about it all the time. He holds a special ceremony for the people who have reached the third chakra, or who have become stuck there."

"So you set the fires," I called, before I coughed. Smoke was hard on the vocal cords.

"Of course! Can't you feel it? There's so much anger and hate in the air."

"There's even more if you're setting the plane on fire," said Tucker, and it sounded so much like me that I nearly smiled. We'd made it. I felt joyful, even though Topaz needed a brain transplant.

Topaz waved her hand. "I wouldn't have let the airplane catch fire. I started lighting incense until I decided we needed more Manipura for a true transformation."

"They blamed that poor guy—" Tucker broke off coughing, too.

"The preacher? Please. I'd never lend him my lighter. He's dangerous, you know?"

She was as oblivious as ever. On my psychiatry rotation, we graded people on their insight and judgement. I usually give patients "impaired," but Topaz had just won the "zero" prize.

"Your fires were out of control." If I kept my voice low, I didn't cough as much. My eyes watered, though.

"Well, I didn't want to tell anyone. You're not allowed to take your lighter out of your pocket when you're travelling. I could've gotten in *trouble.*"

A sharp, short scream rocketed from the rear of the airplane. This time, I turned to look.

When Herc had gotten up to tend to the fire, Staci Kelly had tried to climb out of her seat and escape, literally over her dead husband's body. However, since she was ziptied with her hands behind her back, in heels, she'd pitched into her husband's lap. Then the plane had hit such a steep angle that Joel J's body had tented over her, pinning her in place.

Elizabeth waved to us from seat 33C. She'd silently taken over for Herc, guarding Staci Kelly and keeping us safe.

Maybe Tucker was right. Maybe the good people could still win small victories as we worked in concert to repair the world.

While we sat on the tarmac, awaiting the police, Tucker toasted me with a beer. "So in the end, we had a woman who loved her dog more than people—"

"Not uncommon," I said, thinking of Roxy's silky, black ears. My heart expanded in my chest, making me feel less trapped in the belly of this airplane as I gulped down some apple juice. The juice made me think of Mr. Yarborough, who was still not seizing.

Tucker ignored my segue. "She was willing to kill for her dog. You think she knew that he might have had a family, and even a dog?"

"I doubt she was thinking anything beyond Gideon. Most of us aren't thinking when it comes to things that we love." I glanced at him.

He grinned, and I looked away. It was still so fresh. I'd told him I loved him countless times post-hostage taking, but he'd been sedated and post op and puking for part of it. Not too romantic. This felt like the first time that we could canoodle as well as debrief.

"Right. So we had the dog-loving people killer," he said.

I flinched. Gladys was still calling for Gideon.

"And we had the woman who loved money and fame more than her husband."

"That's even more common." I frowned. "I guess that's why I feel sorrier for Gladys. She seems kind of—well, dumb, and she's going to jail, whereas Mrs. Yarborough will lawyer up. Then she'll get off, or have time reduced because she's mega rich and she looks old and frail."

"And Gideon will end up God knows where," Tucker agreed.

"Oh, yeah, that's right." Pain knifed my heart. Literal pain. Once in a while, I get that, an invisible blade stabbing my most vulnerable organ, like a physical manifestation of heartache. "That's not fair. Oh, my God. I've heard the shelters in Quebec are awful, too. Much worse than Ontario."

We sat in silence. Quebec can't take care of its human citizens who vote and pay taxes, as evinced by its horrendous health care and crumbling schools and roads. Care takes money. Why would they look after dogs in any kindly way?

"I'll see if my parents will take Gideon," said Tucker.

"Oh, wow. Really?"

He nodded. "My sisters want another dog. It's my dad who's been holding out. If my mom and I join in, and especially if I play the wounded hero card, I'm sure they'd take him. I'd take him myself, but..."

We both nodded. Doctors can barely survive residency, let alone take on a dog.

He frowned and turned to me. "Unless."

"Unless what?"

The furrow between his eyes increased. He was staring at me in a way that made me stir in my seat. I licked my lips.

His glance dropped to my mouth before coming back up to my eyes.

I crossed my arms in front of my chest. "What is it?"

"Unless we take care of him together," Tucker said.

I swear my hair shot straight out of my scalp so that it was sticking in the air like a Van de Graaff generator. At least, that's how it felt.

Tucker's eyes crinkled. He suddenly looked like the lighthearted guy I'd met in July, and my heart flipped in my chest like a freshly-landed trout as he said, "Yeah. We don't have time, but we could make it work between the two of us. We could make sure that we weren't on call at the same time. That's what other shift workers do when they have kids."

"Yeah, but how could we hand him off every day? Lots of times, we're both working clinics during the day, and then one or both of us is on call. There's no one to walk him at night." I was struggling to figure out how this would work, and what was going on inside that crazy tow head.

"Well, I bet my family and Tori and Mireille and the others would help, even though it would be mostly us. We'd have to be in constant contact. One of us would do the morning walks, and one of us the afternoons, plus weekends. We're not usually both on call at the same time. Not unless we're on a busy rotation, and we could try and schedule them on opposite times during the year."

"Whoa, whoa, whoa. Tucker—"

He beamed at me. His smile was so intense, I could feel the energy radiating from him. It was the first time I'd seen him fired up about something that wasn't me or some sort of disaster in the past five hours, and I didn't want to destroy his enthusiasm, even though I'm incapable of keeping plants alive because watering them is too much of a time commitment. Sometimes I don't even brush my teeth because I need those seconds to sleep. Meanwhile, he thought we should adopt a dog together. That would be dog abuse.

"My apartment is a little bigger, and my rental agreement allows pets, so you could move in with me."

My heart seemed to still. My mouth flew open. It took me a second to coordinate my words. "Move in with—"

"Right. I know that your building doesn't allow pets, so Gideon would be illegal there. And you're only subletting anyway, right? It makes more sense for you to come with me."

My heart beat so fast, I had trouble hearing my own voice over it. Quebec people tend to live together instead of getting married, which I still find weird—something about rebelling against the church, so they rebel against marriage too, which didn't enter my consciousness until a doctor casually mentioned that he and his partner were finally getting married after ten years and three children. Nevertheless, this was not how I pictured me getting together with anyone. Ryan would have a traditional church wedding with groomsmen and bridesmaids and a giant cake that we'd feed to each other. "Tucker—"

"I know what you're going to say. You've got Ryan."

I closed my mouth and nodded once, miserably.

"Fuck him. You're mine."

I almost laughed, which was about the worst thing I could do. Tucker made it sound so simple, and it wasn't the first time he'd said that I belonged to him. The thing was, I agreed. Whenever I was with him, I didn't want anyone else. Tucker was my sun, my moon, my sky, my air, my earth.

The problem was, I felt the exact same thing when I was with Ryan.

I had two exquisitely, painfully perfect men who wanted me exclusively, and I didn't know what to do. I covered my face because I didn't want him to see me crying, or the growing chasm in my heart.

My shoulders shook, even though I tried to suppress any noise and hide any evidence of tears.

Tucker knew I was crying. It didn't stop him. He leaned toward me, fierce, his breath hot against my cheek. "You love me. I love you. There's nothing else to it. Why do you have to make things so complicated? We're together. We're compatible in every way." His eyes gleamed, and I knew what he was talking about.

The entire lower half of my body twitched.

He glanced down. He noticed everything, Tucker did. "You're coming back to Montreal. You're going to finish the family medicine program before your ER year. We can save on rent until we get married."

"Tucker!"

"I know it seems too soon. I know you want to hem and haw. But listen, babe. You and I could die any second. It's like we're a couple during World War II. Every time we're together, someone dies. Now is not the time to think, 'Ooh, I've got to consider my options for the next decade.' I gave you some leeway while I was getting fixed up, but now I'm a hundred percent, as you can see, and feel, and testify." He kissed me, and I kissed him back. I was smelling him and tasting him, feeling his stubble and inhaling his warm breath while my fingers indented his shoulders.

I loved this guy desperately. What he was saying made an insane kind of sense. Nobody else in the world (okay, very few people) seemed to make a love triangle work. Our society is built on monogamy and loving one person until the end of time—at least once you've sown enough wild oats.

I had two oats, Ryan and Tucker. Tucker and Ryan. If I'd had them sequentially, no one would care. But because I was trying to eat two oats simultaneously, that made me the Antichrist. Or at best some sort of spoiled bitch. My friend Ginger didn't understand what I was doing, and our friend Tori refused to speak to me about it. I was a pariah in so many ways.

The Tucker oat kept on speaking. "This isn't romantic. If we had world enough and time, my love, I would give you hearts and flowers and skywriting and wait until you felt safe enough to make up your mind. But right now, I'm giving you my heart. I'm giving you all of me, while we're both in school, with no fancy ring, with blood all over both of us, with nothing but possibly a traumatized, smelly dog to my name." His face changed, and I knew he was quoting something even before he spoke, but his eyes were tender. He meant every single word that thudded directly into my heart.

"'I give you my hand!
I give you my love more precious than money,
I give you myself before medicine or law;
Will you give me yourself? will you come travel with me?
Shall we stick by each other as long as we live?'"

There was only one possible answer. I closed my eyes and thought of Ryan. His smooth, perfect face and his matching body. His incisive engineering mind. The way he and Roxy had saved my life, mentally and physically. My first love. My first lover. I told this mental image of Ryan, I willed real-life Ryan to know that I did love him and want him forever, and in a perfect world, I would.

Then I opened my eyelids and looked at Tucker, his pupils dilated, his hair flopping into his brown eyes, his cheeks drawn, his hands clenched, and I told him, "Yes."

ACKNOWLEDGMENTS

There are two critical points in every aerial flight — its beginning and
its end.
—*Alexander Graham Bell, 1906*

Thank ye, thank ye, thank ye.

Dr. Katherine Ramsland, the forensic psychology expert whom I
interrogated at Writers' Police Academy 2017. She was so cool that I
read her book, *Forensic Science of CSI*. One case sparked the story of
Death Flight;

Alanis Obomsawin, whose observations inspired this famous
quote: "Only when the last tree has been cut down, the last fish been
caught, and the last stream poisoned, will we realize we cannot eat
money";

Lara Roxxx, who made the decision to live;

Captain Mesaglio, who intelligently and enthusiastically
answered all my flight questions and obtained an expert second
opinion whenever necessary;

Dr. Paul Irwin, who always guides Hope with creativity, humour,
and humility;

my triple board-certified doctor pal, who critiqued the sound of my chest tube, analyzed the physics, and suggested an alternative method for murder #2;

my flight doctor, who checked on details even when double booked between medicine and twins;

Sgt. Ed Adach, forensic detective, who valiantly answers my questions and gave an all-day tour in between his real-life investigations and trials in Toronto;

Loonie Doc, who usually reads speculative fiction, but made an exception for Hope;

author Richard Quarry, who always offers his insight;

editors Erik Buchanan, Su J. Sokol, RN Margaret MacDonald, Karen, and Dawn, who do their best to streamline my work and catch the wild typos;

the fabulous human beings who support Hope by plunking down their hard-earned money and posting their reviews and approval online. Special shout out to #TeamTucker for sticking it out this long, although #TeamRyan knows it ain't over until it's over;

the CBC, the Globe and Mail, The Review, The Standard Free-holder, The Seaway News, the Seeker, The Glengarry News, The Medical Post, Rogers, Carol Anne Meehan, Cogeco's trio of Brenda St. Louis, Bill Makinson, and Gabriel Riviere-Reid, librarians, book sellers, bloggers, teachers, and everyone else who keeps the written word alive;

and of course, my long-suffering family. "Even when you're home, you're writing!" pointed out my son. That's right, babe. Mommy is a beast. I promise to take some time off with all of you this summer. You ground and ignite me.

Though we travel the world over to find the beautiful, we must carry it with us or we find it not.
—*Ralph Waldo Emerson*

ABOUT THE AUTHOR

Melissa Yi is an emergency doctor who has answered the call for help on four different flights to date. On the last one, her children chanted, "Go, Mom! Go, Mom!"

Come join the KamikaSze newsletter team at http://melissayuaninnes.com/. We don't bite, because then we might have to give you Clavulin.

If you leave a positive review for *Death Flight* online, you'll help this novel grow wings.

ALSO BY MELISSA YI

Code Blues (Hope Sze 1)

Notorious D.O.C. (Hope Sze 2)

Family Medicine (essay & Hope Sze novella combining the short stories *Cain and Abel, Trouble and Strife,* and *Butcher's Hook*, which are also available separately)

Terminally Ill (Hope Sze 3)

Student Body (Hope Sze novella post-Terminally Ill; includes radio drama *No Air*)

Blood Diamonds (Hope Sze short story)

The Sin Eaters (Hope Sze short story)

Stockholm Syndrome (Hope Sze 4)

Human Remains (Hope Sze 5)

Blue Christmas (Hope Sze short story)

Death Flight (Hope Sze 6)

Graveyard Shift (Hope Sze 7)

More mystery & romance novels by Melissa Yi

The Italian School for Assassins *(Octavia & Dario Killer School Mystery 1)*

The Goa Yoga School of Slayers *(Octavia & Dario Killer School Mystery 2)*

Wolf Ice

High School Hit List

The List

Dancing Through the Chaos

Unfeeling Doctor Series (Melissa Yuan-Innes)

The Most Unfeeling Doctor in the World and Other True Tales From the Emergency Room (Unfeeling Doctor #1)

The Unfeeling Doctor, Unplugged: More True Tales From Med School and Beyond (Unfeeling Doctor #2)

The Unfeeling Wannabe Surgeon: A Doctor's Medical School Memoir (Unfeeling Doctor #3)

The Unfeeling Thousandaire: How I Made $10,000 Indie Publishing and You Can, Too! (Unfeeling Doctor #4)

Buddhish: Exploring Buddhism in a Time of Grief: One Doctor's Story (Unfeeling Doctor #5)

The Unfeeling Doctor Betwixt Birthing Babies: Poems About Love, Loss, and More Love (Unfeeling Doctor #6)

The Knowledgeable Lion: Poems and Prose by the Unfeeling Doctor in Africa (Unfeeling Doctor #7)

Fifty Shades of Grey's Anatomy: The Unfeeling Doctor's Fresh Confessions from the Emergency Room (Unfeeling Doctor #8)

Broken Bones: New True Noir Essays From the Emergency Room by the Most Unfeeling Doctor in the World (Unfeeling Doctor #9)

The Emergency Doctor's Guide Series (Melissa Yuan-Innes)

The Emergency Doctor's Guide to a Pain-Free Back: Fast Tips and Exercises for Healing and Relief

The Emergency Doctor's Guide to Healing Dry Eyes